More Luck Than Judgment

Nancy Russell

Pen Press

First published in Great Britain

All paper used in the printing of this book has been made from
wood grown in managed, sustainable forests.

ISBN13: 978-1-78003-683-0

Printed and bound in the UK
Pen Press is an imprint of
Indepenpress Publishing Limited
25 Eastern Place
Brighton
BN2 1GJ

A catalogue record of this book is available from
the British Library

Cover design by Seren Stacey

More Luck Than Judgment

CHAPTER 1

'Right at the top,' said Bea, changing into bottom gear, 'the view's amazing.' Rose was smiling lazily in the passenger seat of the silver Peugeot and Bea glanced quickly at her before tackling a hairpin bend on a hill like a house-side.

'You know,' replied Rose, her soft, slightly husky voice sounding faintly amused. 'You've been telling me about all these amazing views ever since we left the outskirts of Leeds – and you're right,' she added hastily. 'It's great, Bea and I'm going to love The Dales.'

'This one *is* a bit special, though,' insisted Bea, as they rounded another tight corner. 'I love it when we get to this last stretch of the journey … a bit like coming home. It starts for me as soon as we leave the A65 and head north. It was a great idea of yours to suggest coming to the caravan – I should have thought of it myself, with this spell of good weather due to go on for a few more days.'

For pity's sake, thought Bea, do we need to be so unnaturally polite to each other? She wondered how soon the holiday would make them relax into something more like it used to be in the old days. Still, she didn't want to go blundering in – she was all too aware that tact wasn't her strongest point. Scorpio was the sign of loyalty, but those born under it also needed the loyalty of their friends – to help them overlook the Scorpion's startling bluntness.

'There's one of those "viewpoints" where we can park, just round this corner,' she told Rose and she signalled right as she prepared to pull over. 'It's well worth stopping for, but the entrance is very close to the bend – you've got to be so careful crossing into … LUNATIC!'

As Bea was swinging the car across the road into the little parking area, an ancient dark green Astra hurtled round the bend towards them and narrowly missed the Peugeot, which skidded into an empty bay in a noisy swirl of gravel. She glanced across at Rose, who had made no sound, but was rubbing her shoulder where the seat belt had done its work.

'Sorry about that.' Bea looked ruefully over towards the road they had just left. 'You wouldn't think they'd allow such an awkward turn-in, would you? But there wasn't a vehicle in sight as I started to turn … and she was driving like a boy racer!'

'Funny,' muttered Rose, preoccupied. 'For a minute I thought she was …' But Rose leaned back, frowning and didn't say any more.

'Was going to kill us? … was certifiable? … was your next-door neighbour? Honestly, Rose, you're doing it again!'

'Doing what?' Rose's voice was rising in protest.

'Starting to say something and then stopping short,' answered Bea, uneasily aware that in the stress of the moment, the politeness was evaporating fast.

'Oh – sorry. But I don't think it could have been her anyway, now I come to think about it.' Rose was frowning as she gazed unseeingly through the windscreen. 'It's term-time and she'd be at work on a Friday afternoon. I … I came across her when I was living near Lancaster last year and she's got an old banger just like that.' Rose seemed perplexed as she turned in her seat to look at Bea. 'It really did look awfully like her and that driver had a mop of curly blond hair too, just like hers. She's married to a friend of … her name's Barbara and she's a teacher – infants.'

'In that case,' Bea answered tartly, 'I hope she's a damn sight more careful looking after other people's infants than when she's behind the wheel!' Bea returned Rose's gaze. 'That's if it *was* this woman – how could you see her properly, anyway? She was gone in a flash.' Reaching down to the shelf in front of her, Bea pulled out a large bar of dark chocolate. She had remembered that it was Rose's favourite. She opened it now, hoping it would serve as a peace-offering.

But Rose had never been one to bear a grudge. She certainly hadn't got Bea's tendency to brood; she was open and easygoing. You could never call her feckless, thought Bea – in many ways she was so organised and she had a very responsible job. But there was no doubt she was *very* laid back. The years since they had been at school together hadn't changed Rose much. In appearance too, she was much the same – she was a pleasingly solid, compact little person with deep reddish-brown hair, very often worn softly knotted behind and she had greenish eyes that you just couldn't fail to notice. Her complexion had a sort of deep glow, an echo of her hair. Someone at school had said she was reminded of her family's pet guinea-pig. Typically, Rose had taken this in her stride and didn't seem to mind.

Bea, by contrast was tall and lithe, her rather serious face framed with cleverly cut dark hair. It was quite a distinguished-looking oval face, with a longish, fastidious nose and a generous mouth. In repose, she habitually looked thoughtful – even sober – but when she smiled and her grey eyes lit up, they softened and sweetened her expression. She sat back now and gazed at the valley below them. She never grew tired of the Yorkshire Dales, though she didn't come to the caravan so often these days – and normally only in the middle of summer. She was anxious that Rose should like the area too and she hoped that once the sharp wind dropped, they would be able to enjoy the promised warmth. Such settled spring weather was unusual enough to alter their plans. Bea's cosy flat in Leeds seemed less appealing for their week together, even though mid-May was a bit early for holidays up in the hills.

Bea wondered why she had never asked Rose to come here before – it was only during the last year or so that there had been that coolness between them and now was their chance to put things right. They sat in silence, nibbling their chocolate and taking in the understated elegance of the view. It was a huge expanse of grey and green, inlaid with ribbons of sparkling water. The pattern of the hills, stone walls and valleys had captivated Bea ever since she spent her childhood holidays here among the grazing sheep and stony streams.

She had stayed in the family caravan at Shawhead Farm every summer. The old farmhouse was now converted to a holiday let and the owners had retired to a small property in the village. Far from growing out of this early holiday home – apart from a brief spell eight or nine years ago, in her late teens – Bea had continued to be drawn to the area. Her parents began to take more sophisticated holidays as their offspring grew up, but her father had helped her buy a smaller, newer replacement for the roomy old caravan, and she kept this in the same paddock, close to the farmhouse. This was when she was just starting her first job and it had provided a wonderful (and cheap) escape at weekends for her and her friends. She had been delighted when the man in her life had clearly enjoyed their time spent up here. Recently though, they had tended to fly off to the sun, using the caravan less.

Today was cloudless and it was hot in the car. Rose wriggled about as she shrugged off her slatey blue jacket. But though it was so warm behind glass, Bea knew the strong breeze up here would be quite chilly. She kept her fleece on and by tacit consent there was no suggestion of getting out. Breaking off another square of chocolate, she pushed the bar along the dashboard towards Rose, who grinned ruefully and shook her head. Unlike Bea, she needed to be wary of putting on weight, though she never made an issue of it, passing off any refusal with a casual shrug. Shortly they agreed to move on. Bea eased the car cautiously out on to the road which, after the steep ascent, now dropped much more gently into a broad valley.

Rose looked about her, clearly appreciating the acres of ewes and lambs that stretched as far as they could see, in fields that were divided haphazardly it seemed, with never-ending grey walls. The river running through the valley was bright with pebbles, which showed up clearly on its shallow bed. They crossed the ancient bridge – no more than a cart's width, with deep triangular refuges for those on foot.

'This landscape's just so different,' she said. 'I'm much more used to the wild moorland … this is just the opposite – not a bit wild, but certainly woolly! It's got a – a *calmness* about it … as if it knows it's been here a very long time, unchanged and secure. We're quite near to the village now, aren't we – I just saw it signposted?'

'Five minutes – up this "bank", over the top, and you'll see the village in the bottom, then we climb up a bit to the farm itself.'

They dropped down to the valley floor, following another small river. The road crossed over this to reach the first cluster of solid-looking cottages. Then it divided to encircle the centre of the village – a gentle slope of grass and paving with several beech trees and a few rustic benches dotted about. The shops stood well back from the central area and they looked interesting and inviting.

'This is it – Little Blaeford!' Bea's broad smile completely transformed her face. 'People seem a bit bemused about the name – Blae is just an ancient word meaning bleak, or grey and of course, it's pronounced like grey … a bit odd, though, because there's nothing bleak or grey about it!'

'No, it's got a mellow look, hasn't it? And it's just as you described it, Bea – but somehow, even more appealing than I imagined. And what a lovely feeling of space! It makes you feel unhurried, somehow – am I making any sense?'

'Yes I know just what you mean – spaciousness and timelessness," said Bea. 'Probably that's why we've always been able to relax here.' They were driving at a walking pace without fear of holding up the traffic, since few vehicles were about just then and the village had a sleepy look.

'That's what I meant by secure – you wouldn't feel anxious in a place like this and it seems completely unspoilt … '

'On the whole, it is,' answered Bea. 'It just manages to be remote enough not to be ... *infected* by the nastier things in modern life. People round here are a pretty independent lot, you know. I've always found that they have a natural politeness, and yet they'd probably tell you they "mek nowt o' trippers" – and they certainly aren't going to alter the way of life that suits them, just to accommodate a bunch of strangers.'

She stopped the car to let Rose look around her. 'We've still got a Post Office,' she said, pointing to a long low building that was combined with an inviting looking general store. 'There's a hotel and a very good pub and there's a craft shop that opened last year and the butcher who's been there forever – oh and the farm shop that we pass on the way up to Shawhead. Then there's a recreation ground down by the river, with a few swings and so on – but that's about as far as tourist attractions go.' She removed the rest of the chocolate from the dashboard and packed it away in her handbag to avoid further temptation. 'I can't see them ever having a caravan site around here – they'd never accept it.'

'Don't blame them,' replied Rose. 'You're lucky then, to have the use of the farm site for your caravan.'

'Yes, I think so. It's tucked well out of sight – Dad planted trees on three sides of our plot years ago so as not to bother Mr. and Mrs. Dyson at the farm. They've grown into a thick screen and Philip and I have put in some birch saplings as well. We've tried to make sure it's not offending anyone, and there's electricity laid on and mod cons, so it's pretty comfortable.' A small group of young women pushing prams passed the car and smiled in a friendly greeting.

'The Dysons, who own the farmhouse, live in the village now and they pop in to open up the caravan quite often when they're seeing to their holiday guests. But I had a card from them – they've taken the chance to go for a short holiday before their first booking of the season in a week or so's time. The 'van might be a bit musty after being shut up for a while, but I always leave one of those low-wattage electric heaters in there on its minimum setting. It'll be fine once we put the proper heating on and open the roof ventilators.'

Rose gazed about her at the stone houses that seemed to have sprung out of a considerable prosperity. 'I love the way they're built – simple, but so stylish and unfussy. They're quietly confident – I mean, they're not trying to prove anything, are they?' She looked across towards the Post Office, where two women were just coming out. Rose twitched Bea's sleeve. 'Look, Bea – just as I'm talking about quiet confidence and unfussiness!'

Bea laughed and waved, as two women passed the car. 'Oh yes, that's Carmen. She does look a bit like a gypsy, doesn't she?'

'But her name isn't really Carmen, is it?'

'No, it's Marjorie Dutton, but most people feel Carmen suits her better.'

'And does she know they call her Carmen?'

'Oh, I expect so. She'd not mind. Probably plays up to it a bit.'

'Even in the city,' said Rose, amused, 'it would be a bit over-done, wouldn't it? Those amazing earrings, and the hair ornament – and those clothes…'

'Pretty flamboyant, yes. But you must admit she's very decorative – handsome seems to describe her best.'

'And the woman she's with? She looks – for a moment, she reminded me of somebody … I can't just think – '

'Her daughter. She's just the opposite, isn't she?'

'But how terrible to be so dowdy, with a mother so – notice-able!'

Bea had a curious smile on her lips. 'Dowdy …don't you think she has a certain something, though? Anyway she doesn't seem interested in competing – or at any rate, not on the same terms!' She fingered the ignition key tentatively. 'Shall we go on now? It's less than half a mile.'

*

Bea ran towards the caravan, key at the ready, and shouted to Rose: 'Quick! Let's get out of the wind. Feels more like winter than spring up here.' She held the door of the caravan open with some difficulty, while Rose hoisted herself and her large yellow grip bag up the portable step into the narrow doorway. It was difficult to do this gracefully. She envied Bea's longer reach and natural agility.

'I'll put the heating on before we fetch the groceries in – it's to be hoped this wind drops soon, or you won't feel you've made a good choice, coming up here! ' Bea threw her bag down at the far end of the caravan and her jacket and handbag joined Rose's on one of the benches. Then she knelt down to fiddle with an electric heater under the end window. 'I'll put the kettle on in a minute, but we have to run the tap a bit first, or the water will be stale. We could leave the unpacking for now, if you like and sort everything later ... but you can put your bag in the main bedroom out of the way. Through that door – the first one ... bit of a squeeze. I thought you might like to have that room and I'll have the smaller one – not that either's very – '

'Bee – eea!' The sound was a long, high, animal-like scream of horror.

'Rose! For Heaven's sake – what on earth have you done?' Bea straightened up and went to peer over the sturdy form in the narrow doorway. And there was just room over Rose's shoulder for her to see it.

On *her* bed. All that came into her mind for a split second was that someone had removed her patchwork quilt, the one she'd made during long winter evenings when she was between boy friends. It had been bundled up along with the duvet, in a corner near the window. Then she grasped reality – the reason for the quilt being on the floor was the man on the bed. He was stretched out quite tidily, lying on his back. There was no doubt at all that he was dead.

*

'Better drink this – sorry I haven't any brandy.'

'Oh, I don't think … I hardly ever touch whisky, you know.'

'Come on, Rose, there's a love – this is no time for being choosy. Anyway, it'd make me feel most uncomfortable drinking on my own in the middle of the afternoon.'

'Thanks Bea. Of course you got a terrible shock too. I didn't realise … I wasn't thinking straight.'

'Let's just sit here a minute until the shaking stops.' Bea cradled her glass of single malt, thinking irrelevantly that this was not the kind of occasion they had had in mind when she and Philip had included it among essential groceries when stocking up the 'van. Her eyes slid towards the bedroom door and she hoped they would not have to open it again. Yet she felt a horrid fascination and a niggling feeling of misgiving. After all, she might perhaps have recognised the man if she had taken a proper look. As it was, she had paused for only the briefest of glances before grabbing the near-fainting Rose and firmly shutting the door.

'Rose, before we phone the police – '

'What!'

'The police, Rose,' repeated Bea patiently. (Rose *must* be in shock, if she hadn't even got that worked out yet.) She fished in her handbag for her mobile, and began to scroll through her contacts for the number of the local police, which she knew was listed there. Then she remembered that there was usually a problem getting a signal in this fold in the hills.

'I'm wondering if it might be better to drive into Blaeborough. We'd have to drive nearly to the village anyway, to get in range, and it wouldn't be much more trouble to turn the opposite way and go straight to the police station in the town. I think I'd prefer to explain in person. What do you think?'

'Bea, I don't want to get involved with the police. Please don't drag me into it. You go if you must, but leave me out of it.'

Bea stood up, finishing the whisky off in one gulp. She eyed Rose chillingly enough to freeze her to the spot, had she not remained bent over her glass, refusing to look up.

'That is charming! Wonderfully supportive. Anyway, you *are* involved, from the point of view of the police.' Bea picked up her car keys from the table where she had thrown them on arrival. 'And while I'm enjoying myself in the arms of the law, what had you in mind for yourself? Were you going to walk all the way home, or did you intend to stay here and prepare us a nice little supper? We could always keep the bedroom door shut while we're eating.'

'Oh Hell! Bea, I'm sorry. You don't know – you don't understand. I just can't go through all the questions and – and everything.' Rose stood up and put her glass on the table, then turned to face Bea. 'If I went home now – you could give me a lift to Blaeborough and I'd manage from there somehow.'

'Well, it's very good of you not to want me to run you home to Darlington while I'm about it. But the police would want to know what I'd been up to, wouldn't they?' Bea put her mobile back in her bag and, picking up her fleece, stood quite still in an attitude of silent challenge.

Rose stared at her and took a deep breath. 'Of course I'm coming with you,' she said in a voice more like her normal one. 'Please try and forget what I said. I realise now that – well, it's the shock I suppose. I'd never normally just walk out on anyone.'

'I know that. It's most unlike you. Shock does funny things to people, but it's just as bad for me, you know. Well worse really, since it's my caravan and my bed!'

'But not your – I mean, if you thought it might – '

'Not my what, Rose?' Bea stopped in the act of pulling on her anorak, to interrupt sharply, while she gazed searchingly at her friend.

'Oh, I was going to say, it's not really your responsibility.' Rose picked up her jacket and handbag. 'Once the police come I mean, and take – and take it away, then you can forget about it.'

Bea made no reply, but waited while Rose put on her jacket. She felt like hitting out again at this further example of detachment from the reality of the situation but, having no strength left for argument, she said quite mildly: 'Ready then? We'd better be off.'

'OK. Well, it's twenty-five past three now. I suppose we arrived about ten past or quarter past – would you say?'

Surprised at this sudden change in favour of practicality, Bea agreed that that was probably about it. Perhaps, she thought as she locked the caravan door carefully and led the way to the car, that *was* the way shock affected some people. You couldn't guess at a person's reaction – even with someone you'd known half your life. They were of much the same age, but Rose in some ways, was the older in experience and had lived abroad for a while.

Apart from holidays and a couple of assignments to the States, Bea had never migrated from her native Darlington any further than Leeds … and then Rose had been married – though that had hardly been a stabilising influence. With typical forthrightness, Bea had warned Rose against rushing into the relationship without getting to know Guy better and apparently the marriage had only lasted a very few months, though Bea had never found out exactly why. When it didn't work out, Rose had reverted to her former name, though keeping the courtesy title of "Mrs." and had picked up her life where she had left off.

Although not very much surprised by the break-up, Bea had been shocked when she realised how brief the marriage had been. But she had come to accept, too late, that she had had no right to interfere. By then communication between them had dwindled to a card at Christmas and last birthday. Relations only began to thaw out as late as January, when Bea had held out a tentative olive branch in the shape of a few days' holiday together. Bea had never actually met Guy – couldn't even recall hearing Rose's married name (and now wasn't the time to ask). She felt that the rift was largely her own fault and she knew that their friendship now needed lots of TLC to survive.

As she started up the car, the shakiness returned, together with a feeling of total unreality. She was glad they were going to see the police rather than telephone, as somehow she was sure she would feel reassured by speaking to someone face to face. Bea drove on autopilot down the farm track, taking the left turn when they reached the road, instead of turning right towards the village. In contrast to the winding lanes round about, this road took them over a long ridge – straight, level and rather boring. But Bea had no recollection afterwards of their journey – all she remembered was arriving in the High Street of the small town.

The normality of the scene came as a surprise. On the right, just after the Cottage Hospital, was the primary school, built in the early 1900's, that she had always found so charming, with its painted frieze of girls in pinafores and boys in breeches. Today, small children were being shepherded home by nodding, smiling parents. The older pupils had not yet emerged from the "Comp." that used to be Blaeborough High School. Any minute now they would be slouching along in small groups, ties removed, satchels half-fastened – even shoelaces undone – an expression of mild rebellion.

The Police Station was on the left between the supermarket and the Council Offices. It was rather old, purpose-built, solid and somehow more comforting than its modern counterpart would have been. They left the car in the small area behind the building and pushing open the heavy door, they sat down on a bench whose upholstery had become flat and unyielding, to wait their turn. An elderly woman was listing what seemed to be an endless catalogue of the wrongdoings of her neighbour's cat, while the civilian receptionist tried to explain that cats were deemed not to be controllable – something Bea had long suspected. A wholly inappropriate desire to laugh was quickly forgotten as Bea recalled the scene in the bedroom, and marshalled her thoughts in preparation for their interview.

'Our turn,' whispered Rose and they went together over to the counter. The cat-lady was busy muffling herself up against the keen wind and Bea felt, quite ridiculously, as if she was trying to upstage her with her own dramatic news. In the event, the rather aloof civilian receptionist received the bald statement that a body had turned up at their holiday caravan, without a twitch of her carefully pencilled eyebrows. After giving their names and the location of the caravan, they were asked to wait, but they had scarcely sat down again before they were shown into an office at the back of the reception area.

The sun was pouring in through old-fashioned sash windows, lending the shabby room quite a cheerful air. A youngish sergeant greeted them pleasantly – even soothingly – indicating two plain varnished chairs opposite him at a desk that had seen better days. He spoke with the local soft accent and he nodded to a WPC, who took a seat a little apart, notebook in hand. The whole procedure was very matter-of-fact – a sort of anticlimax, really. Apart from their names and addresses and a very concise description of what they had seen, there was little more to be done at that stage, the sergeant said.

'We shall ask you to come back to Shawhead Farm with us now, and then a very specialised routine will be set in motion, once we've checked that things are just as you say. Later, you'll be interviewed by a senior officer. If you wish to drive back in your own vehicle, we'll follow you.'

*

'I didn't realise there'd be so much waiting about – it's nerve-wracking, isn't it?'

'Awful,' agreed Rose. 'I know the inspector apologised, but it's horrible to be huddled here in the car while they're in there – doing what?'

'There's such a lot of them – and look at all the vehicles!' Bea burrowed around, looking for the chocolate bar and then pulled her share of the car rug back round her. 'That man in the dark suit might be the police doctor or pathologist or something and I think the older, rather distinguished-looking one who's just driven off is probably the superintendent.'

'Well, the sergeant's quite nice and sympathetic I think, but the inspector makes my blood run cold!'

' I suppose he's cultivated that alarming manner to keep the suspects in suspense.'

'But *we're* not suspects!' Rose looked startled and dropped the square of chocolate she had just broken off.

'Well, he did tell us the man had injured the back of his head – probably police-speak for someone clobbered him. We were lucky there was nothing to see… but as you say, there's no reason why we would be suspects.' Better not make Rose any more nervy than she appears to be already, thought Bea. She said, by way of a diversion: 'I think the ones in the overalls are the SOCO, as on TV.'

Rose had been scrabbling awkwardly on the floor. 'Oh there it is. Thank goodness. Chocolate is such terrible stuff when it gets on to your clothes. Yes – SOCO – it would all be rather fascinating, if it weren't so worrying. They look a bit like the lab assistants at work.'

'Oh, of course – I'd forgotten you're a boffin. Bet you wish you'd never taken that second week off work!'

'It's not quite what I'd planned. And it's getting a bit chilly, sitting in the car like this.'

'That inspector – Inspector Dove (I think there's a touch of black humour about that name, don't you?) – he told me that he's in charge "for the present", whatever that's meant to imply. But I think he was genuinely sorry about sticking us in the car.' Bea broke the last bit of the chocolate and shared it with Rose. 'You can see his problem, though. They can hardly have us in the 'van and his own car's not much bigger, so there's nowhere to put us.'

'Look Bea, he's coming over now.'

*

As the green Astra sped down the hill and turned away at the bottom, to follow the main road that would eventually take her out of Yorkshire, Barbara took a deep breath. She had slowed down a bit after the scare she'd had at the brow of that hill. People really should know better than to lurch across the road like that without warning – silly place to position a "viewpoint" too.

A fleeting glimpse of the passenger in the front of the Peugeot had rung a bell. She hoped she was mistaken. Just what I need now, she thought. Someone who knows me, who might go around saying "and we nearly ran into Barbara – literally".

Most of the last twenty-four hours had been traumatic, but she wondered if she might have tackled the situation better. Thinking over her actions, she felt she had been somewhat cowardly. After all, she had recently completed a course in self-assertiveness and she was confident and strong – though not, she was sure, in an unfeminine way. But what more could she have done? It was useless to brood over what couldn't be changed. She now needed to get back in time, calm down and not draw attention to herself. Then await events, hoping for the best …

CHAPTER 2

'We'll have a bit more room in here, Miss Roebuck.' Inspector Dove apologised again, explaining that a suitable interview vehicle had not materialised. Instead, a large, thankfully warm police car had driven up, just as other transport of various sorts had departed. As the women moved out of Bea's car, two constables began to carry out what the sergeant called "a bit of a checkover" – though he explained that a full forensic search might later be necessary.

They climbed into the roomy back of the vehicle, feeling grateful for the comparative luxury, and Inspector Dove closed the rear door. He then sat in the driving seat, looking rather uncomfortable, with his right elbow over the steering wheel, as he twisted round towards them. 'Sergeant Bamford here will take notes. He already has your addresses and some information on how you spent the last twenty-four hours. I just need to know a few more things tonight and then I, or my superior would like to see you, together and individually, in the morning.'

'You are Miss Beatrix Roebuck and this is Mrs. Caroline Rose Downey? You had driven up from Leeds together this afternoon? And the caravan belongs to you, Miss Roebuck? How long have you had it?'

Bea tried not to wince, as she frequently found herself doing when her first name was revealed in full. Why did mothers have to inflict the name of their heroes or heroines on their offspring? As she listened to Dove half-heartedly, random thoughts flicked through her mind. How would Rose answer if asked for details of her marital status … presumably, there had not been sufficient time for a divorce? Rose had given her address in Darlington without mentioning that it was her stepfather's home and that Downey was her maiden name. Bea supposed that the police would assume it was her husband's surname. Would Rose make all this clear? And did it matter? She became aware that Dove was waiting for her answer.

'About six or seven years,' she said. 'But I've been coming up here with my family ever since I was a small child. We had a big family 'van on this plot … Mr. and Mrs. Dyson , the owners, live in the village. The farmhouse is a holiday let now, you see.'

'And how often do you come here from – Leeds, isn't it?'

'We have quite a few weekends here in the summer, but only when the weather's really good.'

'I see. And you were here last?'

'At the beginning of September.'

'Would the local people expect you to be here?'

'No, Inspector – I think it's the first time it's happened. Even in summer, when I come for the weekend, I never arrive until Saturday. Friday is our busiest day at work and so I often arrange to stay on Saturday and Sunday nights instead. And in a any case, it would be common knowledge that the 'van is normally shut up until June or even July.'

There was a pause, during which the Inspector remained in his uncomfortable-looking position and just stared at them.

'Now tell me,' he said at last, 'when you discovered the body, why did you drive to the police station – I presume you've got mobile phones?'

'Yes we both have of course,' answered Bea. 'But it's difficult to get a signal just here, so we'd have had to take the car almost to the village – it just seemed easier to come along in person. If there'd been anybody at the farmhouse I think we'd have gone there for moral support. As it was, I felt I wanted to talk to someone face to face – and I think Rose was too upset to decide on any course of action.'

'That's right – and I still am,' agreed Rose. 'I'm afraid I just followed Bea's lead. But I think what we wanted most was to get away from the 'van.'

Bea couldn't imagine how all this could be of use to the enquiry. She had assumed when watching mystery drama that such irrelevancies were thrown in to worry and unsettle the witnesses. She was sure that in her case, the tactic was unnecessary. She was unsettled enough to keep a dozen inspectors satisfied.

'Did either of you recognise the dead man?' Bea was jolted back to the on-going questions. She shook her head firmly and replied that she didn't.

Rose also shook her head, then looked squarely at Inspector Dove and quietly but decisively answered 'No'. Again Dove stared hard without speaking. It seemed to be a habit of his – no doubt an effective ploy. Bea certainly found it uncomfortable.

Then he said: 'Now, Miss Roebuck, I'm going to have to ask you to check over the contents of your caravan with me. The body will have been removed, of course.' A glimpse through the car window gave evidence that this was now taking place. 'Mrs. Downey – you need not be present unless you wish to. I take it that you just entered the caravan and dropped your travel bag down where we found it and didn't unpack anything?'

Rose assured him that this was so and explained how she had been about to put her bag in the main bedroom, thus making the discovery straight away. She told them she preferred to wait in the car, and Bea walked with Inspector Dove past the young birch trees she and Philip had planted in the little enclosure when first she brought him up here. The sergeant had followed and was now examining the exterior of the caravan and its immediate surroundings, now cordoned off with police tape which the Inspector lifted to allow her through. The rest of the team, including the two constables, appeared to have dispersed, for the moment at any rate. She found going into the caravan less traumatic than she might have expected, with everything looking normal, apart from the stripped bed.

It didn't take long to check everything in the two bedrooms, living space and tiny bathroom. Nothing appeared to be missing and nothing was there that shouldn't be there. An earring for which she had long given up hunting and a rather tatty blue comb had come to light. There was no sign of disruption. The police search would have been a thorough one of course, but the caravan was all but empty of personal belongings, so that there wasn't much to disrupt. She turned off the electric heater in the living area and checked that the louvre window in the bathroom was still open and that all the overhead "skylights" were shut.

The Inspector indicated that they were now free to remove their bags, which presumably had also been searched, so she beckoned Rose to come over and they stowed them in the boot of the Peugeot. Bea closed down the lid and found the Inspector waiting nearby.

'There's really only one more thing I need trouble you about at this time,' he said, still with that searching gaze that Bea found so unsettling. 'We can't find any sign of forced entry. Do you keep a spare key hidden?'

With a gasp, Bea realised that this elementary factor had not occurred to her. 'Yes – yes I do,' she stammered. 'I'd forgotten all about it – I hadn't even considered how – how he got in.'

'We'd better check it then.' The Sergeant joined them again, but Rose went back to sit in the Peugeot. Bea pointed out the hiding place and they found the key still in its little box. Sergeant Bamford, who appeared to have a faculty for picking things up without touching them, popped the box into an envelope.

*

The welcoming room and the well-equipped bathroom at The Lamb restored both of them to a state where they were able to think a little more rationally. The police were not ready to hand over the caravan to them yet – and Rose and Bea had felt quite relieved at the suggestion of booking rooms in the village. The sergeant had telephoned the only places offering accommodation locally. Mrs. Dodds at "Blae House" was busy with the overflow from a local family celebration and both her two rooms were booked, but they'd had a cancellation of one twin room at The Lamb. The small hotel at the top end of Little Blaeford was comfortable and unpretentious and it had a reputation for good food. Had they been planning a holiday in an old English pub, they would quite probably have chosen this one.

On discovering the easy availability of the emergency key to anyone with a little prior knowledge, Inspector Dove had continued his questioning in the empty snug over a much-needed tray of coffee and biscuits. Bea had been surprised to find it was still only a quarter to seven, as it felt like many hours since they reported their discovery. But the Inspector promised that they would soon be left in peace until morning. Notes had been made of the addresses of all possible "contacts" and he had wanted to know which of them might be aware of the key's existence and whereabouts.

Bea's family knew, for a start. Philip Lander had his own key – Bea suggested that he was best described as her ex-fiancé. (Do people have fiancés nowadays? she wondered. Well, they do if they're involved with Philip! She was quite aware that some people thought Philip a bit stiff and starchy – look at the way no-one had ever called him "Phil".) Then, as well as her parents there was her brother Sam who might know, but was unlikely to take an interest. He had been very scornful about the caravan in recent years and had no nostalgia for past family holidays. Bea didn't think he would boast to his friends about the availability of the caravan and there was certainly no reason why her parents or Philip should talk about the emergency key. Mr. and Mrs. Dyson, who owned the land, also held a key. She explained that they were away on holiday.

Inspector Dove's only reply had been a nod. He had a way of looking dissatisfied with every answer, Bea thought. He had asked Rose whether she knew that a key was kept on the site.

'Well, yes.' Rose had glanced at Bea before answering. 'It sort of came up once in a conversation about being locked out – just casually chatting, you know – and Bea mentioned it then, because they once *did* lock themselves out and that's why they began to keep a spare. Bea said caravans are particularly difficult to get into if you've mislaid the key.' She had continued, in answer to a further question from Dove: 'Oh, it was ages ago. I haven't seen much of Bea for quite a while – I mean, we've both been busy ...'

'Talk to anyone else about it?'

'No, I don't think so – why would I? But things crop up in conversation ... if someone's saying how they wouldn't keep a key under a mat or a flower pot, you might start talking about what would be the best place to hide a key ... but I don't remember anything like that.'

Finally she had confirmed that this was her first visit to the caravan and, in answer to Dove's question about her marital status, she winced as she told him she and her husband, Guy, were separated and that she had no idea of his whereabouts. Then, after a request to meet them in the morning, which was really not a request at all but an order, the Inspector had finally left them.

They arranged to have dinner and then established themselves in their room, which was comfortable and attractively, though simply furnished. The hot showers made them both feel a little more cheerful and they searched their luggage for something decent to wear on this unexpected occasion. As Bea was shaking out a blouse and finding a hanger, her mobile rang. She studied the display for a moment and then turned the mobile off altogether.

Rose glanced across without remarking on the call. 'It's officially murder, then,' she said quite cheerfully, choosing a jade blouse to wear with linen trousers in the palest possible shade of blue-green and examining an exquisite pair of jade earrings to see if they went well with the blouse. Bea reflected that Rose, always resilient, usually recovered from any shock far quicker than she. She gave herself a mental shake and sorted out her favourite black skirt – a beautifully tailored silk and wool, cut on the bias that she's had forever – and a fairly new camel-and-black top. She added, with a twinge of pain, a pair of jet earrings that had been one of Philip's many presents to her. She knew that both of them would probably be very overdressed in the clothes they'd packed for their one "posh night out", but their favourite clothes would help to boost their morale.

'I don't think Dove's actually *said* murder – but with all this "procedure", it can hardly be anything else. It sounds somehow far-fetched, doesn't it?' But Bea had had no doubt of what it was from the beginning. 'Thank goodness there was nothing horrible to see! But really you know, there could be no other explanation – the chance of a perfect stranger getting in and climbing into my bed just for the purpose of breathing his last is too unlikely, isn't it?'

'And considerately removing the quilt!' agreed Rose. 'And putting lots of old newspapers on the mattress to keep it clean – did you notice?' No, Bea hadn't looked long or hard enough to see them. 'But on the other hand why go to the bother of getting the key and bringing the corpse there. Or someone who was about to become a corpse.' She added with a shudder.

'Yes, well – I don't quite see it that way, and I have a feeling the Inspector doesn't either … I think this was someone's bright idea that went wrong. If as you say, the mattress was covered, it was because they were intending moving the body, if we hadn't – ' Bea's voice trembled and faded as she realised that she would never have known about the body if all had gone according to plan. She shrugged impatiently and gave her thick hair a final vigorous brushing, as if determined to tame it. 'Look, I'm not particularly hungry, but I *am* desperate for a drink. Let's go and see what we can find. I'd no idea the Lamb was so promising! I'd thought of suggesting a meal here one evening, as well as my favourite restaurant the other side of Blaeborough … anyway, we might as well make the most of it.'

They chose a spot in a quiet corner of the bar, which was as little modernised as possible and which gleamed with polished woodwork, copper and brass. They began to relax a little as they glanced at the menu, while they sipped stiffish drinks and tried for the moment to forget the reason that had brought them there.

'Aren't you Bea Roebuck?' said a voice nearby, as a rather untidy-looking man was just putting a pint of beer down on the next table. He was of average height and slim build, with bushy, fairish hair and he wore an ancient-looking pair of cords and a navy blue guernsey. Bea thought he looked to be somewhere in the early thirties.

Startled by the normal world encroaching on their unreal – surreal? – situation, Bea responded hesitatingly. 'Yes, I'm Bea, but I'm sorry – I can't place you…'

'No, that's all right – you won't. But I think I saw you last year – you arrived at the farm as I was leaving. I'm a relative of the Dysons – I've just arrived here for a week or so. That's your caravan at the farm, isn't it? I'll be up there later on – my name's Ralph Norman.'

'Oh yes, I've heard your name mentioned.' Bea felt herself unequal to normal social behaviour, as if she had temporarily forgotten the rules. She tried to pull herself together. 'This is Rose Downey. She's er … she's come up to stay for a week in the 'van with me, but – '

'Hello Rose.' Ralph smiled as he turned towards her and continued to hold eye contact. He had an easy warm manner and an expressive, mobile face. 'Let's hope it'll be good hill-walking weather then,' he went on. 'That's what you've come for, I suppose?'

'Well, we *did*,' replied Rose. She looked across uncertainly at Bea, who sighed, and then seemed to make up her mind.

'We'll have to forget the holiday, I'm afraid. You might as well know now – I expect everyone for miles will have heard by morning – '

Rose interrupted her. 'We had the most awful shock when we arrived, Ralph … we found a body. In Bea's caravan. Dead!'

'We don't know how he died, but the police seem sure it's murder,' went on Bea. 'And we've had to answer a lot of questions, though of course we don't know a thing about it.' She felt that she was chattering in a most uncharacteristic way, but this was probably due to release of tension.

Ralph, after listening carefully to all this, had apparently recovered from his astonishment enough to ask: 'Who was the man – do they know? Do *you* know?'

Again Rose looked at Bea, who took a sip of her drink and said: 'No to both questions – that's what's so strange. Well, of course, the whole thing is bizarre – completely crazy. I've still got a sense of unreality and we don't know what's going to happen next.'

'What'll happen tomorrow morning is that Inspector Dove – whose name has got to be a particularly spiteful joke – will come here and start the questions all over again.' Rose had finished her drink and was turning her empty glass nervously around in her fingers.

'We've told them all we know,' added Bea.

'So at the moment – you're staying here?'

'Yes … well, we could hardly stay in the 'van – we couldn't get away quick enough. The police told us they'd probably finish their preliminary work late tonight and of course the body's been removed. Then they'll seal off the 'van until they've completely done with it.'

The waitress – young and enthusiastic – came over to them, asking if they were ready to order. This caused some hasty decision-making. They realised that they had been supposedly looking at the menu for a long time. Ralph told them he wouldn't be eating there, as he was on his way to visit an aunt who lived in the village.

'I'll get fed there as well,' he grinned, as he finished off his pint. 'Overfed, probably, if it follows the usual pattern!' He asked them if they would meet him in the bar afterwards for a nightcap and they agreed, realising that they probably wouldn't sleep anyway, if they went up earlier.

＊

They enjoyed their meal more than they felt they had any right to. They agreed, since this was apparently the only "holiday" they were going to have, to indulge themselves. The Lamb was well-known for game and for all the local produce. Rose and Bea decided not to look at the prices at all. Afterwards, they settled themselves in the same corner as before with a pot of The Lamb's excellent coffee.

'You've been very quiet, Rose.' Bea reached for one of the after-dinner chocolates beside the coffee pot. 'If you're terribly tired we can easily make excuses to Ralph and slip away.'

'No, I'm all right. A bit shattered of course – well, it's not quite that – it's a feeling I can't really describe, because I've never experienced it before.' Rose looked thoughtful as she spooned some sugar into her coffee. 'I'm sure sleep would be impossible. And I keep thinking … you know what you were saying just before we came down from the bedroom?'

'I think I said the Lamb seemed pretty good and we'd struck lucky – seems I was right.'

'No, seriously, Bea. You said something about how the body came to be there and I've been trying to make sense of what you said. And I can't … I mean to say, either the … killer brought someone here who was already dead (and why do that?), or they (he or she) persuaded him to come up here – an even bigger why – in order to kill him.'

'Ah, but you see, Captain Hastings, there is a possible alternative …'

'Hello again! Rose – Bea. How was your meal?'

'Well, we actually enjoyed it. We never thought we would.' They were persuaded to have cognac with their coffee and turned the conversation away from their own predicament by asking about Ralph's connection with the Dysons at Shawhead Farm. He told them that he was a distant cousin and that he came regularly for short holidays.

'It's surprising that we haven't met before, Bea – although I think your parents and mine know each other.' Ralph looked very relaxed as he sipped his brandy and the two women felt their own tension ease a little. 'But I don't often come in the summer because the farmhouse is usually booked up, so that probably explains it.' He told them that he worked in Manchester and found it fairly handy to drive over for a week's walking in the hills.

'Yes, of course I realise who you are now. I think we're both suffering from shock – it's surprising how it makes you unable to take things in properly.'

Ralph looked at them both, speculatively. 'Look here – one of the reasons I wanted to come back tonight, was to ask you what your plans are ... no that's silly, you probably haven't made any plans yet. But what are the police likely to want you to do – stay on here?'

'We haven't thought any further than tomorrow morning's interrogation. What do you think, Rose?'

'Well, I don't think they can actually detain us, can they? If we want to drive back to Leeds, I presume we could, so long as they know where we are.' Rose reached over for Bea's coffee cup and refilled it along with her own. 'Originally we were going to spend the week at Bea's flat in Leeds and make day-trips from there, but this spell of good weather changed our minds. I expect we can revert to that arrangement?' She looked for guidance at Bea.

'Mmm, I think that's the only thing to do,' Bea agreed. 'Although perhaps we may find it better to stay at least another night here.' She looked thoughtfully at her cup as she took it back from Rose. 'There's the caravan to consider. I know it's not as if it had been vandalised, or covered in bloodstains, but somehow I don't think I can just lock it up once the police finish with it and then turn up in a few weeks' time as if nothing had happened. I really don't know...'

'I've got a suggestion to make.' There was something purposeful about the way Ralph put his glass down in the centre of the table. 'There's tons of room at the farm as you know and I think you should move in there for a day or two – it would make sense all round and I'm sure you could do with a bit of moral support.'

As Rose gave her a quick glance, Bea had the impression that this idea would be most welcome – and why not, if it meant they wouldn't be abandoning the caravan (she wasn't sure why that mattered) and they would be on the spot if the police needed to see them.

'Well,' she replied slowly. 'It's a very good idea – but what about the Dysons? How would they feel if you invited two other people to stay?'

'Well, they know you well enough don't they? And if they're told the reason, I'm sure it's what they would suggest too.' Ralph picked his glass up again and cradled it as he looked expectantly across at them. 'Anyway, I had a word with my Aunt just now and she offered to phone them – she's related to them by marriage. She seemed to want to take over – so, if you agree, I'll ask her to call them.'

'I'd like to do that, Bea,' said Rose. 'That is, if you would, of course.'

'Well, yes it's very good of you to offer, Ralph. It would be a bit of an invasion, though – it's not as though you really knew us. Still,' she said, looking over at Rose, who looked serene and unconcerned, 'we might be able to make ourselves useful round the house! That's if the police leave us any spare time...'

'I can't imagine they'll be bothering you much more after the official interview tomorrow. But there'll be the inquest, I suppose ... what time do they want to see you tomorrow?'

Rose shrugged. 'We don't know. The Inspector just told us to be available in the morning as soon as we've had breakfast. I just don't understand what more they expect us to tell them ... oh, why on earth did anyone have to choose Bea's 'van to die in?'

'Doesn't sound as if he had a lot of choice, from what you've told me.' Ralph had a wry smile that looked as if it might often be a feature of his rather mobile face. 'Anyway,' he went on, 'I'm sure that what seems to you like a third degree is nothing more sinister than the "routine" we're always hearing about – they probably follow a fixed procedure that they can't alter.'

'I suppose so,' Rose answered. 'In a way I guess it's a bit like the processes in a laboratory – you run the information through every possible test, even if you have a good idea of what is or isn't really important.' She looked across at Ralph who had raised an enquiring eyebrow. 'It's my job – I work for a firm that does testing for industrial techniques, among other things.'

'That's extraordinary!' Ralph grinned at her. 'That's more-or-less my job too.' He went on to ask Rose about the name of her firm, after which the conversation became somewhat hi-jacked by shop-talk.

A short spell of trying to find the details of laboratory life fascinating was quite enough for Bea, who soon gave up the struggle.

'Look,' she said, as soon as she could find a suitable pause. 'I've got some phone calls to make – they were out at home when I tried before. So I'll do that and then I'll probably be ready for bed, if you'll excuse me.'

'Sorry Bea – it must be terribly boring listening to us talking test-tubes. I'll be right behind you anyway.'

'Yes – sorry,' echoed Ralph. 'Just come over to the farm whenever you're free tomorrow. I'll be there all day. I'm trying to put in some time in the garden … it's always a problem with a holiday house.' Ralph walked over towards the door with Bea. 'Goodnight then – hope you manage to sleep.'

Bea hoped that Rose didn't mind being left to entertain Ralph on her own. But on recalling the exchange of glances she had observed between the other two, she decided that it had been the right decision and unlikely to cause offence. She was very aware that the renewed friendship between her and Rose, which she valued, was still at a vulnerable stage. When she had gone to the States last summer on an extended work assignment, she had left behind a good deal of ill-feeling, having just been told of the lightning courtship and imminent marriage of Rose and Guy. Bea, instinctively cautious, was not one to be carried away by romantic idealism, but she soon knew she had been too outspoken. It was the only serious disagreement in their long friendship.

Bea returned from America to discover that Rose had already been separated, after only four months, reverting to her maiden name. Something cataclysmic must have happened, surely? It was never referred to, but the "I told you so" factor was never far away. Up to the time of the marriage, Rose had appeared to believe that Bea's doubts had come from an unreasoned prejudice: after all, Bea knew less than nothing about Guy. Or perhaps Rose thought that a touch of envy was involved. Certainly it was possible that Philip appeared stodgy to Rose – she might not appreciate those solid and dependable qualities which Bea was missing so much since she and Philip broke up. What a romantic Rose was – so easily led astray by charm! Why, even tonight Bea had caught several exchanged glances … yes, she thought, her absence just then had probably been well received.

When she had pleaded tiredness, it was no less than the truth – even the explaining she was now going to do seemed a tremendous effort. She decided to use the public phone in the foyer: she would have more privacy on her mobile in the bedroom, but her father was slightly deaf and found mobiles more difficult. Her mother had no problem hearing, but Bea hoped to be able to tell the story to her father – it would be done in half the time and there would be no unnecessary demands for explanations which she was in no position to supply.

She gave herself a mental shake and dialled the number – fingers crossed that her mother would be out. She then felt guilty for hoping so. Her brother Sam picked the phone up and in a rare moment of insight, recognised something in her manner which made him ask no questions, and he called Dr. Roebuck to the phone.

Ever since they had had that unfortunate quarrel, Philip had been wondering how, and how soon, he could make contact again. Once Bea convinced herself that she had right on her side, (to be fair, she did not do this hastily) she could be terribly stubborn. He must be careful and go about it in the right way. The timing was important – the method too.

On that Friday evening, urgently needing news of her, he had spoken to Bea's father on the phone. He told Dr. Roebuck that Bea did not appear to be in the flat in Leeds and he had not so far succeeded in contacting her on her mobile phone. However, her parents had no details of her whereabouts; it was assumed that she and Rose would be making various excursions over the weekend. Philip confessed that there had been quite a serious row. The Roebucks were not the sort of parents to take sides - or rather, Bea's mother might well be biased in *his* favour, if anything. He asked Dr. Roebuck to pass on a message, should Bea get in touch and then rang off. He gazed blankly into space for a moment, perplexed and uncertain. It was so frustrating to stand helplessly by, just waiting for a chance to talk to her. But he would have to be patient. All could be lost by rushing into action at this stage.

*

Hearing her father's voice, sounding as every-day sensible as ever, Bea suddenly felt strangely weak and tears sprang to her eyes. She supposed it was some kind of delayed shock. Quickly, she explained their change of plan and outlined the events of the past few hours. Her father was wonderfully reassuring, offering to come down from Darlington in case he could help. But Bea discouraged this, knowing how difficult it was for him as a busy GP, to set off at a moment's notice. She explained that they were going to take up Ralph's offer.

Dr. Roebuck said he had a vague memory of Ralph's family, which included several high-spirited boys. He agreed that there was no real need for him to make the journey for the time being, as long as Bea kept him up-to-date with events. He asked her to text him the phone number of the farm, as the only number he had was the Dysons' new home in the village. That would be easier for Bea, as it was a pay phone at her end. Apart from the inquest, he thought the police would require little more from them. They could discuss at a later date what to do about the caravan.

'Philip rang, by the way,' added her father. 'Not long ago. He asked me to say that he is thinking very hard about all the things you said to him. I think he'd like you to get in touch – he sounded … anxious.' Bea thanked him and rang off after sending love to the rest of the family and promising to give Rose their greetings. As she made her way upstairs, she fingered the mobile phone in the side pocket of her bag, but decided that she was not yet ready to talk to Philip. Let him wait and wonder for a day or two – he took things far too much for granted.

She reached the door of their room and was fishing for the key when Rose came along the corridor.

'Did you make your phone calls?' she asked, as they both flopped down, Rose in the armchair and Bea on the bed on the left, kicking off her shoes.

'I rang my father. It was really good to talk to him. I actually went all weepy on him! But in the end I decided not to ring Philip.'

'Just as well, then – you might have gone all weepy over *him,* and I don't think that's what you want at the moment is it?'

'Hell, no! I don't know what I *do* want. Since we had that row, I've just been avoiding facing up to reality; he's not going to change his priorities – and neither am I.'

'You're both quite strong-willed, that's the trouble.'

'Perhaps so. But he just expects me to be Mrs. Pushover when it comes to where we want to live. My job is as important to me as his is to him, and yet he expects – no, demands that I just tamely forget about my own career and go wherever his profession takes him.'

'Maybe if you let him think it over for a bit, as you are doing at the moment, he'll come round.'

'I'm not at all sure that he will – not in the long term, I mean. I've been kidding myself long enough, Rose. He'll be exactly the same as he's always been – perfectly reasonable until we get back on an even keel and then – wham! He'll start all over again trying to brainwash me.' Bea got up and slipped off her skirt and top, wrapping herself in a luxurious silk robe in an unusual shade of snuffy brown. 'He's been terribly preoccupied lately as well,' she went on. 'I've felt that his mind has only been partly on our problems – it's something to do with his work, I think.' Bea sighed and, sitting down in front of the mirror, began to brush her hair. 'I've got to recognise it, Rose – there's probably no way forward for me with Philip.'

Rose got up and started to rummage through her luggage. 'I'm really sorry,' she said. 'It might be better to find out now, though – before it's become much more difficult to disentangle. I've learned that the hard way.'

'Yes of course.' Bea was feeling her way carefully, since this was Rose's first reference to her unfortunate romantic experience. 'Anyway, this "happening" has taken my mind off my problems a bit … by the way, are you going to ring your parents – they'll get a shock if they see it in the paper?'

'I'll do it tomorrow. They're in Canada – didn't I tell you? They've been away nearly a month now visiting Mum's sister, so I should imagine it's unlikely that they'd hear anything about this. I think they're due back towards the end of next week.'

Bea heaved her travel bag from the bottom of the wardrobe to check that she had all she needed for the night. 'What a pain it is to have carted all this clobber up here when we don't need much more than a toothbrush.'

'If we'd known someone was going to leave a corpse to greet us, we'd have packed overnight emergency bags.'

'Well, I wish we had – it drives me bananas, having this great big holdall …trouble is, in the car, it's just so easy to bring stuff for any eventuality instead of working out what I might need.' She burrowed a little more energetically and then, with a yell of triumph she shook out some silk pyjamas. 'Wouldn't you guess? Right at the bottom! The skirt and my wrap were on top, but I was beginning to think I hadn't packed these.' She dug out the novel she was currently reading and the torn-out page of a newspaper with sudokus and a crossword. 'So, you got to know a bit about Ralph and his job, then?'

'Yes, it was interesting. He does quite similar work to me – linked to industrial processes. I'd like to talk about it with him when I'm not so tired.' Rose went to the dressing table and spread out her belongings on one side of it. 'He says he'll expect us when he sees us tomorrow. I told him we'd be bringing the food that we'd brought along for the caravan and he's going to make a casserole, so we can eat whenever it's convenient. It sounds as though he likes to cook.'

'Great! As long nobody wants me to do the cooking – perhaps I can make my contribution in the garden instead.'

'Sounds as if there's plenty of scope for that.' Rose got up wearily and took her nightdress – a lovely soft, pale sea-island cotton – and a matching wrap, from her bed. 'I'm dead tired, but I don't know whether I'll be able to sleep – shall I have first go in the bathroom?'

'Mmm, fine. I'll just catch the end of the news till you've finished in there, and then I'll get ready for bed. I'm sorry Rose – this wasn't quite the way I'd planned the first day of our holiday.

CHAPTER 3

The breakfast room at The Lamb was a small and pleasant off-shoot of the main dining area, with well-polished old oak and comfortable, spacious seating. This morning it was filled with spring sunshine. The wind had dropped and it looked like a perfect day for walking the hills or even a picnic by the river.

Having settled the bill, Rose and Bea were enjoying their leisurely breakfast. They were very nearly lulled into forgetting that they were on stand-by for the arrival of Inspector Dove, or perhaps "the Super" – or might it be a chief inspector, if that rank still existed? They both owed their slight knowledge of such things to television, so they felt rather uncertain of what to expect in real life. However, as they were leaving the room they caught sight of the Inspector who was seated in the entrance hall, clearly aware that they had been at breakfast, but unwilling to join them. Oh well, at least they'd had their meal in peace.

'Better the devil you know ...' Rose murmured under her breath and Bea hoped that was true. They greeted the Inspector and explained that they had been about to pack their bags.

'They'll be wanting our room, I expect,' added Bea.

'Good morning, Miss Roebuck, Mrs. Downey. You're moving out, then?'

'We've been offered accommodation at the farmhouse – Mr. and Mrs. Dyson's holiday let, that is.' Bea explained how this had come about and assured Dove that they would be around for a few days. He nodded and ushered them into a small room that was normally used by the staff as a servery. As they seated themselves around an ancient and battle-scarred oak table, the Inspector opened his briefcase. Bea wondered if Rose also had butterflies in the tummy – then wondered why she should be so nervous. After all, there was no reason to be apprehensive.

'What I suggest,' began the Inspector, 'is that we get a few essentials out of the way immediately – come in!' He broke off as, with the briefest of knocks, the sergeant from yesterday joined them and sat down unobtrusively near the window. 'I shall then have some telephoning to do,' Dove went on. 'That will give you a chance to pack up here. I presume that will not take more than fifteen or twenty minutes?'

Although this was said with the utmost courtesy and in comparatively mild tones, it was quite clear that there wasn't much scope for disagreement. Resisting the urge to ask what was to happen at the end of the fifteen minutes, they nodded and Inspector Dove went on:

'First I have to tell you that we are now treating this as a murder investigation.' This came as no surprise to the two women, but there is always a mild shock when something unpleasant is put into words, officially.

'This interview is informal,' went on the Inspector. 'But Sergeant Bamford is going to take notes, just so that I have something to refer to. There are a few things we touched on yesterday, that I'd like to explore further. Mrs. Downey – I understood from what you told me that you haven't stayed at the caravan before?' As Rose agreed, he went on: 'So this is your first actual visit, but were you familiar with the general location?'

'No.' Rose's voice gave a clear impression of weariness at the repetition of this theme. 'That is, I've passed through the area once or twice and I've visited Bea in Leeds a few times – but I live and work in Darlington. We were at school together there – Bea comes from Darlington originally…'

'But it was Leeds you came from yesterday?'

'Yes, that's right. I had been visiting friends in Cambridge… I told Sergeant Bamford this yesterday.' Rose glanced at the Inspector, whose face remained completely impassive. Somewhat daunted, she took a deep breath and continued. 'Anyway, I came up by train to join Bea and we grabbed something from the sandwich bar and then drove straight on up here. Inspector, how is all this relevant?'

'Let me try to explain, Mrs. Downey.' Dove paused as the sound of a vacuum cleaner in the passage outside made it difficult for him to make himself heard. As it faded away, he went on: 'The police come into the situation with absolutely no knowledge except what they can observe. The only way we can hope to get to the truth is to have a complete overview of everything and everyone concerned. A lot of the information we collect has no relevance whatever and it's up to us to make up our minds about the possible importance or otherwise of what we are told.' He looked at them for the first time with the hint of a smile. 'We also want to eliminate as many people as possible, quickly – for their benefit and ours.'

Dove leafed through the papers in front of him. 'So – when was this holiday planned?'

'Well, it was *planned*,' replied Bea, 'in the sense that we had agreed to spend next week together – soon after Christmas. But what happened was that Rose was already on holiday in Cambridge during this last week and then she rang up to ask if she might join me a day or so earlier than originally arranged. And since the weather looked unusually good, we decided to go up to the caravan, after meeting at the station, instead of making our base in Leeds, which was the original plan.'

'I believe you said that normally you don't arrive at your caravan on a Friday?'

'I think it's probably the only time I've ever done so, because Fridays are our busiest day – as I told you. But I called in a favour on this occasion because I've always been there until late on Fridays and sometimes I've covered for other colleagues.'

Rose joined in. 'When I rang Bea on the Thursday night and suggested that we visit the caravan, we decided to come straight up here, while the weather lasted – the forecast was particularly good. She said she'd see what her boss said and asked if I could catch an earlier train if she texted me on Friday morning, as soon as she could clear it at work … and so that's what we did.'

Dove asked for the name of the firm of publishers in Leeds that Bea worked for and wrote down their details. He went on: 'Had you mentioned to anyone at work where you were going – it would be quite a normal thing to do?'

'No, I hadn't. All that had been mentioned during the week at work was that I had some leave coming up on Saturday – as I said, we didn't change our plan until Thursday night. Then it didn't arise during Friday morning. I was in a meeting most of the time and I had a bit of a rush getting away to meet the train. The only person I spoke to about my plans was my immediate superior when I wanted to leave early … not in detail, I just said I had a friend arriving for the weekend. I was quite surprised that it took so little persuasion – but I suppose they felt they owed me,' she added.

'I see. And no neighbour, cleaning lady, milkman – anyone like that – knew your plans?' Bea shook her head and Dove paused a moment, staring over their heads at a photograph of the local hunt, meeting outside the Lamb. Turning to Rose, he said: 'What about you, Mrs. Downey?'

'Well, I told my friends when I arrived in Cambridge that I was going to spend the coming week with a friend, but not the exact time and not the actual place, or anything… well, I couldn't tell them *where*, because it hadn't been planned then. The subject never came up after that.'

'I see – thankyou, Mrs. Downey.' He went on, addressing them both: 'I can tell you that it is highly likely that the death took place during the night before your arrival.' Both women uttered little gasps, even though they realised that this made it neither more nor less distressing. 'From what you have been telling me, it doesn't seem that anyone in your circle of friends and acquaintances would normally expect to find the caravan in use. We had hoped to eliminate quite a few people, but unfortunately we can't rule anyone out for that reason. We don't know the man's identity at the moment. The cause of death has not yet been confirmed, but I am able to tell you that he was hit with some force on the back of the head and then placed as you found him.'

Dove nodded to the Sergeant, who made a brief call on his mobile phone, merely giving his name and murmuring, 'progress?' and 'OK'. He ended the call and told the Inspector that everything would be ready. Dove then dismissed the Sergeant and stood up.

'We need your co-operation in our efforts to identify the body,' the Inspector said as he began to gather up his papers. 'You have told me that yesterday, quite understandably, you took one horrified look at the deceased and then shut the door of the bedroom. And neither of you then went back for a further look?'

He paused and they shook their heads firmly.

'Right. I suggest that you lock your bags in your car when you have finished packing and leave the car in the yard here. Then we would like to take you down to the mortuary for a more careful look – just in case he reminds you of somebody.'

*

'Perhaps it's just "routine",' said Rose, as they hurried along the corridor to their room. 'And the same goes for the way they keep asking the same questions over again.'

'I expect so,' sighed Bea wearily. 'But I do think once is quite enough to look at the body – I was just beginning to feel I could put that experience behind me.' As Rose unlocked the door, they both went in and, grabbing their luggage, hastily began repacking.

'Yes, I know – but if it's got to be done, I just want to get it over with. It was a dreadful shock at first, of course, but then I realised that it couldn't...' once again, Rose's sentence petered out.

Bea bit her lip. This wasn't the time to lose patience with Rose, who after all, had been quite supportive and philosophical since they'd been at The Lamb. 'Yes,' she said helpfully. 'Couldn't what?'

'I – um, I just meant that I realised that it was only a dead body, after all – it couldn't hurt anyone.'

'No, but it's not the sort of thing, however harmless, that one is just going to accept as a little local difficulty at the start of a holiday.'

'It doesn't help it to go with a bang,' replied Rose from the bathroom where she was retrieving her belongings. 'I was really only trying to be positive – because to be honest, I'm probably dreading it even more than you.'

Bea took a final look around, twitching over the duvet on her bed to double check and then zipped up her travel bag. Rose opened and shut some of the drawers, though clearly she hadn't used them and, putting in her vanity case, fastened her bag. 'Come on then,' she said with a smile that was only slightly forced. 'Let's earn some Brownie points by taking even less time than we were allowed.'

There was no sign of the Inspector when they arrived downstairs, so they took their luggage out to the little yard at the back reserved for residents. They were surprised to see a uniformed constable near the back entrance. He was talking to a small group of youngish men and women and it did not look to be a particularly friendly chat.

'How have they got to know so quickly?' wondered Rose, realising at once that these were members of the press.

Swiftly, they locked their bags in the boot of the car and escaped back inside the hotel, to find the inspector waiting for them. He suggested that they leave through the kitchen and down a narrow alley, where a police car was awaiting them with Sergeant Bamford at the wheel. They were whisked thankfully away without, on this occasion at least, being asked to tell a waiting world "what it felt like to have a corpse in my bed".

*

The Cottage Hospital in Blaeborough was on the right, just as they approached the town. A complex modern wing had been added, with a sizeable car park at the front, but it was to a yard with high walls, behind the original stone building that the police car headed. The small mortuary turned out to be less alarming than they had anticipated. Their TV-sourced notions had prepared them to be chilled. The single-storey Victorian building was very different from the modern, super-efficient examples depicted in dramas and, if not exactly cosy, it had a lived-in, everyday sort of atmosphere. Together, they were led into a small shabby room. Bea had assumed that she and Rose would experience the ordeal together, but Sergeant Bamford told Bea that he would take her along first, after he had taken their finger-prints. Doing that now, he explained, would save them a trip to the Station.

During the journey from The Lamb, Bea had noticed that Rose was covering her agitation well. But there was no doubt that she *was* agitated and Bea wondered whether Rose had always been subject to such variations of mood – was it only these very unusual circumstances which had brought this about? Rose appeared to swing from an attitude of almost callous detachment to a state of apprehension that seemed equally inappropriate. After all, they were very much on the fringe of the actual crime – only associated with it by a bizarre coincidence.

'If you're ready, Miss Roebuck …' Sergeant Bamford's comfortably rotund figure rose from the table and he packed away his equipment. There was no sign of Inspector Dove, but a WPC came in to look after Rose, who sat at the table, staring after them with a slight frown on her face. Then a squarely-built man with greying hair and hazel eyes appeared from nowhere and was introduced as Chief Inspector O'Neill.

Bea followed O'Neill and the Sergeant down a corridor – its battleship quality linoleum and its lincrusta and anaglypta were unchanged probably since the reign of Edward VII or before. She was aware that they were getting nearer to the business end of the mortuary. 'Just follow your nose,' she thought. The room she was led into smelled of cleanliness and, she supposed, formaldehyde. She was glad that she would not have to be there for more than a few moments. An attendant stood by the trolley, with its sinister passenger and, after a swift enquiry from O'Neill, she nodded and the sheet was drawn back. Asked to take her time, she looked more thoroughly at the man she had barely glanced at previously.

He was, she thought, in his thirties and had very dark hair and a short, well-shaped beard. His skin was deeply suntanned. To Bea, who had never seen a corpse before, he did not even look dead and yet his face seemed to have a strange marble-like quality, especially around the forehead, which was high. The hair had thinned slightly on the temples and the face as a whole was very good-looking – though Bea, fastidious as ever, detected a slight coarseness in the features. She had certainly never seen the man before. She looked at O'Neill and shook her head decisively.

As Bea turned to follow the Sergeant up the corridor, O'Neill drew her towards a little alcove and the Sergeant waited for them nearby. 'Just one moment, Miss Roebuck, before we leave you in peace.' His smile was pleasant and disarming, but Bea felt apprehensive, wondering what he wanted.

'Can you tell me anything about Mrs. Downey's husband? It seems to be rather a touchy point, and we haven't been able to persuade her to talk about him …'

'Oh, I see – well, it *is* rather a sensitive matter. She was married last year but they were only together for a few months – it was a disaster.' Bea shook her head slowly. 'I'm afraid I don't know anything about him … I was out of the country at the time and never met him. All I know is that his name is Guy and I think they met abroad.'

'Do you know where?'

'No … Well, I have an idea it might have been in Mauritius. I think she said he either worked there or was brought up there. But

I've only heard it mentioned once, in passing and I'm not even sure I've got the right place. As you say, she won't talk about it … that's all I can tell you, I'm afraid.'

O'Neill thanked her and then, with Sergeant Bamford still in attendance, he took her back to the small room where Rose was waiting and then he gently asked Rose to accompany him. His bedside manner, thought Bea, was soothing – a great improvement on Inspector Dove's unbending correctness, which made her uneasy. She even felt that under the formality was a sense of menace, however hard she tried to tell herself this was illogical. It's not what he says, she thought. It's something indescribable in his manner.

As the Chief Inspector and the Sergeant left, the WPC returned. She smiled and offered Bea the inevitable cup of tea, which arrived promptly, complete with official-looking biscuits that actually tasted more interesting than they looked. Then the policewoman went out at the far end of the bare little room, but left the door ajar. This door appeared to open out into a large office space with several staff at work. The nastiest bit was over now, Bea thought, wasn't it? No need to dwell on it. After all, it wasn't as though it was someone she knew and cared about. She hoped Rose would also be able to put the experience behind her now that this duty had been performed. Then they might be able to get back to normal and the police would presumably leave them alone.

Rose seemed to have been gone for quite a while and Bea passed the time in trying to think of scenarios to account for the dark stranger, as she found herself calling him in an uncharacteristically fanciful way. A possible explanation started to form in her mind and she was deep in thought when the door was suddenly pushed wider, startling her. She prepared to get up, but then realised that it was not Rose – only a young woman in civilian clothes, who stuck her head around the door as though looking for someone and then withdrew.

Bea forced her mind away from the subject of the murder and on towards the days ahead: perhaps they might even be able to enjoy staying a day or two at the farm, if things worked out well with Ralph. They would have to come to some kind of arrangement with Mr. and Mrs. Dyson about payment, since the holiday lettings were after all, run as a business. Bea had wondered about the advisability of moving in with a stranger – but then, Ralph wasn't really a stranger at all. He was a relative of the Dysons, and her parents had known of his family for as long as she could remember. She liked what she had seen of Ralph. He had an air of quiet dependability and a touch of old-fashioned formality of which, she thought wryly, Philip would approve.

Well, it helped that Rose seemed keen on the idea (where had she got to?). Bea felt it important not to raise any objections on grounds of prudence, which might run the risk of further resentment on Rose's part. It had been inevitable that Rose would be hurt by Bea's attitude to her marriage. The coolness that ensued was understandable and Rose was really behaving very generously now – well, particularly since Bea had been proved right. It was important never to let Rose feel she was being reminded that her friend's warnings were justified.

At long last, Sergeant Bamford's voice could be heard in the corridor outside and he and Rose appeared behind the WPC, who put down another tea-tray and left. Rose sat down, looking very white. She had that almost greenish tint that sometimes shows in her type of colouring and she sipped her tea rather shakily. The Sergeant asked them to wait just a minute or two and then the Chief Inspector would like a final word before they were driven back.

As soon as they were left alone, Bea turned to Rose. 'What is it? You look shoc … er , rather upset?'

'Do I? Well, it is a bit shattering, isn't it? I've never seen a – a corpse before.'

'You were in there a hell of a time. What was going on?'

'Oh, I wasn't in the mortuary room, or whatever it's called, for very long.' Rose finished her tea, took a second biscuit and poured herself another cup. She gestured towards Bea with the teapot, but Bea explained that she had already had some tea. 'There's a little office next to it and that's where I was, with this O'Neill guy. He was quite nice, in a way, but he kept on with more questions – going back over things I'd answered already.'

'What sort of …' began Bea. But the Chief Inspector came in at that moment. He wanted to know details of their immediate plans and their telephone number at the farmhouse. Bea didn't know this offhand, but she and Rose had already given their mobile phone numbers. The Chief Inspector said that Mr. and Mrs. Dyson were being contacted, as owners of the site and the farm number could be obtained from them. He asked Bea and Rose to advise the Sergeant before they moved from the farm and he also told them that when the identity of the deceased was known, the police would inform them. The inquest had been fixed for Tuesday at two-thirty in the village hall and they would of course be required to attend.

'An incident room is being set up,' he told them. 'It will be in the old schoolhouse on the Blaeborough Road, not far from Shawhead farm. You probably know it. If you remember something, however trivial – or if any other information reaches you, please call in at the incident room, or you can telephone us there. The Sergeant will give you details."

They were taken back to The Lamb, to pick up their car. This time, they encountered nothing more threatening in the yard than the rather fine tabby cat, which they had noticed previously, washing its face in the deep window embrasure of the hotel lounge.

Bea drove slowly out of the village street, lost in thought and unaware for the moment of the sun on the river, the peaceable sheep, the drystone walls and the rich green slopes. Then she slowed down. 'There's an old pub that I rather like at the other end of the village, The Fleece – what about a drink? I could certainly do with one.'

'Ooh yes! The sooner the better.' Rose was more like her usual self now, but she still had a tremor in her voice. 'But why not at

The Lamb – it's grown on me since yesterday,' she went on, as Bea turned the car round in a gateway. 'Gosh – only yesterday – it seems a lot more.'

'Oh, you'll like The Fleece. It's one of the places I'd hoped we'd be visiting while you're up here.'

Rose nodded and smiled, at the same time looking rather uncomfortable. Bea thought she had a slight strain in her voice as she said, 'Just what we need – a comforting country pub. I feel a bit fragile. That wretched man kept on asking me about things I knew nothing about.'

'What sort of things?'

'Well, he kept on about had I been here before and was I sure …' Here Rose hesitated.

'Go on, Rose.'

'He said was I sure I hadn't seen that man before … that's so silly, isn't it? It's not the sort of thing you'd have any doubt about – so why did he keep on?'

'And you haven't any doubt?'

'No, of course not. Why do you say that?'

'Well, it would account for your being so jumpy … and you *were* trying to duck out of seeing the police yesterday.'

'That's perfectly natural.' Rose showed signs of becoming agitated again and Bea cursed her customary directness, wishing she had been more tactful. 'It's just the shock and everything,' explained Rose. 'Not everyone has your iron nerve, you know.'

'Sorry! I'm being unreasonable. Of course you were in shock.' Bea turned the car into the pebbled yard behind The Fleece and slid it into a convenient space. As she switched off the engine, she turned to Rose. 'Did the Inspector say whether they can get any closer to the time when the man might have been killed?' she asked.

'Well yes, he mentioned it – but they're not a lot closer. He said the police now think he died after six o'clock on Thursday evening and before six a.m. on Friday. It seems a very wide range, doesn't it? But apparently they can't – or won't – be more specific.'

Bea tried to work out the implications of this news, but failed.

'Oh, and he said to tell you they'll be finished with the caravan by tomorrow ... .'

'Well, that's a help, anyway. Some of my old walking gear is in there, along with other odds and ends that I'd like to have, now we're staying a few days,' said Bea, opening her door. 'Can you fish my handbag from behind your seat when you get out? I threw it in with my coat and it fell down. You've got your boots and so on in your luggage, I hope?' she added.

'Yes I have – and a hell of a drag it's been toting it all around on the train.'

'No use coming up here without, though.'

They locked up the car and approached the old inn. Rose said it looked very attractive and unusual. It was covered with creeper and set among trees – quite a contrast to the rather austere local style. Bea led the way through an inviting-looking porch to the lounge-bar on the left. They found a table between two long-settles, near a wood stove that was quite welcome in spite of the spring weather.

'D'you mind getting the drinks in, Bea?' Rose said, fishing for her phone in a handbag that was nearly big enough to be a small weekend case. 'If the signal's OK here I really must try to get a message to Mum and Dad, just in case some well-meaning busy-body has thought of getting in touch – you never know.' She looked towards the bar. 'I think I'll have a brandy. I feel I could very well develop a dependency if I were to experience anything like this again.'

'Me too – I hope we shan't be given the chance. By the way – you'll probably have to go out to the yard to get a signal. I've tried in here before.'

Bea fetched the drinks and sat back in the old-fashioned seat, leaning her head against its high back. She quickly became aware of voices on the other side of the settle, one of which she seemed to recognise, though she couldn't quite place it. It niggled at her, as she wondered which of the few local people she knew would sound so familiar. About to get up and fetch a menu from the bar, she checked hastily as the words drifted over to her.

'Don't think I haven't noticed that *he*'s back again up yon.'

'Mum!' This voice was quiet – a rueful protesting sound, with a slight whine. 'Have you come up here in your lunch-hour just to interrupt my work and give me the gypsy's warning?' Bea gave a start … perhaps by association of ideas, she now knew whose voices these were.

'I've come here because every time I call in at your house, Geoff's hanging around – '

'Well, that's not surprising – it's where he lives, isn't it? And he's working nights at the moment, so he's likely to be about quite a bit … what've you got to say that you can't say in front of him, anyway?'

'Rhona, I don't have to spell it out, do I? Or at least I shouldn't have to. I saw you there on Thursday … one of these days you'll go too far and Geoff – '

'Geoff's all right. He's as mild as milk, is Geoff, always has been.'

'Well, you mark my words ….'

'Mum, I'm going back to the servery – it's starting to get busy. There's nothing for you to be worrying about … and anyway, what were you doing up that way yourself?'

The reply was inaudible and Bea caught sight of Carmen's daughter hurrying off in the direction of the bar-meals counter. Two words in the conversation she had overheard had set her thinking: "up yon" had been an expression she had picked up from the local children years ago. It had a very specific meaning – Shawhead farm and the few isolated cottages in the lane not far away. She wondered whether to mention it to Rose, who was just returning.

'Sorry to have been so long. That my drink? Thanks.' Rose took a sip of her brandy and then continued. 'I couldn't get hold of them – bit of a relief, really. They were bound to want to know all the details. So I sent a rather long text, which had to be carefully thought out, not to alarm them. It should keep them at bay for a bit. Eventually though, they'll be phoning to know what's going on …'

'Won't they just! I'm surprised my mother hasn't got back to me yet. She'll want to know all the details – and then have them over again. It will be no end of a story when she's finished telling her friends – that's why I wanted to talk to Father last night, when I was pretty sure Mother would have gone to one of her classes or committees. I expect he's put a gag on discussing it – it's what usually happens. You'd think, being a GP's wife, she'd have learned to be to be discreet!'

Bea pointed to the menu. 'They're doing bar meals … shall we have something to eat here – it's half-past twelve? We can hardly arrive at the farm looking as if we expect to be fed.'

Rose looked as though she found the suggestion unwelcome. Surely, thought Bea, it can't be because she's in a hurry to see Ralph again? Oh lord – what am I going to do if she gets involved in another headlong romance? If I try to steady her down, I'll be the interfering jealous friend … ex-friend!

But Rose had recovered her composure and agreed that it would be much better to avoid getting there at a meal time. They quickly decided on the Caesar salad, which Bea recommended. She asked Rose to give the order at the buttery next to the bar, while she herself popped into the loo.

Rhona came forward as Rose approached, and Bea, crossing behind them on her way to the ladies' room, glimpsed a strange expression flicker for a moment over Rhona's face. It could have been surprised recognition. It might have been fear, even. Here I go again, thought Bea – my imagination's working overtime.'

*

Philip, having received all the news from Bea's Mother, expressed amazement and concern, whenever he could get a word in. He was disappointed that Bea and Rose were intending to stay at the farm instead of coming up Darlington, as he had hoped they might. Who was this guy Ralph, anyway? He was sure Bea would be much better off at home for a few days after the shock of her discovery. But at least he could phone her there – her mother would help him to make contact.

'Give it a few days', he told himself. 'If I phone her after she's had some breathing space, with any luck she'll relent – all I need is a chance to apologise and see if we can arrive at a compromise.'

He wished he could turn the clock back and do many things differently. But surely, his relationship with Bea was sufficiently well-founded to be salvaged? He would do his best – the rest was up to her.

CHAPTER 4

As they drove up the lane towards the farm, the paddock to the left of them looked innocent – nothing at all sinister about it. Bea thought of the caravan behind its sheltering trees, and wondered if she would ever want to stay in it again.

'Who's that?' asked Rose, pointing to a corner of the paddock by the wall. Twice they glimpsed the figure of a man as he walked between the birch trees, before he went through the far gate and disappeared over a neighbouring field. He was tall and broad, perhaps thirty-ish, with a shock of light brown hair. He was dressed in shabby jeans and a check shirt and he looked as though he could have been one of the local farm workers.

'I think it might have been Geoff Collins. Wonder what he's been up here for?' Again, Bea thought about telling Rose of the conversation she had overheard in The Fleece, but on reflection she felt that it might stir up needless trouble. Instead she said: 'I bet he made a detour through the paddock so that he could inspect the scene of the crime. Not much to see, is there?'

'Who is he then – this Collins bloke?' asked Rose as they pulled into an attractive cobbled and mossy courtyard.

'He lives in the village. I think he works as a porter at the Cottage hospital and he's married to Carmen's daughter, Rhona. People reckon he's a very long-suffering husband, but you can't believe everything you hear, can you?'

'You mean, this Rhona's got a bit of a reputation? Her mother certainly looks – well, looks more the part. But *she* ... '

'Ah yes, well Carmen isn't what she appears at all. She's a very respected figure in the village – leading light on the Parish Council and runs all the Church functions. She works part time down at the farm shop – we passed it just now on the way up if you remember. We'll go shopping there and you'll meet her – a blameless widow!'

'Here's Ralph, look. Hello – we're just coming.'

Ralph came out from the porch to suggest that they unload the car and then leave it on the gravelled area round the back. Rose stared up at the house, which was plain and square, but with the elegance she had come to expect. The windows were well-proportioned, with many panes that twinkled invitingly in the afternoon sunshine. It seemed that few alterations had been done – nothing to spoil its character. Its setting was ideal for larger parties, as there was plenty of space outside at front and back and a lawn at the side of the house big enough for an impromptu game of badminton.

The broad oak door stood ajar, propped back by a tall copper ewer containing some late tulips – big yellow ones – and some dark greenery that Rose couldn't put a name to. Ralph gave them a hand with their baggage and conducted them through to a big, homely-looking square kitchen with a flagged floor. There was an old-fashioned dresser with a great many blue-and-white plates of various designs – compatible rather than matching – and a large scrubbed table.

In answer to Ralph's query, they told him they had already eaten at The Fleece, so he suggested that they should sort out their rooms. He lifted the latch of a narrow pine-boarded door to reveal an enclosed little twisty staircase. In spite of their protests, he grabbed both of their bags and swung them easily up to the landing.

'The backstairs,' explained Ralph, dumping the bags on the floor between two doors that stood ajar. 'I've always wanted to live in a house with backstairs!'

He showed them two attractive low-ceilinged rooms with window-sills almost at floor level. They were furnished simply, with pine cupboards and bright modern fabrics. Ralph said there was a small bath and shower tucked away there, to supplement the big old-fashioned bathroom off the main landing – up two steps and through an archway.

'That's the newer part of the house – but still pretty old,' he told them. 'Through there, as well as the big bathroom, there are two children's rooms with bunks, and then the big one I always have. Downstairs there's a family room that sleeps four, with its own shower etc. and a wonderful drying room – a "must" for hikers in our climate! ' He explained that a local woman had been in that morning to prepare the rooms.

'She comes in to clean when the house is let and sees to the changeovers and so on. The Dysons always arrange for her to pop in and tidy up while I'm here and she'll be in a bit extra now there are more of us.' Ralph turned towards the archway. 'When you've sorted yourselves out, come down and if you haven't had coffee after your meal, I'll make some now. Mrs. Holroyd has made a one of her fruit-cakes – they're very special, and she always brings one up when I stay here. But you might prefer to sample that later on. She believes that nobody gets fed properly in cities – or in the South, of course. In fact, practically everywhere outside Little Blaeford, come to that!'

'It's a lovely old house, isn't it?' said Bea, picking up her grip bag. 'Of course, I've been in it plenty of times, but only in the living room and via the front door.'

'Thanks very much, Ralph. Coffee would be great.' Rose added, raising an eyebrow towards Bea, who nodded. 'We can unpack properly later, so we'll be down in a minute or two,' Rose called after Ralph. He was making off down the main staircase, which was quite grand, with a fine curved banister rail – a contrast from the very plain but beautifully proportioned surroundings.

'That back room's a bit small to hold a double bed,' Bea heard Rose say, as they went from one room to the other, inspecting their various merits. 'Would you rather have the twin room at the front?'

'Not specially. They've both got marvellous views, but I particularly like the outlook at the back – if you don't mind my having the double bed? Those old-fashioned shutters are nice, aren't they?'

'Mmm – so practical, really. You feel both cosy and safe with them closed at night, and those heavy iron bars in place. You can get a modern version of them – I can't think why people don't use them so much today.'

'My parents have got them, though – original ones, I mean – have you noticed them?' Bea put her grip bag down in the back bedroom. 'You go down when you're ready, Rose and I'll follow shortly. Don't wait – get on with the coffee!'

Bea ran a comb through her hair. If nothing else, she told herself, her well-shaped hair was never a problem, thanks to both nature and the skill of one of the best hairdressers in Leeds. A first class cut was one of her few extravagances. She drifted over to the window and dropped on to the low window-seat, gazing at the fields of sheep with their lambs. But this calm scene did not manage to stop her thoughts returning to various niggling ideas which kept revolving and surfacing in turn.

Just as Ralph had appeared in front of the house, she had been talking about Carmen and Rhona. She had been on the point of telling Rose of the conversation she had heard in the pub, and then something had made her change her mind. Would she then have asked Rose if she could explain the look that Rhona had given her? Had Bea imagined the look? Would it be wiser to avoid questioning Rose, who might feel she was being got at? Could it really be Ralph that Carmen had been talking about?

But no-one had been staying at the farm on Thursday evening – would Rhona know which day Ralph was due? And what was Geoff doing in the paddock? Perhaps he had come to see Ralph about some logs, or something like that. She could ask Ralph, of course. And why was all this worrying her? None of it was her affair. The body was not her affair either, though she supposed it would be around in their minds at least until they knew who it was – maybe until the murderer was caught.

How long had she sat here asking herself daft questions? She had only intended to be a minute or so. She got up and headed downstairs, where she found the others in the kitchen, looking domestic and cosy over the coffee pot.

'Sorry to be so long. I got carried away with the view from my window and forgot the time.'

'Apparently we've just managed to avoid the press again, Bea!' Rose brought another cup from the dresser and indicated a chair at the kitchen table.

'They were milling around the place in good time this morning,' Ralph said. 'I think I convinced them that I couldn't tell them anything because I wasn't here at the time of the crime – then they wanted to know about your whereabouts and I told them you'd gone home!'

Ralph grinned. 'I said I thought you lived in Clitheroe – that should keep them off for a bit – so they just took some photos of the caravan and eventually sloped off.'

'I was telling Ralph about our interviews this morning,' Rose said, as she poured coffee for Bea. 'The police have been up here too – asking where he was, taking fingerprints and so on … . we had to produce alibis for the whole of Thursday night, Ralph.'

Rose passed the cup to Bea as she went on: 'Well, I was in Cambridge of course, and Bea – luckily, a friend slept in her little spare room that night.'

'That sounds OK then – you've given them all they need.' Ralph appeared to be considering a second cup of coffee, but seemed to abandon the idea.

'Yes, but then why do they keep on at me about "am I sure I can't give them any clue about who the man was"? I suppose it's because they haven't been able to find out anything about him, and – '

'I don't think so, Rose,' Ralph cut in quietly. 'They have some strong leads by now and it looks as though they know who he was, or they very soon will.'

'They can't do! They said they'd tell us when they know.' Rose stared at Ralph, shocked and unbelieving.

'Don't be upset, Rose.' Ralph spoke very gently. It was a soft, pleasing voice and for the first time, Bea thought she detected a faint Scottish flavour to it. 'I'm not just saying that to stir things up – it's obviously not been verified, or you'd have heard.'

'Where've you heard it from?' asked Bea, wondering if Geoff could have told him.

A rueful grin appeared on Ralph's tanned face, as he answered 'Mrs. Holroyd!' He went on to explain: 'Her husband's a constable – the village bobby, I suppose.' Ralph seemed to decide on more coffee after all and poured out the half cupful that remained in the pot.

Bea had a hazy recollection of a P.C. Holroyd, though she hadn't made the connection in the earlier conversation. She looked enquiringly at Ralph, who smiled and shrugged.

'Things leak out … but it's no big deal really. It's about to be cleared for the media, I gather, so you'll hear officially very soon. Apparently they are pretty sure no-one else had been inside the 'van recently, apart from the corpse – '

'And the killer!' interrupted Bea.

'And the killer, as you say, yes. But they're still not ruling out the likelihood that a woman is implicated in some way.'

'How do they make that out?' asked Rose. 'She'd have been in there with him, wouldn't she?'

'Well I gather – piecing together the hints Mrs. Holroyd was offering, they reckon she might just have arrived at the rendezvous when they saw or heard somebody coming. She may have run off and hidden – perhaps secrecy was more important to her than to him.'

'Yes, I can see how that could be,' said Bea. She finished off her coffee and Rose looked speculatively at the coffee pot. 'Say they were just about to go into the 'van. He's just opening the door, so when she bolts, he stays there ready to cover with some silly tale and give her the chance to get out of the way.'

'That scenario works particularly well if say, she was local but he wasn't. But anyway it's all speculation.' Ralph took the lid off the coffee pot and peered into it. 'I'll make some more,' he said.

Rose asked whether an actual name had been mentioned.

'No, but Mrs. H. says they've been making enquiries in the Lancaster area.'

'Isn't that where you were for a while, Rose?' asked Bea and then wished she hadn't – Rose wouldn't want to dwell on her short time with Guy.

'Oh – er, very briefly. Not long enough to get to know people there.'

'Well, you've missed the chance,' murmured Ralph as he got up to fill the kettle at the far end of the big room. 'Too late to claim acquaintance now!'

Rose gave him a startled look. 'What does he mean?' she muttered, as the noisy tap drowned her voice.

'For Heaven's sake, it was just a joke – not all that funny, but – ' Bea stopped, as the tap was turned off.

Ralph put the kettle on the hob and then went to the back door. 'Just remembered something,' he said. 'If one of you will see to the coffee, I'll get the fuel in for the Rayburn. I meant to do it earlier on.'

'I wish it *was* funny – laughable, I mean.' Rose looked as if she were about to cry.

'I know – it's horrid. But let's not keep on pressing Ralph about it – he'll wish he'd never asked us here.' Bea smiled encouragingly at Rose, who nodded and went over to wait for the kettle to boil. Then she came back, putting the replenished coffee pot on the table and sat down.

Ralph returned and put a hodful of coke down next to the range. He poured his own coffee and offered the pot to the others. 'While you are both getting settled – unpacked and whatnot,' he said, 'I'd like to go and chop up some logs. There's lots of well-seasoned timber out there, but it needs reducing to fit the wood-stove in the living-room. By the way,' he added. 'I spoke to the Dysons earlier today – they rang up after hearing the news. They were very concerned about you both and they thought this arrangement was the best thing you could do. You can argue later with them about the business side of it – but I doubt if they'll agree to any rental. So feel at home, or feel like any other holiday guests.'

Rose smiled her thanks. 'About tonight's meal,' she said. 'I know you've prepared something, but if it will help I could make a salad and sort of put it all together. And I could make a tart or a crumble, if you've got anything to go into it?'

'Great! When I'm working out of doors, it's really good not to be responsible for meals as well. I'll show you what I've made, and as to the tart – well, you'll find bottled and frozen fruit of every kind; they always have more than they know what to do with. It's always the same in the country, isn't it?' he added. 'You get a glut and you can't even give it away, because all your neighbours have got a stack of the same thing, especially when it's plums … oh, and I've just remembered, we've got some fresh cream too. Bloke from the village brought it up – '

'You don't mean Geoff?' put in Bea.

'That's him. I saw him wandering about near the paddock and when I went over to him, he said he'd brought some cream up – it was a present from his mother-in-law. She works part-time at the farm shop just down the road, before you get to the village. I suppose it was her way of sending sympathy to us all. She's incredibly kind is Carmen, she mothers everybody – though you'd never guess, to look at her!'

'Yes, I know. She and her daughter seem to have reversed their roles, in a way don't they?' Bea leapt on this unexpected chance to look for possible answers to the suspicions that had arisen during their visit to the Fleece. She tried an exploratory probe, but she hadn't had time to choose her words. Trouble is, she thought, I'm just not good at this sort of thing. She found herself saying, rather obviously: 'Have you seen Rhona at all this year?' and then wishing she'd never spoken.

Ralph did not appear concerned. 'I've not seen her this time,' he said evenly. 'She used to turn up here quite a lot with some excuse or other. But I think the message has finally got through – she's given me up as a bad job.' Ralph chuckled. 'Geoff is an amazingly patient chap – it's a wonder he hasn't strangled her before now!'

'They say he's a sort of gentle giant, don't they?' put in Rose. 'Just as well then …'

'Hardly a giant – in another age I'd say he'd be called a *gentleman*. Anyway, where have you heard that?' asked Bea rather sharply.

'You told me … didn't you?'

'Oh, perhaps I did – I say far too much sometimes.'

Rose picked up the cups and started to clear the table, telling them she intended to inspect the freezer and store cupboards with a view to doing a bit of cooking. Bea said, in that case, as soon as she'd unpacked, she was going to put on her oldest jeans and her tatty walking shirt and see what needed to be done in the garden.

*

Bea was enjoying herself. She had found a barrow in the shed, along with a hoe and some small tools. She was now well into a largish bed, with a satisfying pile of weeds in the barrow. She realised though, that life in the Leeds flat had left her out of condition and after a while, she felt a blister starting – maybe there were gardening gloves here somewhere. Straightening up warily, she examined the damage and decided to get a plaster before her finger got worse. She sat on the bench outside the back door to take off her walking boots, which had doubled as gardening footwear. Then she went up the twisty backstair to her room, where she found a suitable plaster among the minor first-aid items in her luggage. Glancing out of the window, she could see Ralph put down his axe and take a beer from Rose, who sat on a log while he drank it. She realised that it was getting time to stop and get cleaned up. As soon as she had put the tools away, it would be a good idea to have a really hot shower, as she was beginning to feel stiff.

As she set off downstairs, she heard the telephone ring in the hall. About to go and call Ralph, she turned back, as she thought of the shoeless journey across the yard and around the utility room lean-to. Instead, she picked up the phone. The voice replying to her "Hello?" was rather breathless – almost, she thought, flustered. 'Oh – er – sorry! I seem to have the wrong number.'

'Who did you – ' began Bea, but the caller had already broken off the connection. Although she heard very little, the voice reminded Bea of someone … reminded her, she reckoned, of lunchtime at the Fleece. 'And what,' she asked herself, 'was Rhona ringing up for unless to speak to Ralph? And Ralph has made his own position clear. So he said.'

*

'Are you coming?' called Rod from the garden. Her husband's voice sounded mildly exasperated, but resigned.

'In a minute,' Barbara shouted back through the kitchen window. 'I just want to catch the news headlines… '

'Whatever for? It's all the same old political stuff – or ghastly news about fighting and mayhem.' The voice came closer to the window. 'I'd have thought,' he went on, 'we had enough to worry about right here in the garden, without looking for trouble on the radio.' He leaned over the windowsill, his head through the open sash, his glasses, as usual, slipping down his nose, his expression both irritated and conciliatory at the same time. 'I want you to come and have a look in the greenhouse. I'm not at all happy about those tomato seedlings … '

'In a sec.,' said Barbara firmly, seizing the portable radio and taking it into the downstairs loo, where she turned it low and stood with her ear next to its speaker … Surely, she thought, I should be able to have two minutes' peace here.

There it was. She hadn't missed it, although it was only a very brief item, close to the end of the bulletin: no name – merely the information that the body of a man had been discovered in a caravan in a rural area of Yorkshire. The police were treating it as a suspicious death.

Barbara turned off the set, remembering to flush the lavatory and then she shut the door noisily. 'Sod the greenhouse,' she said under her breath. 'I just can't be fussing over a few tomatoes, when there are far more important things to think about.' But by the time she went out to inspect the tomatoes, she had herself well under control.

*

The evening meal was a great success. They were all hungry by the time they had finally finished their various activities, and had enjoyed baths or showers before meeting up for aperitifs. They laid the long table in the living room, which had been kept as far as possible unchanged since the time when it had served as the comfortable heart of a prosperous farmhouse. It was a large room, lit by several well-placed lamps, and the polished oak gleamed invitingly.

The atmosphere felt almost festive. Rose and Bea had called in the village on their way up from the Fleece and bought a couple of bottles of what Rose described as "educated plonk" and a very ripe melon, which Bea said was the only culinary item she was capable of selecting and dealing with. They seemed to have decided tacitly to forget about the events that had brought them together. It was no effort – perhaps for the moment, they really had forgotten. Once or twice while she was upstairs getting ready, Bea thought about her intention to ask Ralph more about what the police had asked him. It surely couldn't have been anything more than the standard questions, since Ralph hadn't even arrived at the farm when the murder was supposed to have happened. However, the right moment didn't seem to come.

The melon made a successful start to the meal and Ralph's casserole was a triumph. After an interval, while conversation flowed easily, with Ralph recalling some amusing incidents from previous years at the farm, they started on Rose's tart (and Carmen's cream). Just as they were doing so, the telephone rang and Ralph excused himself, shutting the hall door behind him. They could just hear muttered tones for a moment or two and then he came back and sat down.

'Wrong number,' he smiled, pouring cream liberally. Bea glanced at his face as he spoke and felt that slight lurch of misgiving that she had experienced earlier. Although he had been on the phone for a very short time, he would by her reckoning, have had enough time for a brief message.

'Oh, that reminds me,' she said as casually as she could. 'There was a call this afternoon. I took it when you were both outside. That seemed to be a wrong number too.' The others carried on eating and if she had hoped to catch a guilty expression on Ralph's face, she was disappointed.

'This is where I miss the dishwasher,' Rose remarked as they were clearing away the dishes. 'I'm afraid I'm spoilt.'

Ralph told her that the reed-bed system of drainage installed last year, had to be treated sensitively. 'It's very good environmentally ... but no dishwasher I'm afraid – I guess you can't win on all counts.'

So there was quite a spirited argument over who should wash up, with all of them trying to ensure that they pulled their weight. In the end, it was agreed that the women would do the washing and drying while Ralph put everything away, since only he knew where it went. He offered to make coffee too. After that they played Scrabble for a while, but they all admitted that they were shattered, and Bea was thankful not to be the first to disappear this evening as well as last night.

*

Rose woke before Bea was up next day and went to tap gently on her door. She stood at the window as Bea, not long awake, sat up and accustomed her eyes to the gentle sunlight. It was a slightly hazy morning, which promised a superb spring day. At last, they began to feel as if they were on holiday and Bea tried to put aside any doubts about Ralph – she had probably let her imagination take over anyway, due to the unusual circumstances. Dressing quickly, they went to the kitchen and hunted around for bread, milk and coffee. Rose found bacon and eggs too, so that when Ralph came in at the back door, breakfast was well on its way.

Ralph seemed to relish his cooked breakfast and Bea found that she enjoyed hers – though she never ate a "proper" breakfast at home. Rose, of course, always had a remarkably healthy appetite wherever she was. Finishing off his egg with a piece of delicious local bread, Ralph said he was sorry to have to introduce an unpleasant subject. He had had a call from Inspector Dove.

Rose flinched as the Inspector was mentioned, but all she said was, 'He's rung already? 'It's only a quarter to nine now.'

'Actually,' replied Ralph, 'he rang last night. Do you remember that "wrong number" during the meal? Well, I didn't want you bothered then – we were having such a relaxed evening … I reckoned you'd both had enough for one day.'

'Oh, that was nice of you! You were right, we had had enough, hadn't we, Bea?'

'It was very thoughtful of you, Ralph.' Even as she spoke Bea could hear how pompous and stilted she sounded. She realised that she had been unjust to Ralph, as it now turned out – thank Heaven she hadn't said any more than her slightly pointed remark, last night. But even now, she didn't feel entirely easy with him, in spite of her good intentions. 'What did you tell the Inspector?' she asked.

'Oh, the usual sort of thing – you'd both gone to bed early with a sleeping pill. Anyway, he wasn't bothered. He just said he had a bit of information for you and he'd give you a ring in the morning.'

'Oh, right. Let's hope it's not another grilling this time.' Bea pulled a wry face and went on: 'By the way, Ralph, what sort of things did Sergeant Bamford want to know when he came up here?'

'Same as the stuff you complained of! Oh, it wasn't that bad – where was I on Thursday stroke Friday – you know. It's all sorted out anyway, give or take a bit of checking on their part.'

'Hope we're not going to waste half the day waiting for this call,' Rose had finished her plateful and was now tucking into toast and honey. 'It would be nice to go off somewhere – it's such a promising day. It's hard to believe that it snowed only a couple of weeks ago, isn't it? Did you have any around Manchester, Ralph?'

Ralph looked as if he was having difficulty remembering. 'Yes, a bit, I think,' he said absently. Bea felt a lurch of recollection, painful and nostalgic, at the mention of the recent snow. It had started suddenly while she had been in a country pub with Philip. They had driven up to the gateway to the Dales from Bea's flat in north Leeds. It was the last occasion when they'd met – ending up unable to resolve their conflicting points of view. They had been enjoying a delightful meal and then while they drank their coffee, an issue from the past which they had both believed to be over and done with, somehow re-introduced itself. They had come to an impasse, both refusing to budge. The memory of the unseasonable late snow, confronting them as they emerged into the night, seemed now to fuse in Bea's mind with the ugly and harmful image of their quarrel.

It was a bleak journey back in every way, especially when the car became stuck on a steep hill. There was only an inch or so of snow, but on the untreated road, it was enough to be a hazard. Philip, always a belt-and-braces type, had made sure that his car was well-equipped after hearing snow warnings on the radio. In the event, he didn't need the shovel, but he'd brought a couple of old sacks as well, and these were invaluable in helping to get a grip ... 'Get a grip, Bea!' she admonished herself and pulled herself back to the present and Ralph's voice.

'... pack a picnic if you want, while we wait for him to ring. Is there any more coffee in the pot?'

Bea poured some for him. 'I suppose,' she said, 'we could ring up the police station ourselves. I'm afraid I'm a bit of an ostrich about all this. I feel it might just go away if we keep our heads down long enough.' She also tried to push away the thought of how glibly Ralph had dealt with last night's phone call, but that uneasy feeling hung around. Even though it was done for the best of reasons (apparently), the fact remained that white lies, at any rate, came easily and fluently to Ralph.

*

The call from the police station, when it came, was only a message to say that the Inspector was on his way to see them and to give them an update personally. If this attention should have been flattering, Rose and Bea did not seem to appreciate it.

They had long finished breakfast, planned their day out, prepared a simple packed lunch and were sitting again round the kitchen table, deciding against yet more coffee, by the time Dove arrived. Ralph made an excuse and disappeared outside. The Inspector first told them what they had already surmised: the man came from a village close to Lancaster.

'His name,' went on Dove, 'was Arthur Gurney Wharton, aged thirty-four – an employee of a firm making paints and allied products.'

Rose and Bea received this news in silence and awaited any further disclosures.

'We are now in a position to confirm the cause of death.' Dove was by this time seated at the table, having refused an offer of tea or coffee. 'He was hit on the back of the head with something large and flat and the blow was sufficiently hard to kill him outright.' Once more, a quirky and inappropriate urge to giggle took hold of Bea. He means "blunt instrument", she thought, but he's trying to avoid the cliché. She controlled herself in time to hear what he was saying.

'We are trying to find relatives of Mr. Wharton, but this is taking rather longer than we would have expected.' Dove paused briefly, almost as though he had anticipated some help in this matter. Then he was ready to take his leave. They could now enter the caravan if they wished, he said. Bea could use her own key, while the police retained the spare.

They thanked the Inspector and to their relief, he got into his car and departed.

'Well,' sighed Bea. 'Are we supposed to feel any better for knowing all that?'

Rose was gazing through the window to where Ralph was filling in the time stacking some of the logs he had cut up yesterday. She turned at last and looked at Bea. 'Did you notice how Dove kept staring at me? I find that very unnerving.' She got up and went towards the back door. 'I'll tell Ralph we're ready, shall I?'

And that's that, thought Bea, as Rose went into the yard, seemingly unmoved – even indifferent. Except for the touches of paranoia that kept cropping up when the Inspector was around, or even when he was mentioned. Obviously, that was all it was – Rose simply had a bit of a "thing" about Inspector Dove. Another good theory gone wrong! In fact, she hadn't really had a theory at all – it was just a feeling of something hidden behind the freckles on that frank, open face that was one of Rose's most charming features. Rose had seemed a bit more shaken than would be natural, even given the nastiness of their discovery. Well, Bea supposed she must have read too much into it.

Maybe Dove had been picking up similar messages too, also mistakenly ... he had questioned Rose rather a lot. And then her interview with Chief Inspector O'Neill had lasted longer than Bea's – and yet surely if anyone was involved, it would be the caravan's owner, not a guest who was a stranger to the area?

The sooner I get out into the cleansing fresh air the better, thought Bea – I need a mental detox. Her favourite pair of boot-socks was in the caravan, along with her trekking pole and the very small rucksack, which was all she would need. She'd better get them now, so as not to hold the others up.

It was not the ordeal she had expected. She noticed that the little low-wattage heater that she always left on had done its job – there was very little evidence of mustiness. She went into the main bedroom to hunt for the socks and the little rucksack. They were in the bottom of her wardrobe just as she had left them after her last visit and the few items she always left on the dressing table were apparently undisturbed. Even the digital display on her small radio/recorder was still telling the right time.

She wondered whether to take the radio back home with her. It was a bit special, that radio – she had had it ever since her last year at school, a present from her first boyfriend. She had been touched when Josh had brought it back from a school skiing trip to Austria. He couldn't have had much money, but he'd chosen to spend it on her. And it was such a clever little set – you could preset it with a start and stop time, if there was a programme you didn't want to miss, or you could use that facility as an alarm. Perhaps he'd traded it for something else – they were always doing "swaps", so he may have got a bargain!

'Never mind,' she said aloud. 'It really *is* the thought that counts – I must be a bit sentimental, after all!' She picked up the little piece of electronic wizardry, that was still set as she had left it last time, to start at quarter to eleven each evening. She remembered now: Philip had had to return to work and she wanted to make sure she didn't miss "A Book at Bedtime" – a fresh serialisation was due to start that evening. Foolishly, she'd then forgotten all about it, and had jumped out of her skin when the programme came on just as she was getting into bed. She now turned the switch to manual. At first she thought it wasn't working, but on turning up the volume, she caught the end of a comedy show.

This reminded her that, once more, she was wasting time – she seemed to have a tendency to day-dream lately. She jumped up from the end of her bed where she had perched and hurried back to the house to stow her treasure in her room. Quickly packing a few necessities in the rucksack, she joined Ralph and Rose in the yard, where they were loading his car – a comfortable but unremarkable estate – certainly no status-symbol.

'Thought we'd better take my car – just look at all this gear,' said Ralph, stowing rucksacks, picnic, waterpoofs and boots into the vast rear area. 'Rose tells me Dove's put a name to your corpse – he's a morose sort of chap, isn't he? The Inspector I mean, not Arthur Gurney Wharton!'

Bea agreed. 'He sort of *looms,* doesn't he? And those amazing eyebrows, with the rather threatening overhang!'

'You can see why I find him a bit fierce,' Rose said with a grimace. 'But it's too nice a day to worry about him. By the way, Bea,' she added. 'Ralph got rid of some more reporters while old Dove was busy tormenting us – don't know how he did it … '

Ralph grinned. 'Easy!' He opened the front passenger door, and Bea got in, after noticing that Rose was already climbing into the back seat. This was a relief, as Bea feared it might be rather pointed to suggest that she sat in the back. It was a help that Rose was being so sensitive.

They set off, Ralph explaining that he had suggested a not-too-strenuous walk starting along the riverside, if Bea agreed. Rose wanted to call at the farm shop. 'We could do with a few apples and perhaps bananas.'

'It will be practically lunchtime when we get to the start of the path, so I think it might be better to eat by the river and do the main walk after – not ideal, I know.' Ralph pulled up the car outside the farm shop and Bea volunteered to get the fruit while Rose went to look at the small butchery counter. It was a very attractive, well-stocked shop in a purpose-built wooden building and it seemed to depend as much on local trade as on the holidaymakers, since prices were modest.

Bea made her choice rapidly, adding a bag of pears, which she was particularly fond of. As she and Rose brought their purchases to the counter, where Carmen was on duty, she introduced Rose, carefully giving the name as Marjorie Dutton, before Rose had a chance to put her foot in it. They thanked Mrs. Dutton for the cream, saying how timely the gift had been.

'Cream?' said Carmen, looking a little puzzled. Then: 'Cream. Oh yes I remember now. Geoff said something – well, you're very welcome I'm sure!'

Back in the car, Bea once more kept her own counsel. She had already jumped to entirely wrong conclusions, with her nasty suspicious mind. So what – if Geoff wanted an excuse to go up to the farm and indulge his ghoulish whim – what did it matter? And the cream had been delicious.

'Just morbid curiosity,' she said. Then she realised that she had spoken her thoughts aloud. 'Sorry – I'm mulling over the various events, and the fact that people doing their shopping seemed to stare a little. The sort of thing you get when there's been an accident – it's only to be expected.'

*

'You went up there with some cream, then?'

'What are you on about?'

'Why did you want to be taking cream up to t'farm?'

'Your Mam gave it me for them.'

'That she didn't!'

'Ask her then.'

'I just did!'

'Oh.'

'Yes, "Oh" … it's supposed to be her half-day today and she called in not half an hour ago on her way home – I'd only just got in myself, we've been real busy over lunchtime and I didn't get back till after three. She said it wasn't her that asked you to take it – it was your idea, that. And I want to know why.'

'Why what?'

'Aw, come off it Geoff, now you're being silly.'

Rhona knew her easy-going husband had a facility for stonewalling – the kind of obstinacy that often goes with that slow-to-rouse type.

'We-e-e-ll.' He drew out the syllable until it contained all the scorn he could muster, which wasn't a lot. 'I can go up there if I like, can't I? Just wanted to take a look, like. See what it were all about.'

'Well, there'd be nothing to see… I can't tell what you thought you'd see.'

'How do you know what there'd be?'

'Because it's common sense, that's what.'

Geoff sat down at the kitchen table, his attempted cockiness dissolved. 'They want to talk to me, Ro.' His voice was quiet now, little more than a mumble. 'That constable from Blaeborough that came doing the house-to-house. He said there'd be a routine visit from someone – sergeant or an inspector. But I don't think it *is* routine, Ro.'

'Course it is. Why should they pick on you?'

' 'Cos they think *you've* been up there, Rhona.'

'That's rubbish and you know it!'

'That's as may be, but it's what they think. And if they think *you've* been up there, then they think they know why *I've* been up there, see?'

How long this laborious trading of short stabbing sentences could have gone on would be difficult to gauge. But the doorbell rang and Geoff went rapidly to answer it. Both Sergeant Bamford and Inspector Dove followed him into the living room.

Geoff gestured vaguely towards the cretonne-covered chairs and sofa, grouped round the fireplace of the biggish room that served as a dining- and sitting-room in the comfortable ex-council house, but the two policemen remained standing.

'There are just a few points we would like to be sure about, Mr. Collins, connected with your movements between six o'clock on Thursday night and six o'clock on Friday morning last. If you wouldn't mind just stepping out to the incident room just up the road, we think that will be the most convenient way to clear it up.'

CHAPTER 5

Whenever Bea found herself walking in a threesome, she had always found it slightly tricky. Unless there was a very broad path, allowing three abreast, someone always got left behind while the other two chatted, trying with difficulty to include the third. It was even more awkward if her companions were a couple. If she walked beside the man, it seemed to be asking for trouble to squeeze his partner out. Leaving the man out was almost as bad: if the two women chattered in typical fashion, he was probably left wondering why he had bothered to come at all. Clearly, the couple would feel uncomfortable about leaving *her* as the odd-man-out! She wondered whether she was over-sensitive about this – other people probably didn't give a damn. Among her regular walking friends was a gay couple with whom she could relax, as the problem didn't seem to arise.

However, the path they were following at the moment was a single-file track, so she did not have to worry about whether it looked pointed to leave Rose and Ralph together. Soon they would leave the river, where a short steep climb would cut talking down to a minimum. Rose was leading, since she was not nearly as long-legged as the others and she was in danger of being outpaced. They were soon at the top of a sort of cliff which overhung the river, giving them a fine view over the valley towards the hills. Ralph had binoculars with him, while Rose had her camera at the ready and Bea produced the bag of apples, as they all flopped down just off the path.

Bea lay back on the soft turf, finding the sun surprisingly hot and she felt that she could fall asleep if nobody disturbed her. The low murmuring voices of the other two was also rather soporific.

'You can see the village quite clearly from here.'

'You can actually see the farm as well … look – up on the hillside, just above those trees.' Ralph handed the binoculars to Rose. It's what the name means, you know … '

'Shawhead Farm?'

'Yes – a place at the head or top of a small wood.'

Bea half-opened one eye. As she had imagined, their heads looked so close that they could almost use the glasses at the same time – Rose using the left lens and Ralph the right. I wonder … she thought. Was it accidental? But after watching for a moment or two she concluded that any one with half an eye (which was what she was using) could see that there was nothing accidental about it.

She sighed. 'Nothing to do with me,' she chided herself under her breath. She rolled over with her face close to the sweet-smelling turf, and drifted off almost at once into one of those strange daytime snoozes. She dreamed that a sheep was stuck in a hedge and she was attempting to free it. But the stupid sheep didn't want to be freed. It stared out from its entanglement with a defiant glare, stamping its foot in that strangely petulant way that a ewe will do when in a challenging mood. Then the sheep assumed vaguely human characteristics, which soon began to resemble Rose.

She could only have been asleep for a matter of moments, because when she opened her eyes again, Rose was still busy with the binoculars.

'Look Ralph – look over at the farm – here take the glasses. Over there, by the paddock. It looks like that man we saw yesterday … Geoff something? I wonder what he wants.'

Bea also wondered what he wanted at the farm; but whatever it was, she thought it must be connected with Ralph, since it would be known locally that he was staying there. Could there be some kind of link between Ralph and those two, Rhona and Geoff?

'Yes,' she heard Ralph's voice. 'It is Geoff, I think. Perhaps he's brought another pot of cream!'

He sounded detached and indifferent.

'What's he doing?' Bea asked, sitting up and stretching.

'Don't know. He's round the far side of the caravan now.' Rose had the glasses again. 'Surely he shouldn't be nosing about the farm, should he? Would the Dysons want him around like that?'

'Possibly not,' replied Ralph. 'But without knowing more, it's difficult to do anything about it. It may well be that he has some good reason for coming and the Dysons may be quite happy about it. You've got to be so careful in a small community – and we're only holidaymakers, with no right to interfere.'

'What sort of reason had you in mind, Ralph?' asked Bea, as they struggled to put on their rucksacks.

'Oh – rabbiting, or something like that.'

'He doesn't seem to have a gun,' objected Rose.

'Well … snaring, then.' He held up a placatory hand at the outburst this received. 'No – only joking, honestly! I'm not going to worry about it,' he went on good-humouredly. 'Unless of course there's another corpse, in which case he'd be the very first suspect. Or perhaps he's planning to steal the 'van.'

'Oh, thanks, Ralph. I don't know which would be more inconvenient.' Bea grinned at him. 'Mind you, the 'van has been in that position for years; I think anyone who managed to move it deserves to keep it!'

'You might be relieved to have it stolen, after what happened,' said Rose. 'Surely it won't feel right again – sort of tainted?'

'I think that's true, Rose. At the moment, I can't really imagine using it again. I'll have to talk to my father – see what he thinks. Not long ago he was talking about improvements – extra insulation and so on … but I'm not sure it'll ever feel the same.'

'Right. Ready to go on? Shall we carry on as far as the old shepherd's hut – you'll know that, Bea – and then back down to the river?' Ralph turned to Rose. 'Do you want to take the lead again?'

*

They came back to the house around half-past five and Rose offered to organise a meal, intending to cook the lamb chops they had bought at the farm shop. 'Something a bit more basic than last night, I'm afraid and – Bea, we'll have to work out a system for any food we use. Perhaps just replacing whatever we take will be the most straightforward?'

'Yes,' put in Ralph. 'That's more-or-less what I do when I'm here on my own. We don't have to replace bottled plums and things like that though. But as far as what we buy – and the booze of course – we can organise a kitty or something.'

'OK, we'll do that from now on. That way, nobody feels hesitant about having a drink if they want one.' Bea saw the flaw in this as soon as she'd said it, but she just hoped no-one among them was about to develop alcoholic tendencies.

'Let's have one now then, as soon as we get this kit off,' Ralph suggested. 'It's been a really good day, hasn't it?' He emptied his rucksack and showed the others where such things could be stowed, in the big cool, slate-floored room, which in former times had been a spotless dairy, where the churns and separator had been. The sinks and sluices were still usable, and the room now made an excellent utility and laundry room with a washing machine and a creel, and still there was plenty of hanging space for their gear.

'I have to admit,' went on Ralph, taking their waterproofs to put on the row of hooks above the boot-racks. 'I don't always enjoy walking in company. Sometimes people sort of invite themselves along – sorry, I don't mean you of course… and I still miss my dog – a Springer spaniel called Flossie. She died at a ripe old age around Christmas time. But today helped to get me back on track …I really enjoyed it – hope you have too.'

'Thoroughly,' Bea was able to say with true enthusiasm. 'Now, before I get changed, I just want to pop over to the caravan – something I forgot.'

73

It was no trouble going there this time. Almost back to normal, thought Bea, but she stepped rather warily into the main living area and looked carefully around. There was no sign of anything having been disturbed, yet Bea was unable to get rid of the idea that there was something a bit fishy about Geoff's apparent interest in the caravan. Could anyone get in? Well, the murderer could presumably, if he'd made a copy of the key. The emergency key had been there, waiting to provide the pattern.

'But only,' she muttered to herself, 'if someone told him about the hiding-place.' It wasn't as if the key had been under a plant-pot or dustbin. It had been buried in a little mustard-tin wrapped in plastic, under a patch of shrubs. He would have to dig up the whole enclosure – assuming he knew there was something to be found.

Bea took a quick look round the bedroom, just to set her mind at rest. Everything was in place. The absence of bedclothes was a slightly eerie reminder of what had happened. She glanced at the cupboard in the corner. Surely she had left the door ajar as usual, when she came to the 'van earlier? It was something she always did because of a tendency to damp at this end of the 'van, but it was shut now. She kept the little tubular greenhouse heater close beside it. She touched the heater now; it was switched on. But had she fastened that door herself?

Well, she couldn't be sure. After all, her normal routine might have gone slightly awry while her mind was preoccupied. She shivered slightly. If someone had been in the 'van, then that person must be the murderer with the copied key. The police still had the emergency key and she had the other. Why would anyone else want to get into the van to take nothing and to do no damage? Could the murderer have forgotten something which the police, so notoriously thorough, hadn't discovered?

Should she tell the Inspector? If only she could remember about the cupboard door … but the more she thought about it, the more uncertain she became. At least, she thought, if I just told him *that* – that I'm simply not sure, it would pass the responsibility on to him.

Back at the house, nobody was about as she went through the kitchen and up the backstairs to her room. She washed quickly and slipped into a respectable pair of trousers and a clean shirt, ran a comb through her hair and went down to the kitchen. This time Rose was at the sink, busy with some vegetables. She did not seem to be getting on with her task very urgently, for Ralph was standing close behind her with his head close to her shoulder – presumably advising her on the best way to scrub carrots. Bea bit back a sardonic remark and enquired if there was anything she could do to help and was there a sherry going.

Ralph joined her at the table with the sherry bottle and Rose stopped her efforts for a moment, wiping her hands on her apron, to take her glass. They both looked very pleased with themselves, Bea thought, as people tend to do on discovering that they've both been bitten by the same bug.

The meal was a pleasant affair. They had decided to eat quite early, as they were all hungry. After they had washed up and had coffee and Ralph had put on a CD of some of the jazz that he and Rose had been choosing together, Bea began to wonder whether she should make some excuse to leave the others on their own. It would be difficult to avoid elephantine tactfulness though, and she was still wondering – and trying to suppress silly niggling thoughts about the caravan and its cupboard door, when the telephone rang.

'It's for you, Bea,' said Ralph, coming through from the hall and shutting the living room door firmly.

Bea started in surprise, since no-one knew the number of the farm. Then she remembered that her father had mentioned that he would like to have the number, the other night and in the end she had decided to text it to him. She hurried off and was filled with pleasure and relief at hearing his voice. Her mother, apparently, was out at one of her numerous committees, but had insisted that he should ring the farm. Of course he had heard the reports on radio and TV, giving the name of the victim, but not much else.

'Yes, well that's about as much as we know too,' Bea told him. 'The inquest is on Tuesday, but the police don't really seem to know anything much themselves – why it happened, or what he was doing there …'

'Don't you believe it! By now, it's highly likely they know all those things and much more, but they're not going to tell you.'

It was then that Bea remembered that her father had at one time long ago held the post of Police Doctor, though nowadays he did only his normal work as a GP in a small and rather old-fashioned practice.

'Anyway,' went on her father. 'I shouldn't think there's anything for you to worry about – you and Rose.'

'No-o,' answered Bea rather doubtfully and she found herself outlining briefly her impression that someone – presumably Geoff – had got into the caravan. 'Though I'm not even sure I *did* leave that cupboard open.' She sighed and glanced anxiously towards the door. Sounds of conversation, laughter and music reassured her. 'I think I'm getting neurotic, Dad … but I keep wondering what Geoff's got to do with everything and then I've even felt suspicious about Ralph … and Rose seems as if she's bothered about something, but is putting a nonchalant face on …'

'I think all this is understandable Bea. You've had a nasty shock and you're a bit over-anxious. It might be an idea to have a word with this man Dove – just tell him that Geoff's been hanging around the place. You can contact him at the incident room, can't you? He'll be quite used to people expressing their concerns. In that way, you'll have handed over the doubts about the caravan to him, and as for Ralph – well, what sort of a person is he?'

'Considerate – kind – unflappable. Not outstandingly good-looking, but attractive in a healthy outdoor sort of way. And I think he's taken a shine to Rose.' Bea had dropped her voice, although the house was old enough to have soundproof walls and doors, and she could only just hear the faint sounds of the music still playing.

'And that bothers you?' Dr. Roebuck had managed to pick up something in her tone that was less than enthusiastic.

'Only because she's impulsive. She's made one bad mistake, she's on the rebound and he's just the type … she's probably had enough of the smooth, handsome type (because I rather think that's what Guy was – almost flashy perhaps). But we're all thrown together in rather unusual circumstances and really we hardly know him. And then Rhona Dutton (that was) has been around, I gather … oh, don't take any notice of me, I'm being silly.'

He didn't pursue this, but went on to tell Bea that Philip had been asking for the phone number at the farm, because he knew she wouldn't have a good signal on her mobile. Bea refused to allow her father to supply this and then promptly regretted it. However, pride would not let her go back on what she'd said.

As they were about to end the call, Dr. Roebuck asked: 'Oh by the way, your mother said the name Wharton rang a bell, but she couldn't think where she'd come across it – thinks it could have been some friend of yours … '

'Of mine? … no, I don't think so.' Bea frowned. 'Well, it's not like Smith or Jones, but it isn't *that* unusual – not likely to be the same person, is it? Perhaps we shall know before long.'

'Bound to. Well, I've passed it on. The rest of her message was of course to give you her love and to tell you to stop worrying and look after Rose.'

'Well, tell her I'm not worrying! As for Rose, she won't thank me for anything like that – she seems to be doing very nicely. Honestly, Dad!'

'Mother knows best,' replied her father in as irritating a voice as he could manage. Bea found herself laughing as they said goodbye, wishing he were around to cheer and relax her with his common sense.

In spite of her denial to her father, she was tempted to telephone Philip, but once more she decided against it. She stood for a moment, looking down the hall and through the clear square panes above the broad front door. The sun was almost set and a few low rays played on the white paint and tiled floor. It was the sort of house she would like to live in, but on the other hand, it was essentially a country house and she would never want to do full-time rural. She sighed, as if she found the thought troubling.

As she returned to the living room, Bea felt this might be the opportunity she needed to excuse herself for the rest of the evening. She gave them an edited version of the phone call and then said she wanted to write some letters.

'Do you think there's any writing paper around, Ralph? I've got friends in the States who are owed letters and I could make a start … any sort of paper will be all right.'

'I've seen a pad in a drawer here, I think. A bit basic, but no doubt it'll do. There might even be envelopes … ' He rummaged through the top drawer of a tall chest of drawers and soon produced the pad and envelopes. As he handed them to Bea, he wore a slightly puzzled look.

'Something wrong?' asked Bea.

'Oh, not really – just that I was reminded of something I'd mislaid. I had my sunglasses with me yesterday when I went out to chop wood and I was sure I'd put them back in the case. But I found the empty case on the kitchen window-sill later … I put the case in this drawer, so I'll know where it is when the specs turn up. I'll have to have a good look round outside tomorrow … I've got a bit of a thing about mislaying my belongings – it bothers me. Now, have you got all you need? Are you coming down for a nightcap later?'

Bea said she would almost certainly have a self-indulgent soak in the bath and then go straight to bed. Rose, who had been reading in the window seat until the fading light had made her put down her book, said she wouldn't be late either.

Bea found it rather a relief to be on her own for a little while. She was used to being alone quite a lot and needed generous helpings of her own company.

That's one reason Philip and I have normally got on so well, she thought. He does understand the need for personal space – even, she added venomously to herself, if he *is* still in the Stone Age about women's careers. She felt a surge of the fury she had experienced during their fierce and uncharacteristic battle in which neither would give any ground. He was thoroughly stubborn and unreasonable. She had also noticed that he had been a bit on edge for some time recently, but she had quickly learned not to allude to this. She wished, none-the-less that he was here to confide in. He was able to see things in the round, giving a more detached view than even her own level-headed shrewdness could offer.

There was a small satinwood table between the two bedroom windows and after closing the curtains, Bea now pulled this out under the light to serve as a writing desk. She sat on the pretty little upright chair, with its hand-worked cushion and wrote for an hour or so without stopping. She had always been a prolific letter-writer – enjoying this better than talking on the telephone.

The written word had always been very special for her, which was probably why she had chosen a career in publishing. She realised that most of her contemporaries regarded the use of the postal service as an idiosyncrasy and thought her a walking anachronism. Even so, she normally used the computer for the actual business of writing and it felt a little strange to be using pen and paper – and terribly slow.

Soon after ten o'clock she got up, stretching her long arms. She put the chair and table back near the window, lifting the curtain to gaze at the night. The stars were so bright here in the dark countryside and it was very still and beautiful. Even so, the question of whether there had been an intruder in the caravan still picked at the edges of her mind. Sensible, she thought, to follow her father's advice and have a word with Dove – then she perhaps would be able to forget about it. The trouble was that her father made it sound rather like a friendly chat and Bea wasn't at all sure that the Inspector did friendly chats. He was too aloof and forbidding. She certainly hadn't any firm facts to offer him – only an uneasy feeling, after Geoff's unexplained visits.

Bea made her way across the landing to the main bathroom, where she had been tempted by the huge old-fashioned tub, armed with every luxury she could find for bathtime bliss. She could hear music floating up through the open living room door, and over the banister she caught a glimpse of Ralph disappearing in the direction of the kitchen.

Rose's voice called after him, 'Ralph … yes, I will have one after all – sorry!' Ralph's tone had the easy, comfortable matiness of old friends, as he sang out, 'Women!' – and the fond note in his voice was unmistakable.

The bath was soothing, but still the same thoughts circled endlessly. As soon as she pushed Geoff to the back of her mind, up popped Rose. Not long ago Bea had come to the conclusion that her ideas about Rose were pure imagination, as she recognised the old Rose, drifting happily through life, paying only superficial attention to anything that had no direct bearing on her own concerns. Even so, there were inconsistencies: on several occasions there had been odd reactions – as if she were personally involved. Then, seconds later, all would be normal – but there was still something closed in Rose's habitually transparent expression. What was it that was worrying Rose?

After a long bath, she made her way back to her room. She thought she could hear the music still playing downstairs. Before she settled down to sleep, she decided that tomorrow she would invite Rose just once more to confide in her – she'd have to risk upsetting her. But she would also look for an opportunity to slip down to the incident room – perhaps Sergeant Bamford would be there. This was a more comforting prospect, and with that in mind, she fell asleep surprisingly quickly.

*

In the morning, Ralph declared that he wanted to go to Blaeborough for various items for the garden and to take the chain-saw in for sharpening, as he had promised the Dysons he would do. He offered to pick up anything needed at the supermarket and suggested he might call at Clem Counter's – probably, he told them, the best butcher in Western Europe. When Rose said she had thought of getting a chicken, Ralph said that Clem's chickens had all been known personally to him and bore no resemblance to the birds in ordinary shops.

'I'd quite like to have a look round the village,' said Rose. 'And perhaps call in at the farm-shop as well. D'you want to come, Bea? If not, perhaps you could drop me off there, Ralph?'

Bea said she would be happy to go with her. There was the Craft Centre to visit and she had some shopping of her own to do. The decision about meals she left to Ralph and Rose, who at once began an expert discussion which, though impressive, was of little interest to her. Then they all paid into a kitty, and as soon as that had been arranged, Ralph drove off.

Rose had some clothes to wash before setting off, so Bea said vaguely that she wanted to catch the post and she set off in the car with her letters. But she ignored the post box, which she passed as she drove into the village and went to airmail them at the post-office. She then hurried back to the incident room on the Blaeborough Road not far from the turning to Shawhead.

The building had been a tiny schoolhouse and Bea wondered why it had been built outside the village. It was situated among a small group of dwellings that had been farm cottages. Some had been "improved", for better or worse, but one row of several terraced cottages was empty and in various stages of dereliction – evidence of the tremendous change in country living. Presumably, there was no longer a need for farm workers to live close to their work in tied cottages that were damp, cramped and inconvenient. And in any case, there were far fewer farm labourers today. Bea noticed that one unoccupied house still had its roof more-or-less intact, but once the first of those huge stone roof-tiles shifted and the rain began to creep in, it would join its neighbours before long. Sad, she thought, that they had not been rescued and new purposes found for them.

As she approached the schoolhouse, nowadays used for evening classes, as a polling station and also for concerts, she rehearsed with a certain trepidation, what she would say when she saw Inspector Dove. It was an anticlimax (and a relief) to be told that the Inspector was not there at the moment. Sergeant Bamford was available, however and Bea relaxed as she waited in a small interview room. But not for long; she heard voices beyond the door and realised with dismay Inspector Dove must have returned. He greeted her courteously enough.

'Mrs. Downey all right, is she?' he added. 'Got over the shock now?'

Bea made suitable noises and then went on to explain that of course, what she had to tell him would be of no consequence, that she was afraid she was wasting his time and that really she should not have come at all.

'Miss Roebuck,' cut in the Inspector, as the Sergeant made himself even more unobtrusive than usual in a corner, 'why don't you just tell me what has brought you here and let me decide whether you are wasting my time?'

'It's noth – it's just a feeling I had.' Bea was struggling, unused to being incoherent. 'I went to the caravan to … to get some walking gear … ' well, she told her conscience, I *did* go to get my walking gear, on my first visit. 'and I had a strong impression that someone had been in there … since you finished with it, I mean.'

'Can you tell me what the signs were that gave you that feeling?'

'Well, nothing out of place, or anything like that.' Bea went on to explain about the cupboard that she usually left open, thinking as she spoke how pathetically slight this all sounded, now that she put it into words. 'I just thought someone had been there – but I can't see why they should. You've obviously searched it, so it would be too late, if anything had been left behind.'

Dove did not reply for a moment. He looked at her, as if deciding whether to answer this.

'A guilty person's judgment is often distorted,' he said at last. 'He (or she) needs increasing reassurance and will risk returning quite unnecessarily. But if anything *was* amiss – something unnoticed, or apparently quite innocent – it would represent a continuing danger, in case someone suddenly realised its significance.' Dove gave her a penetrating look from beneath the eaves of his overgrown brows.

'Well, I'd looked around before, of course, and nothing occurred to me then … unless it was something I might only notice if I were staying there again?'

'Possibly, or it may be that there's another reason for this kind of visit.' The Inspector did not enlarge upon this but left Bea wondering what sort of reason there could be. 'Have you seen anyone up there – hanging around – calling on some pretext?'

Reluctantly, Bea explained about Geoff's visits. His appearances at the farm had been the trigger for her suspicions. It would be foolish to try to cover up for Geoff, but she felt very uncomfortable all the same. Dove raised his useful eyebrows enquiringly towards the Sergeant who replied: 'Fully questioned – I'll get the file for you,' and slipped quietly away.

'The local people have all been thoroughly examined,' Dove told her, as he took the file from the Sergeant. 'In this case, because of your concerns, I will tell you that this man, Mr. Collins, was on night shift (you may know that he works as a porter at the hospital in Blaeborough) – during the entire material time. This information is confidential and I'm only giving it to you because I feel it might prevent you from feeling anxious, or nervous, since he's a neighbour of yours.'

'Thankyou,' answered Bea. She felt mortified and was about to apologise when Dove went on:

'However, we can't ever be one hundred per cent sure. I should like to take another look myself at the caravan in your presence … no, Miss Roebuck, I am *not* humouring you!' For the first time, Bea saw the suggestion of a smile, lurking around those rather fierce eyes. 'We follow things like this up and we try to keep an open mind.'

Dove arranged to come up to the farm at three o'clock that afternoon. Bea was just leaving, when the Inspector said, 'By the way, we are still hunting for relatives of the dead man – hoping they'll help us to find out why he had come here. We know he was married and we shall soon know who his wife is – or was. That sort of thing is normally very simple nowadays – but in this case, tracing the record of the marriage has taken longer than usual. Pass that on to your friends, Miss Roebuck. I'm sure they'll be glad to know we're making progress.' The Inspector looked as though he was about to enlarge on this, but all he said was: 'So worrying – the unknown – I always think.'

Bea said goodbye and drove off up the lane. Why had the Inspector offered all that information about the dead man's wife? She was convinced that what he said had been carefully planned, intending to reach its target. As she shut the car up and walked across the yard, her head was bent in thought, her mind in turmoil.

*

'You've been up yon again, Geoff!'

'Up where?' Geoff knew as he said it that it wouldn't wash. It was his mother-in-law nagging him this time – as if Rhona and the police weren't enough. Margie usually left him alone unless it was something drastic. She must be fretting then. Well, so was he, but it wouldn't do to go around showing he was bothered.

'Farm,' said Mrs. Dutton, who didn't believe in wasting words. 'You want to keep away from there. Folks'll get ideas.'

'Let 'em. I've done nowt. Nor our Rhona hasn't – oh, I know what they're thinking … I'd have to be blind and deaf not to.'

'I know, Geoff.' Mrs. Dutton spoke more gently. 'But if you keep putting in an appearance right where it happened, it's just going to spur them on, like. If you've done nothing – and I'm sure that's right – just lie low and let it blow over.'

'Aye.' The soft local affirmative somehow said more than "yes". It carried a rueful, sighing overtone, as he acknowledged the sense in what she was saying.

'Well, think *on*! ' With this rather telling local way of saying "remember", his mother-in-law closed the subject. 'I'll just leave this,' she added, pointing to a plate covered with foil, which she had placed on the kitchen table. 'I know our Rhona never seems to get much time for baking these days – working all hours. Any road, I've been making pies, so I did an extra one for you.'

When he had thanked her and had seen her setting off in the direction of the farm-shop, he went back into his garden where he had been busy digging. However, even hard manual work failed him this time as an antidote to anxiety. The nagging thoughts recurred and pestered him – like the gnats that he kept shooing from around his head.

Why did the police seem to be suspicious of him, in spite of his having told them he was miles away at the time? He felt defeated and defenceless. What more could he say or do? They had such a clever way of putting things and he couldn't think of the right words to answer them. Always loyal, despite being sorely tried so often during his years with her, he found it natural to deny all possibility of Rhona's involvement up at the farm. But self-preservation was also natural and now he wondered whether it would be wiser to let people think whatever they wanted. If the worst came to the worst, he told himself, at least they'd think I had good reason …

Exhausted, yet unable to rest, he jabbed his fork ever more viciously into the dry earth.

CHAPTER 6

Bea was glad to be on her own with Rose, not only because she wanted to talk to her. She was finding the threesome a little bit wearing, even though she liked Ralph and found him easy company. But it would be nice to do what she and Rose had originally intended – to spend time together recapturing the friendship they had before Rose's marriage, if that were possible.

They had driven down to the village and parked the car on one of its broad cobbled verges. As they strolled through the main street, they spotted Rhona on the other side of the road outside the General Stores. She waved and continued towards The Fleece. Bea was reminded of a fleeting picture in her mind from the other day – surely there had been a look of recognition, just for a second, when Rose had approached Rhona at the buttery. What was it that Rose had said the day they arrived, when they saw Carmen with her daughter in the street? She couldn't remember now, but there had been the same feeling that Rose was holding something back … no matter how much Bea told herself that this was her imagination taking over again, the impression persisted. She had dithered long enough. There was only one way to resolve it.

'Rose,' she said slowly, as they stood outside the Craft Shop. 'Are you sure you've never been up here before?'

'What d'you mean, am I sure? I'd know, wouldn't I?' She turned towards the window, gazing at some small wooden animals that looked as if they might be local work. 'Anyway, what is all this? It would be no big deal if I had.'

'It would if you'd told the Inspector you'd never been near.'

'Oh – the Inspector! I honestly don't see why you're bothered about him, Bea. As long as I had nothing to do with this killing, then ... well then, he may feel he has to ask the questions, but I don't feel that I have to go to a lot of trouble to answer them. Not if my answers have no bearing on the case.'

'But Rose, they might have ... you just can't tell. Even I can see that he needs absolutely all the information, so that he can form a judgment – '

'Well,' said Rose crossly, 'he can form his judgment without *my* help'. She then turned to Bea and smiled with that disarming change from cloudy to sunny that was so typical of her. 'It's after eleven,' she said. 'We can get a coffee here, can't we? Let's go and grab one now, or it will be too late.'

They spent the rest of the morning looking around the village, calling in at the ancient church and then they set off for Shawhead Farm. They had bought fresh bread-rolls in the village and Rose remembered that she wanted to call at the farm-shop on their way back – she wanted some of the local eggs and something from the delicatessen counter, recently installed.

'That'll cover any eventuality – whether Ralph comes back for lunch or not.'

They were the only customers just then. Two groups of what were probably weekending families on their way home from self-catering cottages went out, weighed down with boxes and bags. Carmen was serving on her own, but seemed to be enjoying coping with a sudden busy spell. She was as friendly and talkative as ever and while Bea was wondering how to broach the subject, she immediately began to talk about the murder, which no doubt was the sole topic on everyone's lips in and around the village.

' ... Never had anything like this round here before and the police all over the place. Looking for the weapon, they are.' Her voice was low and pleasant, her speech gently accented – the language of the Dales at its best, and quite at odds with her appearance. 'We've had them calling round all times of the day, asking questions ... then coming round and asking 'em all again!' Carmen was putting their purchases through the till swiftly and efficiently all the while she regaled them with the exciting but unwelcome events. 'Over and over,' she went on. 'Where were you, where was he, why did you do that? Well, you'll know all about it – I expect you've had the same and worse.'

They agreed that there had been a lot of questioning, most of which seemed pointless. Carmen continued, as if she found it a relief to talk to fellow-sufferers.

'You'll have heard they took a shovel away?' Bea and Rose who had not heard, waited, feeling sure that they would soon have all the information they could wish for.

'Not from us, mind. Not from me, or our Rhona. But Billy Goss – you know Billy – him that owns this shop and the farm? Anyway, he says they took a shovel from that shed down by the road, just as you turn in ... well, he's got ever such a lot of junk in there. He says he didn't even know there *was* a shovel. And they gave him a receipt – said they were taking it away for elimination purposes ... but Billy, he said they must have had a good reason ... and it was all they did take, as far as we know – and he hasn't had it back yet.'

'Then,' she was well into her stride by now. 'They've fairly grilled poor Geoff – our Rhona's husband, you know.' Carmen took a carrier with a smart logo on it and deftly filled it with their shopping. 'He was on nights down at the Hospital and nowhere near Shawhead that night. But would they give up? Had our Rhona in tears and even Geoff was a bit bad-tempered over it. They really seemed to think that Rhona knows something about what happened and it didn't make any difference when I told them she comes up to me of an evening if Geoff's working – unless she's at the Fleece, which she wasn't that night. What can we – ?'

At this moment another gaggle of customers came in and saved Bea and Rose from having to think of a reply. With a smile and sympathetic wave, they withdrew, thankful not to have to gloss over the obvious possibility that Rhona didn't necessarily go straight home from her mother's at the end of the evening.

Bea suggested that they go up to the farm by the "back lane", a turning on the left just after the shop. 'It's actually quite a bit shorter that way and it's much nicer than the main road – but the lane's very narrow and twisty, so we don't use it a lot.'

They were now driving between high walls, getting occasional glimpses of the sloping fields that fell away to the right, but with a lovely sheep-filled hill rising to their left, and only an isolated cottage here and there.

'Whose idea was it to come the pretty way?' asked Bea, grinning ruefully when she had to back up for a Land Rover and trailer. She got a friendly wave from the driver as she pulled into a passing place. Just opposite was a dwelling that looked to be on the brink of dilapidation.

'Look Bea – what a shame! That's such a lovely cottage, but it's been let go. It'll soon be a ruin.'

'I know. It's sad, isn't it? It's not a tied cottage you see, or the landlord would have obligations. It's owned by a funny old boy, Mr. Birch – oh, he must be well in his eighties. He's a stubborn old curmudgeon, and he won't let his family move him, or even improve his living conditions.'

'Oh, I know that one! I've got a Granny like that. You sort of admire them of course, but all the same, they're a real pain to deal with.'

'Yes, well he is, from what his daughter says. She lives over towards Blaeborough, but I've come across her on occasions like the village fete – she's usually one of the helpers there. She says she and her husband have been worried about security, with him living so far from the village – it's a safe area, but we have had rowdies up here from the cities once or twice, bent on causing trouble. It's really quite isolated, apart from that old farmhouse you can see further up the hill there. Apparently he was persuaded to let them fit two external security lights, but even then the ungrateful old codger made a fuss because the front one disturbs him if anyone comes up the lane. And that can't be very often.'

'No, but the house is right on the road, isn't it?'

'Well anyway, Renee – that's his daughter – said they'd have to get it re-sited away from his window.' Bea looked up towards the eaves, where the lamp was fixed. 'Doesn't look as if it's been moved yet, though ... and that, along with the phone they put in, is as far as he'll let them go ... I wonder where he is,' she added. 'I don't think I've ever been up here on a nice day and not seen him sitting in his porch.'

They carried on up the narrow road, taking a right fork into a stony lane. Rose looked thoughtfully at the bag of shopping on her knee and remarked that Carmen had obviously had more than her fair share of the police's attentions. 'None of it's her fault, after all.'

'It's a shame,' agreed Bea. 'Carmen's such a good sort and I honestly don't know whether she's aware of how widely Rhona's reputation has spread. OK, there's one in every village, I suppose, but it's a pity it has to be her daughter.' Bea turned left and they were now in the upper end of the farm track. She explained that they had cut out the main road altogether.

'I wondered where that funny little lane led to,' Rose said, before returning to Carmen and her problems. 'I thought she really seemed to believe what she told us about Rhona – though that seems impossible.'

As she was getting out of the car, Rose went on: 'I hope for her sake that it's all above board. I thought it was just ... ' Once again, Rose's conversation drifted to a standstill and Bea, though curious, was careful not to quibble. There were other matters that would have to be tackled, and there was no point in souring the atmosphere beforehand.

Ralph had not returned when they let themselves in at the back door. He had indicated that he was quite likely to stay and have a pie and a pint in the town, especially if he ran into anyone he knew. Bea helped Rose to prepare a simple lunch, which they took to a sheltered spot in the garden. There was a little breeze today, which had felt quite sharp once or twice as it blew down the village street, but the sky was blue and it was quite hot in the corner they had chosen.

Although Bea was impatient to discuss the snippets gleaned during their encounter with Carmen, she was determined to avoid anything that might seem to Rose like pressure. Very soon her patience paid off as Rose soon turned to the subject of the latest news heard in the shop.

'Of course,' she murmured, 'that shovel could have been taken out – or put in for that matter – by almost anyone. The shed's right on the road and it didn't look as if they bothered much about locking it up – the door was nearly off its hinges.'

'But the police must have been looking for a shovel or something similar in the first place … they said a heavy implement, didn't they? It could have been taken at any time, I suppose, and returned when it suited.'

Rose spread pate thoughtfully on her roll. 'On the other hand, if you were setting out to kill someone I shouldn't have thought you'd go looking for anything like that as a weapon. It's more the sort of thing you'd pick up in the heat of the moment, just because it was lying around handy …'

There was a pause, as they poured more coffee. It's now or never, thought Bea. She yawned and stretched her long arms over her head, waiting until Rose had finished fiddling with her cup and spoon.

'I went to see the Inspector this morning.' She said it casually, but was afraid that it would not be received in the same way. There was silence for a few moments. She found herself noting almost unconsciously how the sun had brought out a few more freckles on Rose's face. Not too many – just the right number! As she awaited a reply, Bea was imagining how these – combined with Rose's natural charm, her glow and her green eyes – could well have a stunning effect on men.

'Why did you do that?' Rose answered her at last, quite mildly and reached for another roll.

'Several things were worrying me. First, I'd been concerned about Geoff coming up and hanging about the paddock. So I went to the caravan last night to take a look. I don't know what I expected … but when I went into the main bedroom, I noticed the cupboard door was shut – the little one in the corner by the window, that I always leave open.' Bea spread a little pate absent-mindedly on her roll as she explained briefly about the damp spot in that corner.

'It's easy to be mistaken about that kind of thing.'

'Yes, I know.' Bea looked perplexed. 'I'm not a bit sure, so I hesitated about mentioning it to officialdom. But I've felt so uneasy, Rose – and after all, they'll know whether I'm imagining things, won't they?'

'So what did Inspector Beetlebrows say when you told him?'

'Well, he didn't laugh at me, or even fob me off. He seemed to want to look into it, even though they'd officially finished the search – he'll be coming round later on. But you'd think anyone would realise that the police will have found all there is to find?'

'Not a guilty person.' Rose was tucking in heartily to her lunch, quite untroubled by doubts or worries, it seemed. 'If you're trying to cover something up and you're getting anxious, you don't think it out sensibly. You get into a panic about some insignificant thing – feeling sure it will mean something to other people, just because of what it means to you.'

'And I suppose that nine times out of ten, other people haven't noticed anything.'

Bea took a bite of her roll in a half-hearted fashion. Somehow, she was having a struggle to take an interest in food.

Rose nodded vigorously. 'It's like someone who's having an illicit affair. They walk down the road to the love-nest, feeling terribly conspicuous – as if their secret was written all over them in large letters. But usually, as far as anyone else is concerned, they're just going about their normal business.'

'That sounds like the voice of experience,' Bea said, with a grin.

'I'll tell you about it one day.' Rose sounded quite ready to confide her secrets at some future time, and yet there was a hint of evasion which did not escape Bea.

It was no use. She just had to find the answer to the most urgent of her nagging doubts. She decided to go in with both feet.

'Something else has been worrying me, Rose – worrying me more than anything else.' She took a deep breath and looked across at Rose who was calmly on her third bread roll. 'You *have* been here before, haven't you?'

Rose looked over towards the yard, where some sparrows were enjoying a dust-bath. She sighed deeply. 'Yes,' she said at last, her forehead furrowed in an expression that was rueful, but in no way apprehensive. 'I'm sorry, Bea,' she said. 'I had no right – '

'To hell with rights. That's not what's bothering me. Or rather … I'm not thrilled that you felt you had to keep it from me. But I'm mainly concerned that you've put yourself in a difficult position with your friend Beetlebrows.'

'He's the least of my worries. Why should he find out anyway? It's none of his business.'

'I'm afraid it is, you know,' said Bea gently. 'I imagine that very soon he'll know all about everyone in this village, and beyond. He told me rather pointedly that they're following up the dead man's relatives – looking for his wife, he said – and he particularly asked me to pass that on to you and Ralph.'

'Perhaps he hasn't got a wife – she's clearly not around.'

With what Bea felt was a superhuman effort on her part, she avoided telling Rose to use her common sense. Instead, she said patiently, 'They'll have contacted everyone who knew him, and they've obviously been told that he had a wife, from the way Dove looked when he was telling me. It was very – very sure and to-the-point and it seemed as if he was trying to give me a message for you. So they'll be checking records and they'll discover who she is, whether it's relevant or not. Don't you see that, love?'

Her quiet, unchallenging tone must have struck the right note. Rose grabbed Bea's hand in a gesture of capitulation.

'All right, I'll tell you about it – hang on a minute!' A persistent fly was hovering round the pate-smeared plates. Rose stacked everything quickly on the tray and took it to the kitchen. Bea wondered if she was being evasive again, but Rose returned straight away and sat down, looking determined.

'It was just – oh Bea, I've managed to put last year and all that happened … out of my life. I'm not sure now whether coming here was a good idea, but I felt that it was a way to – sort of prove to myself that it was over and done with … to lay the ghost.

'When all this happened, I thought keeping a low profile was the answer and I've been able, most of the time, to wipe out any connection – in my mind, I mean. And so far I've sort of stood aside from it all, as if I was watching a play.'

'Yes, that explains a lot … look, Dove said he'd be here around three o'clock. It's nearly that now, so we haven't long to talk.' Bea looked into Rose's troubled face. 'But he's going to find out about Guy – and it won't look very good.'

'About Guy? You knew, Bea? Right from the beginning?'

'No, not from the beginning … but I was gradually becoming more certain. And even when Dove gave us his full name, it only threw me for a moment – I just assumed that Guy must be a nickname or whatever. On the other hand, you never turned a hair when he said the body'd been identified, and that made me waver for a moment!'

'Well I was ready for him – I'd realised what he was going to say. But Bea, I didn't – '

'It's all right, Rose – I know you know nothing about what's happened. You don't need to tell me that. And the police know you came from Cambridge and that I met you off the train. You were with friends the night before …'

Rose sighed deeply. 'If only it was that simple,' she said.

'What do you mean? Look Rose, for God's sake tell me the lot. We've messed about long enough and Dove could be here any minute. You may suddenly find them asking awkward questions – the only mystery is why they haven't already … '

They both froze as they looked in the direction of the lane. It was mostly hidden by the trees at the end of the garden, but they had heard the car's engine and they glimpsed a flash of silver through the trees. Ralph's car was dark blue.

'Go upstairs, Rose – go in that way, round the other side – till he's gone. Time enough to talk to him when we've sorted things out a bit. Let's hope he hasn't got the full story yet. Go on, hurry … and for God's sake keep out of sight!'

Bea was confident that the Inspector, who had been parking his car round the opposite side of the house, could not have seen that somewhat undignified departure. She got up unhurriedly from the table, thankful that it was now innocent of the tell-tale meal for two, and came across the lawn.

'Good afternoon, Miss Roebuck – all on your own today?'

Bea smiled. 'It's nice sometimes to have the place to yourself, don't you think?'

She led him round to the paddock. She had committed herself now, so she hoped that Rose didn't start nosy-parkering about and show herself at a window.

As she opened up the caravan, she wondered why she had ever thought of discussing her misgivings with the Inspector. She was sure it had been a mistake and getting him up here seemed quite pointless and a bit embarrassing. However, she showed him the cupboard that she always left open and the little greenhouse heater beside it. He made no comment and they went on to look at various cupboards and drawers. All was in order, as Bea knew it would be.

Taking a look at the tiny shower room, Bea stopped short in the doorway. Her eye was immediately drawn to the shelf above the handbasin, on which was a pair of glasses. They gleamed in the light from the window above – stylish alloy-framed sunglasses, sitting askew on top of a tooth mug, over which they had been hooked by one "arm". Remembering that Dove had cautioned her not to touch anything that might be out of place or unfamiliar, she backed out of the small space and called Dove over.

'Those glasses aren't mine – on the shelf – and I'm sure they weren't there last time I looked in here … ' Even as she spoke, she remembered the glasses Ralph had complained of mislaying. Her heart gave a huge thump as she considered the implication.

Dove had the glasses in a plastic envelope as he emerged.

'You don't recognise them at all? A man's sunglasses, it seems.' She shook her head.

'They were not here when we did our search … but do you think you could have overlooked them when you were in the caravan recently?'

Bea was uncertain, but thought it unlikely. That meant – what did it mean? And should she mention the loss of Ralph's sunglasses to the Inspector, or wait until she knew more about this particular pair.

'I'm trying to remember. You see, I didn't go into the shower room yesterday, I just looked around in the bedroom. That was when I noticed the cupboard door. And before that … but that would mean – '

'I shouldn't start guessing about it yet, if I were you.'

'But – if Geoff Collins did come looking for something and accidentally left the glasses – '

'Whatever Mr. Collins was, or was not doing here the other day, Miss Roebuck, I think you can be fairly certain that he neither overlooked those glasses, nor attempted to retrieve them.'

Bea had to make what she could of that. Dove was ready to leave it seemed, without any mention of Rose, so she had no wish to detain him. He told her that someone would be along later to finger-print the 'van once more, after which he thought Bea would be able to hold both keys again. He also reminded her that she and Rose would be required at the inquest the next day, in the village hall. She nodded and went slowly back towards the house, thoroughly confused and anxious.

She would have to ask Ralph about his glasses. Dove had seemed to imply that they were not connected with Geoff. But they couldn't be Ralph's – he would hardly have drawn attention to his loss in that case. He had been wearing them on Saturday and the case had been left outside on the kitchen window sill. So he said.

She fastened the paddock gate and stopped, staring blankly at the house, as she reached first one conclusion, then the opposite. Rose had said it wasn't "that straightforward", just as Dove arrived. Were the police still checking *her* story? Had they already done so, and for some reason they were waiting before they pounced?

She turned left, through the back yard and went into the big friendly kitchen, with its ancient pine dresser which was impossible to keep clean and tidy, but which was so comforting and welcoming. She would go and find Rose, she decided and she would simply pour out everything, including all her doubts and suspicions. Whatever that wilful woman might have been up to, Bea was perfectly certain that it was no more than foolishness.

When she found Rose, she was stretched out on her bed, fast asleep.

'I don't know whether to hit you, or fetch you a cup of tea!' Bea said when she finally managed to waken her. 'There I am, perjuring myself for you, worrying myself into a decline, because you're up to something – oh yes you are! … and you're going to tell me all about it right now, Rose. I'm sick to death of worrying about other people.'

'By "other people" I take it you mean me. You've no need. I can take care of myself – '

'Well, I don't just mean you, as it happens. There's Ralph as well,'

'Ralph! How do you mean, Bea?' There was a sudden and most unaccustomed sombreness in Rose's voice and she sat up suddenly. 'Where does Ralph come into it?'

'I wish I knew. Probably not at all.' Bea plonked herself on the edge of the bed. 'But ... well, you know last night, when he said he'd mislaid his sunglasses?' She paused, then saw that she now had all Rose's attention. 'A pair has just turned up in the caravan.'

'What? But you can't think they're his! He was wearing them on Saturday ... in any case, how could your possibly think – '

'It doesn't really matter what *I* think. Dove was with me when I found them ... it probably took his mind off looking for you! Anyway, did you see Ralph wearing them when he was chopping wood – you were out there – and what were they like?'

Rose swung her legs out of bed and fished for her sandals. She picked up her creamy cashmere sweater from the bed, straightened her hair as she passed the dressing table and led the way down to the kitchen. Bea, determined not to lose the momentum, followed closely and stood beside her as she filled the kettle, her expression making it clear that she was waiting for an answer.

'I'm trying to remember,' said Rose. 'The harder I try to picture him, the more uncertain I am.'

'Can't you recall whether you thought he looked good in them?'

But as Rose shrugged, Bea went on: 'Well, *I've* no recollection at all, but I'm probably not he most observant person in the world, particularly when I've got something on my mind. And I wasn't there most of the time when he was busy with the wood – I was round at the front of the house, if you remember.' She took two mugs down from the dresser, as Rose fetched the teapot and some milk.

'We'll have to ask him. It'll be a bit embarrassing, but he – '

'I'm not sure we should ask him,' Bea interrupted.

'You mean, it would sound too – offensive, as if we're suggest-ing ... '

'No love, I mean ... OK, we're sure it has nothing to do with him, aren't we? But even so, Rose – think!' She plonked herself down opposite Rose at the table. 'If he *was* implicated in any way, and we told him we'd spotted something like that, we'd ... '

'What the hell are you talking about, Bea? You're off your trolley! You know perfectly well that what you've just said is a load of garbage!' Rose's indignant voice rose in both pitch and volume, just as they became aware of a shadow over the doorway.

Ralph grinned at them. 'Nice of me to get out of your way so you can enjoy a good row in peace!' He put down a largish box of shopping on a worktop. Despite her colouring, Rose was not often seen to blush, but she managed it this time. She occupied herself with the teapot and Bea hoped that her confusion was less obvious from where Ralph stood.

'My fault,' Bea said cheerfully. 'I said something outrageous. Do you want a cup of tea?' she managed to add quite tranquilly, but she wondered how long Ralph had been within earshot.

'No – I'd like a great big mugful. It's been a bit of a day.' Ralph's voice sounded a little weary. 'Is there any of Mrs. Holroyd's cake left?'

'In that tin … bring a knife. You were a long time. Did you meet a lot of people you know?' Rose was now recovered and sounded as serene as ever.

'No I didn't.' Ralph sat down at the big table and accepted a mug of tea. 'That is, I did see a guy I know in the pub at lunchtime, but then later, when I was about to get into the car in the High Street, Sergeant Bamford caught me. He'd apparently been trying to get me on the phone this morning. He asked me to go to the station and go through my statement again. It took quite a while in the end.'

'Why did they want you to do that?' asked Bea quietly, while Rose sat motionless, with her mug poised in both hands.

Ralph shrugged. 'It seems that my information about Thursday night has been queried at the other end – in Manchester, I mean, where they've been checking up. I was in the lab until eightish. I'd been very tied up with a project for quite a while and I wanted to finish it off so that I'd be free to come up here. I've had to bring the last of the writing-up with me, even so.' He took a sip of tea and opened the cake tin. 'After that I was at home.'

'On your own?' asked Rose, drinking her tea composedly.

'Some of the time, yes. But Henry Bloom, a bloke from the lab, called round. He'd got some sort of mental block with the work he's doing and he wanted to discuss it. He didn't leave till about a quarter to one – I thought he was never going! That's why I didn't get my own stuff finished – annoying, but apparently it should put me in the clear because, now they've got the pathologist's report, they have a pretty precise idea of the crucial time.

'But the problem is,' Ralph went on, between bites. 'They've asked Henry to confirm, but the silly sod can't remember whether that was Wednesday or Thursday.'

'But that's ridiculous!' Bea could not imagine anyone not recalling events of less than a week ago. 'He *can't* not remember!'

'Henry could! That's the trouble. He's your original absent-minded boffin! He certainly isn't trying to be awkward. If he says he can't be sure, then he can't be sure. He's really one of those frighteningly honest people who create waves of chaos around them wherever they go. So of course he had to tell the police he was uncertain. Doesn't help me a lot.'

'That's really tough,' said Rose. 'Did nothing else happen – a phone call or something that would clinch it?'

'Well, yes. Peter Mason, who lives in the flat below me – he came up quite late to see if I'd got a luggage strap I could lend him. He was only there for a minute or so, but the point is, he came while Henry was there, so that would –'

'Settle which evening it was,' interrupted Bea. 'Now, if you're going to say that *he* doesn't remember which evening it is, I simply won't believe it.'

'It would have to be a conspiracy to frame you,' suggested Rose flippantly.

'It's all right to joke about it, Rose, but it's actually bloody annoying. The police tend to cling on if they once feel there's some doubt. The whole point is that Pete *will* remember coming up to the flat – the day'll be fixed in his mind because he told me he was off to Nepal on a research assignment the following morning – that's what he wanted the baggage strap for. But so far, no-one has been able to contact him.'

'Well Ralph, all you need in that case is to know the day he was leaving – from the travel agent or his family … '

'Sounds easy enough!' Ralph reached over to the teapot and poured himself another mugful.

'It doesn't work though. He told *me* he was off the following morning, but I was still at the door letting him in when he said it, and Henry was in the sitting room and didn't hear him. You see, as far as the police are concerned, Peter might have begun his packing a day or two before he set off – after all, he wasn't just dealing with a casual bag for the weekend. It's the sort of thing you might have to prepare for well in advance – all the stuff you're going to need out there. According to Sergeant Bamford, they asked Henry if he recalled anything Peter said about his trip – "leaving in the morning", or something of that sort. And – you've guessed it … '

'He didn't remember that either!' chorused Rose and Bea.

'But when this Peter comes back – or when they manage to contact him … ' began Rose.

'Oh, right. I don't think there's any problem about that, it's just a matter of getting in touch. But in the meantime I'm on their list of people with a local connection and a doubt about their activities. And he was going to some remote places where he might not even be able to charge up his mobile – it could be a while before we're in touch with him.'

Bea was frowning into her empty mug. 'Apart from all that, Ralph, there's no reason for the police to connect you to the dead man, is there?'

'There's no connection,' answered Ralph firmly. 'Only I get the impression – the police are very cagey of course – but they give you the feeling that they are looking for local knowledge behind the crime. It's what we thought ourselves, isn't it? Why else would it have happened here?'

Rose was frowning as she considered their original assumptions in greater detail. 'Well, if the dead man – '

'Wharton,' put in Bea.

'If he was only incidental' went on Rose, ignoring her. 'I mean, if he simply got in the way ... suppose there was some kind of crook who needed a hideout, or a meeting place – maybe someone who had stayed at the farmhouse and knew all about the caravan.'

'Why on earth go to all that trouble?' asked Bea. 'It's fairly isolated, and yet a stranger in the area would be conspicuous. There must be hundreds of better places, and more convenient.'

'Well, we don't know that yet, do we? OK, perhaps I'm not explaining it very well.' She lifted the teapot and looked at the others, but they shook their heads. 'What I'm saying is that if he was only a *coincidental* victim, who he is – his identity, I mean, is not important.'

'Except to Mrs. Wharton and any little Whartons,' objected Ralph.

Rose sighed deeply. 'Are you going to let me finish? It's your theory that I'm trying to support.'

'Sorry,' said Ralph meekly.

'I mean that, as far as the *victim* of the crime goes, it could have been anybody who happened to be in the wrong place at the wrong time. But the murderer – involved in something criminal – was probably conducting his operation round here because it's a place he knows well.'

'Yes,' said Ralph. 'It could be a bit like that, though it doesn't explain how Wharton came to be at the caravan in the first place, or why. I had a rather different scenario in mind, but on similar lines.

'As you say, somebody round here could be a sort of catalyst – causing a murder to happen, but not really involved in what's gone on. And of course, the police are investigating all known connections with that catalyst and most of them will probably be innocent.'

'Bea stood up and took the mugs to the sink. Turning to look at Ralph over her shoulder, she said, 'You know something, don't you ... you know what happened?'

'No.' His voice was quiet and he went on evenly: 'I don't know what happened. But let's say I've got a pretty good idea how it might have been … what triggered it.'

'Well go on then,' urged Rose. 'You are going to tell us, aren't you?'

'Not at present. I might be horribly wrong. I've got to think it through … I think I'll have another go at the wood in the yard. Chopping wood usually helps me to think.'

Rose looked as if she was about to argue with this, but then she just stared after him and turned to walk purposefully towards the fridge.

'I'd better think about how I'm going to cook this very well-brought-up chicken then,' she said.

CHAPTER 7

'I'll help you then,' offered Bea, seizing the box of shopping and beginning to unpack it at the table. 'Just think up some nice idiot jobs to keep me busy while you master-mind the dinner.'

'There's no need, you know. I'm quite happy doing it on my own and I haven't decided what I'm going to – '

'I know there's no need to.' Bea stacked the vegetables carefully in one corner of the table ready to take them into the larder after Rose had chosen what she needed for the meal. 'I'm sure you can manage beautifully without me. But you have a choice: either I give you a hand – polish the carrots or dust the lettuce or whatever and you tell me about Guy, or I sit and watch *you* do it all, and you tell me about Guy.' She now moved over to the fridge, shuffling its contents around to make room for their purchases.

'Time,' Bea said firmly, 'is running out. If the Inspector finds you before you go and seek him out, it's going to look very bad.'

'He hasn't come up with anything yet. And it's been three days now.'

'Yes, well you've been bloody lucky. There's obviously been some kind of delay, getting the info. But there's no way he won't find out. Rose *please*!'

Rose had been washing her hands at the sink and she now went to dry them with an air of resignation.

'All right, Bea. It will be a relief to talk, really. But let's sit down, I can do the supper later.' She picked up the vegetable knife absently and looked at it as though she wondered what it was. Pushing it into her apron pocket regardless of possible damage, she sat down with her elbows on the table and her chin in her hands, while Bea took a chair opposite to her.

'Back to the beginning, Rose – Guy's name …'

'Is Arthur Gurney Wharton.' Rose sounded as if the name was choking her.

'I was a bit thrown at first because you referred to him as Guy – but it soon became obvious.'

'Well, he wasn't keen on being Arthur – I know it's fashionable lately, but … anyway, he used a version of his middle name.' Rose absently prodded the brown paper bag of carrots with her fore-finger and seemed surprised when it developed a hole. 'Just after we got married, we'd driven off one weekend, meaning to find a country pub to stay at and he asked me where your caravan was. I'd mentioned it to him at some time. Well, I remembered the name of the village and he insisted on coming to look for it, because we were somewhere north of Blaeborough and it wasn't far. I didn't know just where the caravan was, but we were coming along that minor road to the north of here and spotted a caravan surrounded by trees, but just visible across the fields. Funny we should find ourselves in the only spot you can see it from … I knew it was bound to be your 'van from your description of its position and the trees you'd planted and everything.

'Well, we went on into the village and had lunch at the Fleece and when I was coming back from the loo, I saw him laughing and joking with … with Rhona. At the time I didn't think anything of it. But I wonder now if he'd met her before. She seemed to be giving him the come-on, but I wasn't concerned – I must admit, I … she – '

'She didn't seem much of a rival?'

'Doesn't sound a very nice thing to say, but yes, that's true – and in any case we'd only been married a few weeks. I was hardly dwelling on the possibility of the "other woman".' Rose smiled wryly. 'I should have done of course, because very soon after that

I discovered that he habitually behaved like an absolute alley cat … everyone knew except me, of course.'

'I know,' said Bea softly. 'It might have been different if all this had happened in your home town, or a place you'd lived in for a long time, where people knew you and cared. But there would be no-one to tip you the wink as soon as you got to know this guy – no pun intended, sorry.'

'Well, of course – *you* did! You tipped me off – or tried to.'

'Yes, but that's different – it wasn't because of anything I knew about him. I was an interfering old bag, if you like – but it wasn't a case of *who* you were marrying: I just didn't feel you'd given it time …'

'And of course, you were right,' sighed Rose. She now picked up the bag of carrots by her right hand and, taking the knife from the pocket of her apron, began to trim them. 'I can see it all now, but not many people behave rationally when they fall in love.'

'Well, go on.'

'After we'd had lunch in the pub garden – it was a beautiful day – we decided to go up on the hills. But Guy wanted to see your caravan first. It was easy to work out how to get to it from the village. He said we might be able to borrow it for a week, or something like that. So we went and had a look. There was nobody at the farm apparently. But Guy has – had – a funny nosy streak and he couldn't just take a look and leave it at that. He peered in at the windows and then asked if there was a key kept nearby, in a shed or something.'

'So you told him?'

'Without thinking, I just remembered how you'd joked about getting locked out that time and I quoted you.' Rose looked at the growing pile of trimmed carrots as though she wondered how they had got there. 'You'd said, "but anyone bent on getting in would have to know it's the second clump of heathers on the right and then six inches behind it". I think now, that he was filing that fact away for future use.'

'You didn't think it a strange question?'

'Yes, almost immediately afterwards – I'd just answered mechanically. Then I got this feeling that he might go and dig up the key there and then ... and I sort of realised that we were quite out of order and tugged him away, back to the car. We went off walking after that and had a lovely afternoon and I forgot all about it ... oh!'

'What's up? Is there something else?'

'No ... well, it's just occurred to me that he asked me – not then, much later – about you. At the time, it seemed as if he was just interested in what your job was and so on.' Rose paused with her fist on the table and the knife sticking straight up in the air 'And you know that he met Philip a couple of times? Guy came over to Darlington to see me, soon after we first met – you were in the States then of course.' Rose went to the sink and came back with a pan of water for the vegetables (she had now started on the potatoes, as if she needed to occupy her hands while she talked).

'The first time, we met Philip by accident in a pub, so of course I introduced them. I mentioned Philip's job, as you do – and Guy seemed very interested in that. He'd had a few drinks by then and I remember him saying "So you're in a commercial practice ... do you ever come across industrial sabotage?" and Philip laughed and said he thought Guy meant industrial espionage and that he'd encountered all sorts of weird and wonderful crimes. They seemed to get on rather well. Didn't Philip tell you about it?'

'Not that I recall ... funny that. But then, Philip has a few friends that he seems to keep more-or-less to himself and from time to time he'll go off – just disappear for a couple of days. He never says very much about it afterwards. It's this personal space thing – we've both got it. Sorry, you were saying ... did they meet again?'

Bea got up and took the gin bottle from the shelf and waved it questioningly towards Rose, who nodded.

'Good idea! Yes, they met when Guy came over the next time. After that, we got married while we were on holiday abroad and then of course I went to Lancaster ... that's odd though.' Rose frowned, as if something had just struck her. 'Once or twice after that, I thought I recognised Philip's voice when I picked up the phone. Only it couldn't have been.'

'Why couldn't it?'

'Well I asked Guy, of course and he said it was someone from work,' replied Rose as she reached for the chopping-board and began reducing the potatoes to cubes with unusual vigour. Before Bea could point out that what Guy said proved nothing, Rose continued. 'But I was telling you about Guy being interested in the caravan. One of the things he wanted to know about was your normal arrangements for going up there. So I told him you went there in summer, on Saturdays and Sundays and never during the week because of work. He said did you often spend your annual holiday there and I told him I didn't think so. I still thought that he was thinking of a holiday for us …'

'Very handy – all that information!' Bea set a misty, ice-clinking glass in front of Rose.

'I'm so sorry, Bea.'

'It's not your fault, not at all. Only this silly cover-up you've been staging – '

'Not a cover-up at all! I just didn't want to drag it all up again. I thought, if only I could keep out of it somehow… all right – I haven't been seeing straight. I realise that now.'

'But what really gets me, Rose, is how you could see his body – your husband's body, for Heaven's sake – and manage never to let on to me, let alone to the fuzz – '

'But it wasn't *like* that… Bea, I didn't *know* it was Guy!'

'WHAT ?'

'How can I make you understand? To start with, Guy didn't have a beard when he and I were together. And then he'd got this very deep suntan. The dead man had, I mean.' Rose frowned and pushed the now full pan away from her.

'And as well as that, when I found him I only took the very briefest glance at him – in the half light – the curtains were drawn, remember. I even wondered if he might be Indian, or something … I just had the impression that he was very dark.'

'Are you asking me to believe that you didn't recognise him at all?'

'No - o … not quite that. It all happened in a split second.' Rose stopped and put her head between her hands, oblivious of the floury potato-starch that clung to them. Then she looked at Bea and took a deep breath. 'Just as I opened the door, I – well, you know how people say, "I thought for one horrible moment…"? Well, that's exactly how it was. The next second, I wondered what could have made me think like that – it was simply a dark-skinned man with a beard who somehow had a fleeting look of Guy. Then after that my feelings fluctuated – one moment I thought it *could* be him and the next, the idea seemed ridiculous. That's why I got so upset. It was always nagging at me and I kept on trying to recall what I'd seen – so as to be absolutely sure.'

Bea didn't doubt that Rose was speaking the truth. Indeed, the opposite was harder to swallow – that Rose had known it was Guy from the outset and had covered up so determinedly. It also explained the curious changes of mood.

'But when you looked the second time, at the mor … hospital?'

'Oh of course, when I saw him in the mortuary, with those big bright lights – and taking my time – I knew then. And somehow, there was a sort of pallor beneath the tan … but you see my difficulty then? If I said who he was, I thought the police would want to know why I'd not said so before. I had only a few seconds to make up my mind and after that it was too late – I was committed. They'd never believe me – I just couldn't cope … '

'You should have told me. Of all the … you know I'd have helped.'

'Yes I do. Thanks Bea – and look … you've really been great. But just for now, if you don't mind, I think I'd like you to leave me to carry on with the meal. I need something practical to do and I need to be on my own.'

Bea nodded and got up, turning towards the door. 'I'll go and have a bath before supper. I do my best thinking in the bath.' She paused at the door. 'And by the way, don't – ' she stopped, realising that Rose probably couldn't take much more bullying. ' … Don't forget to wash your face – it's covered in potato starch!'

*

Philip was still in Darlington, keeping himself occupied at work and putting in a lot of extra hours. He was biding his time with all the patience he could muster, certain that it was the only hope of success. He had been in constant touch with Bea's Mother, who was delighted to chat with him at any time. He had listened carefully to all the news, though there wasn't a lot. He would ask her father, next time he had a chance, to make a gentle request for him to visit the farm. There was nothing active to be done – often, he felt, harm was done by trying to move things along, when patience was the better strategy.

The local police, in answer to a query from Blaeborough, had visited him. This didn't surprise him, as his closeness to Bea would indicate a connection, however tenuous, with the caravan. He was asked about the current state of his relationship with Bea and he gave them a frank picture of how things stood.

They wanted to know where he was at the time of the murder. As it happened, this was particularly straightforward for him because he had been in Harrogate at a conference for four days that week. It finished on Friday afternoon. His hotel bill was available and he had attended the conference meetings every day. The evening ones were late finishing and ended up in the bar. He'd explained that he was present at meetings on both Thursday night and Friday morning. He'd told them that he knew how people often slip away from such large gatherings, but that he was confident there would be several colleagues who would remember. He found it all rather tedious, but he responded courteously to the questioning. As a solicitor, he knew this was standard practice – there was no point in objecting, even though the questions could seem quite offensive to an innocent person. All in all, thought Philip, it had been just about what he expected.

*

When Bea had used the main bathroom the other night, she had felt a bit guilty about the amount of water she'd used – probably a whole tankful. She had taken a child-like delight in the great bath, which stood in the middle of the room on its claw feet. She wondered if the first plumbed-in baths were put in the middle of the room, rather than against the wall, simply because no-one thought of positioning them differently from the old hip-baths, or whatever they had replaced. The other feature that she thought was great fun, was the fireplace – quite a big, imposing one with a pretty wooden surround. Instead of the chimney being blocked off, a coal fire had been laid in the grate – unlikely ever to be lit, but it gave the impression that on a cold evening it would roar in competition with the bath taps. The small utilitarian bathtub in their own quarters was definitely a come-down. However, the hot suds were just as enjoyable.

On reflection, she found that Rose's story came as no great surprise. However, she wasn't any nearer knowing just how to tackle the problem, which never should have arisen in the first place. She tried to shrug off her exasperation at the way Rose had needlessly invited trouble. Getting cross about it wouldn't help, but possibly some action first thing tomorrow might lessen the impact. Rose might get a rap over the knuckles, or worse, for concealing the truth (wasting police time?), but they couldn't think she was further involved, since she was far away at the time.

So tomorrow morning Rose must be brought, kicking and screaming if necessary, to the incident room and she must tell her story in full as soon as possible, before the inquest in the afternoon. Actually, she thought, I don't think I'll have much trouble with her now – it may be a relief on the whole.

As she was adding more hot water, she heard the back door bang. Ralph coming in, she supposed. She had discovered that this bathroom, added to the house quite recently over the kitchen, was the one place where voices occasionally could be heard. Always curious, she had wanted to know the reason for this. The sounds seemed to be coming from the direction of the airing cupboard. She had investigated this, moving the cleaning things over – and had found an inadequately sealed space where the pipes ran down through the floor from the tank. As she turned off the tap now, a murmur, continuous and urgent, reached her through the half-open door of the cupboard, over which she had thrown her towel.

'Sod it!' she muttered to herself. 'Just what I didn't want to happen.' Earlier, it had been on the tip of her tongue to warn Rose not to tell Ralph. She cursed herself now for the wrong decision. 'Still,' she consoled herself. 'She probably wouldn't have taken any notice.'

Why, she wondered, would it be better not to tell him? She could see no reason when she analysed it. But it was all part of treading carefully, where Ralph was concerned. She felt that was important. He had appeared to be very open about the difficulties with his alibi, but still it seemed unwise to take him so much on trust. There was, for instance, the matter of the sunglasses... Well, that was probably silly, since he had brought up the subject himself when he had no need to.

'Unless of course,' she murmured aloud, 'he was convinced when he said that, that he *had* mislaid them in the yard, with no thought of where else they might be.' Well, she was determined to find out; she would mention the glasses in the caravan and then watch his reaction closely.

Rose had made an excellent dish from the locally farmed chicken. She had clearly found cooking therapeutic – they both complimented her on the potato croquettes, which bore no resemblance to the readymade, frozen ones. But in the event, the meal took second place to the conversation (conference?) which accompanied it. They finished the main course and then, by common consent they began to discuss the situation in earnest. As expected, Ralph had listened to Rose's story earlier, so Bea did not have to hear it all over again, and Ralph offered to go with Rose to the police station.

'Or we can all go, if you think it's better.' Ralph clearly didn't want to look as if he was taking over.

'Bit of a crowd – it might look as if we're making too much of it.' Bea would have preferred to go with Rose herself, but it was really Rose's decision and perhaps she, Bea, had interfered enough. 'You decide, Rose and let us know in the morning. We need to sort it in good time – you haven't forgotten about the inquest in the afternoon, have you?' As Rose shook her head, Bea went on: 'I was thinking … although it wasn't a very bright thing to do, it's probably not very serious, is it? After all, they know where you were at the – "material time", I think it's called …'

'That's just it! *I* know where I was, but – '

'For Heaven's sake, don't tell me *you've* got friends who don't know one day from another as well? I just don't believe I'm hearing – '

'Keep your shirt on! It's not like that at all.' Rose passed her empty plate to Ralph, who was stacking them, rather absent-mindedly, at the end of the table. 'Ralph, you don't know about this, but I was staying with friends, Howard and Celia in Cambridge just before I came up here on Friday. They're very old friends, just back on leave from the Middle East, where Howard's job is, and I'd been with them since the previous Saturday. Well, on Wednesday morning, they had a message from Howard's sister in Fakenham. She had to go into hospital quite suddenly – and they've got two young children.'

'You mean your friends went off to look after them?' Ralph asked.

'Ye Gods – what rotten luck,' breathed Bea.

'For me it was, yes. Howard's sister's all right, though – I got a text from them on Thursday evening. Anyway, they were both free to go – both on leave from work – but it meant the end of my holiday with them. Celia suggested that if I wanted to have another day or two in Cambridge, I was welcome to stay in the house, as long as I learned how to do the burglar alarm …'

Bea interrupted again, but this time in a very quiet voice, measuring her words. 'When you telephoned me, you said nothing about your friends going off. I would have thought it would be perfectly natural to mention it in passing – either then or when we met up later.'

'Oh hell.' Rose looked embarrassed. 'Yes, of course it would have been. Natural I mean – in normal circumstances.' She looked even more uncomfortable. 'But you and I, Bea – we'd only seen each other once since we'd …'

'Fallen out?' put in Bea helpfully.

'Well, we hadn't exactly fallen out. I don't think so, anyway. But things had been a bit dodgy. I realised you'd been right and I was looking forward to joining you, but I was afraid that if I said I was staying on alone, it might look as if I was expecting you to alter your arrangements to suit me. I felt it would be a bit of a cheek, you see. So I just thought I'd sound you out about coming Friday instead of Saturday, but without mentioning any strong reason to do so.'

'Yes,' Bea nodded. 'I see. We've both been walking on eggshells a bit, haven't we?'

'So presumably,' put in Ralph, trying to keep them on track, 'there is no-one to vouch for where you were on Thursday, right through to whatever time you caught the train – or even until you apparently got off it at Leeds?'

'Oh, that's a bit steep – *apparently!* I was on the platform … I saw her get off.'

'I'm not doubting either of you, Bea.' Ralph's slow thoughtful tones gave an impression of quiet reliability, which made Bea think she would have to be very sure of her ground before she questioned his own movements. 'And I'm certain that Rose travelled on that train just as she says. But the police are going to say all these things I'm saying and worse, so it's as well to have a little practice now.

'The fact that you don't drive a car should rule out any chance of your being implicated,' he went on. 'You could hardly have rampaged all over the county murdering people if you were dependent on a rural bus timetable! But I'm surprised they haven't tackled you already about your alibi – and about Guy.'

'Mmm. But in the case of Guy, there's not a lot to connect me to him. We got married during a holiday abroad – did I tell you that? I've even wondered whether it was a proper legal wedding, because obviously they've had some sort of delay getting hold of the records … Then I moved away at once when we split up and didn't even wait to sort things out legally. I cut all ties – not that there were many ties, because I only lived in the house near Lancaster for four months and then I went back to Darlington, reverted to my maiden name – '

'But kept the "Mrs.",' Ralph smiled enquiringly at her.

'Yes. I can't really give you a sensible reason why, Ralph. It was instinctive, it told people in Darlington who'd known me forever just what had happened.'

'Perhaps it was also to deter predatory males?' Bea said light-heartedly, hoping it wouldn't be taken for sarcasm.

'Not exactly. I felt at the time that it helped to make my situation clear. Then I didn't have to go around explaining that I'd been married, or that I was just a bit married – and I just couldn't face up to all the trauma of divorce – not yet. It had been … rather … rather horrible, our so-called marriage. And now I'm a widow!' Rose's voice trembled and Ralph looked sympathetic, while it crossed Bea's mind that the concept of widowhood had only just occurred to Rose.

'I see what you mean about avoiding explanations.' Compassion for Rose made Bea hasten to back her up. 'If you're Mrs. Bloggs and Mr. Bloggs isn't around, people don't like to ask questions. They get the idea that you probably wouldn't welcome any prying.'

'That's exactly how I felt!' Rose smiled wanly. 'Anyway, to go back to Howard and Celia … they left in a rush, of course, so if the police have been calling at the house and asking neighbours, it's quite likely they've not got much further.'

'But that won't hold them off for long. I'm surprised they haven't asked for your help with their whereabouts already. Want some coffee?' Ralph added. 'I'll go and make some.'

'I put cheese and biscuits on a tray in the kitchen and there's fruit … ' Rose began to get up from her seat, but Ralph waved her back and turned towards the kitchen.

'Perhaps,' said Bea, 'they were going to ask you about Howard and Celia this afternoon – if you'd been around.'

Ralph stopped in the doorway. 'This afternoon? Were they here?'

Well, this was something Rose hadn't got round to telling him about. Running away from the Inspector and skulking upstairs wasn't perhaps the kind of thing she wanted to dwell on, thought Bea. But Rose only said: 'Bring the coffee in, will you Ralph? Then we'll tell you about it.'

Ralph had lit the wood-stove earlier and they drew chairs round it. The evenings were quite chilly in spite of sunny days and they enjoyed its roaring comfort. Bea turned on a softly-shaded lamp and the room seemed a lovely peaceful place. If only it were truly peaceful, she thought. But they'd better get on with Rose's story, then perhaps they could try to enjoy the relaxing atmosphere. As she was considering how to get Rose started again, Ralph came in with a tray and forestalled her. He left the tray on the table and sat down by the fire.

'What's this about this afternoon then? Did Dove call here, or did you go down there, Bea? You were a bit concerned about Geoff Collins coming around, weren't you?'

Yes, thought Bea, a perceptive man – kind. As long as he's not a murderer, that is.

'I was a bit. And I had an uneasy feeling that somebody had got into the 'van. Mostly intuition, I suppose, but a cupboard door wasn't left as I usually leave it. So I popped in to the incident room.' Bea tried to make this sound as casual as possible.

'Haven't the police been back to the 'van then? Mightn't they have moved things?'

Bea shook her head. 'I think they finished before I went the first time, to get my walking things. Anyway, Dove would have said. I told him how I always leave the cupboard open, with the little heater on, otherwise it gets damp in there.'

'So what *did* he say?' asked Ralph, pushing his chair a little further back from the fire.

'He's the most inscrutable person I ever met. He was just the same about the sun – ' Bea stopped abruptly. Ralph's easy manner had encouraged her to chatter on, forgetting that she was not yet ready to broach this subject. Too late now.

'About the *son*?' Rose was puzzled, and Ralph merely waited for Bea's explanation, polite and self-possessed as usual.

'Oh,' Bea found herself saying quite easily, just as though the episode hadn't niggled at her all day. 'It was just some sun-glasses that were in the 'van … I couldn't remember ever seeing them before – but of course, you sometimes forget – '

'What were they like?' asked Ralph quickly.

'What were the ones you lost like?' countered Bea, suddenly and uncharacteristically losing her caution. But Ralph did not seem at all put out by her bluntness, answering willingly – even eagerly.

'Metal frames … photochromic lenses – you know, the ones that darken. Have you got them handy? I can soon tell you if they're mine.'

'The Inspector took them away with him.' Bea was surprised at how detached Ralph sounded. How did he imagine the specs had got into the 'van, supposing they were his? 'They were silvery-grey metallic and, yes, I think they might have been the sort that darken, but I didn't handle them. I found them in the shower room, at the back of the washbasin.'

'Yes.' Ralph frowned as he considered this. 'Well, that's odd, but … they do sound like mine, and mine are still missing.'

'I thought you mislaid them in the yard when you were chopping wood.' Rose seemed anxious to help him off the hook. 'And you found the case out there … so you must have had them on Saturday.'

'That's what I thought. I still think so. But your memory can play tricks sometimes – as you said earlier, Bea.' Ralph got up and helped himself liberally from the cheese board, while Bea poured coffee. 'Still, I'm sure I remember taking them off. I'd worked up a hell of a sweat (I'm not as fit as I thought) and the glasses kept slipping down my nose, so I took them off and put them on a roundel of wood. Then later I forgot all about them and was quite surprised to find the empty case on the windowsill and no sign of the glasses – but they would hardly have ended up in the caravan.'

'I should think there are an awful lot of glasses similar to those – they'll turn up I expect,' said Rose, dismissing the subject as apparently unimportant.

'Mrs. Holroyd will be coming in the morning,' Ralph said, totally without relevance, it seemed. Bea had come across more adroit ways of changing the subject and felt like saying so. But then he went on, 'She offered to come midweek, to keep us up to scratch. She can get a lift here on a Tuesday with her husband … so I suggest that you both fade tactfully into the background and let me see if I can do a bit of discreet digging. It's surprising that there's been no fresh news.'

'Surely there'll be something soon.' Rose looked over to the TV set at the other end of the big room that served as dining, sitting and everything-else room. 'I was going to suggest that we put the telly on. It looks a bit ancient, but I see there's a digibox, so it should work …'

'It's fine, I think – though I hardly ever bother with TV when I'm here. I've had the radio on for the news, but I don't think they're interested any more, after those first two items were broadcast. Try it anyway … we can wash up later. You never know – they might have caught him by now.'

'Or her,' said Bea. Ralph and Bea cleared the last things from the table and stacked them. They returned in time to find a picture just appearing. Rose started to fiddle with the remote, but Ralph warned her to leave it alone, just as a fresh news item began. A photograph was flashed up which the newsreader told them was of Arthur Gurney Wharton. Rose shuddered as a reporter said that the police were anxious to speak to Mr. Wharton's estranged wife. She might have an idea why he was in the area. Ralph took the remote from Rose and seized her empty hand as they all stood around to hear that the police were following several leads and were confident that they would very soon have more information. As the item ended, they looked at each other without speaking, and then by common consent the TV was turned off.

'Tomorrow – ' began Bea.

'You'll have to – ' Ralph started at the same moment. 'Go on Bea. You have first shout.'

'I was just going to say, tomorrow Rose, first thing … you're not going to try and duck out, are you? It'll only be worse if you don't offer the information – and then there's the inquest in the afternoon.'

'Just stick to the true facts when you talk to Dove– it won't be such an ordeal as you might think. One of us will be with you – take your pick.' Ralph looked into her face, concerned and persuasive. 'It's not as if they suspect you or anything like that. It's a technicality really … They can only say you should have told them before – oh, who on earth can that be?' he added as the doorbell rang.

The women left Ralph to answer it and he came back into the room followed by Inspector Dove and his Sergeant. They addressed themselves to Rose.

Sergeant Bamford spoke first. 'I'm sorry to call on you so late, Mrs. Downey – Miss Roebuck,' he nodded in Bea's direction.

'There are several points we'd like your help with, Mrs. Downey. It's taken longer than we expected to chase up a few items, but we can't make any more progress now without your assistance.'

Rose had gone rather pale beneath her suntan, but she received this statement calmly. 'Perhaps we could talk in here …' She looked at the other two and Bea thought she and Ralph should excuse themselves and go and wash up. Or maybe one of them could stay with Rose for moral support?

This dilemma was soon resolved, as the Inspector said firmly that it would be best to hold their discussion in the incident room. 'All the files are there, and I shall need to record our conversation.'

'What do you want to talk about?' Rose was stalling.

'We need you to help us obtain confirmation of some of the details you've given us,' said the Sergeant vaguely.

'Can I come with her?' Ralph obviously felt that this was no time to be discussing who would go along with Rose. He sounded confident and reasonable and the Inspector made no difficulty about this, though he pointed out that Ralph might be waiting around quite a bit.

'In that case,' answered Ralph calmly, 'I'll bring something to read.' He picked up the paperback he had been reading recently and popped it in his pocket. 'Bea, will you be all right on your own here for a while?'

It was clear that, where Rose was involved, Bea was to take second place and far from resenting this, Bea found that she was comforted to find Ralph so willing to take the strain.

'Of course,' she answered, smiling in what she hoped was a positive and optimistic way. 'There's the washing up to do, while you two are skiving.' This rather feeble pleasantry was well received, indicating that the others were aware that she was conveying her feeling of solidarity in a tricky situation.

Rose and Ralph took their coats from the hooks in the passage and, picking up a spare front door key, they followed Sergeant Bamford and the Inspector out to the waiting police car, leaving

Bea to lock the door behind them. She went into the kitchen and stood for a moment, looking at the remains of their supper. She'd better get stuck in and not allow herself to think too much. But before she started, she suddenly felt it would be good to talk to her Father. It rapidly became an urgent need and she found herself holding her breath in case it should be her mother who picked the phone up.

It was all right. There was her father's reassuring voice on the line, saying that her mother had gone to bed early with a headache. 'You'd better tell me all about it,' he said, before she had had time to say that anything was wrong. 'I can tell something's up. If you put the phone down, I'll ring you straight back – it's a pay phone, isn't it?'

Bea went through everything and left nothing out. Her father didn't waste time in saying how foolish Rose had been. Instead he told her that, as there was nothing useful to be done at the moment, she must therefore do nothing.

'Whatever you do Bea, you must resist the temptation to tamper – or "edit" things. No creative talent needed here – just stick to the truth when asked or you will certainly get into deep water and every time you adjust your story, your credibility fades. Well, that's really the message for Rose, not you, since she's the one with the credibility gap, isn't she? Mmm – a bit late for advice, but if anything comes up about meeting her train and so on, don't either of you fall for cooking up a story, because it won't work.

'What about this chap Ralph?' went on Dr. Roebuck. 'Is he to be trusted?' Before Bea could answer, he continued. 'I wouldn't pay much attention to those sun-glasses you told me about. Clues like that only happen in TV dramas. I think it all sounds just a bit too obvious, myself.'

Bea asked him why he thought that, but Dr. Roebuck didn't seem inclined to expand on his reasoning, merely observing that the police didn't miss much. Before hanging up, he gave her a message from Philip. 'He very much wants to go down to see you, Bea, and I promised to ask you how you feel about it.'

'Oh, I ...' Bea sounded doubtful and confused.

'Don't put him off for too much longer, my dear,' said her father gently.

'I'll think about it Dad.'

She felt much relieved that at least she had someone to confide in and, sending her love to her mother and Sam, she put down the phone and went to make a start on the piled-up dishes. This looked like enough work to provide all the therapy she needed.

*

It was twenty-five past twelve when she heard the key turn in the front door. The wood stove, which she had stoked from time to time, had burned down to glowing embers. She must have dozed in her chair. Hastily, she threw on a few small, very dry bits of wood and closed the fire up, while opening the vents, so that by the time they appeared in the room, the quick rekindling showed a welcoming blaze.

Rose looked drained and Ralph ushered her to the fire. He fetched a bottle of wine and a glass (had he already learned that Rose was not keen on whisky?)

'Can I get you something, Bea? I'm going to have a Scotch …'

'Oh – yes, Scotch please…. Sorry,' she yawned. 'I seem to have had a bit of a zizz … didn't think I could drop off with all this going on.'

'Well, at least they let me out again.' Rose gave her a wan smile, as Ralph went to pour the whisky. 'Bless you for keeping the fire in. Magic.'

'Do you want to tell me what went on?' asked Bea.

' "Went on" just about sums it up. I thought they'd never finish. Of course, they weren't asking questions all the time. They had phone calls to make, checking and re-checking, presumably with their oppos in Cambridge.'

'They started with this alibi business,' put in Ralph as he came through from the kitchen. 'They had finally got in touch with

Howard and Celia. It seems nobody knew they were away from home, so they had been calling on them and telephoning – they'd lost quite a bit of time that way – '

'That made them a bit fed up with me,' Rose said. 'There were a few dark hints about being obstructive. Then they wanted to know if I could think of anyone who had seen me while I was there on my own.'

'Surely somebody must have?'

'Well, no Bea, they needn't have.' Rose held out her glass to Ralph, who had left the bottle close by. He took it from the hearth and replenished her glass. 'You see, their house – Howard and Celia's – it's one of those largish Victorian semis. You know the sort … high garden walls, trees and shrubs, enclosed and hidden, with a way out at the back into a lane … and more high walls. Well, the only time I went out, apart from in the garden, was to the shops once and then to the station – about ten minutes walk via the back lane.'

'So it would be possible to be there for days without anyone noticing, especially if the neighbours are mostly young professionals, out all day,' said Ralph. 'The Cambridge police had checked with the neighbours to see if they'd seen Howard or Celia – or Rose, of course – but nobody had.'

Rose said: 'I told them why I hadn't explained to you about being there on my own – '

'How did they take that?'

'Difficult to say. That's perhaps the worst thing about them … that deadpan look. You haven't a clue what they think.'

'Then,' Ralph took up the tale. 'They took her through her movements from the time Howard and Celia left the house, right up till the moment you met her at Leeds station.'

'They backtracked several times as well, and in the morning they'll make enquiries of the rail staff.'

'After that, they finally got to the major issue of why Rose didn't tell them who she was, who the dead man was and so on… and why she wasted dozens of valuable man-hours. It hasn't exactly made her popular.'

'Well, you can't really blame them for that … they might have been days ahead but for this.' Bea found it impossible to ignore her innate sense of fairness as she recognised the enormity of what Rose had done.

'Oh, don't rub it in,' sighed Rose wearily.

'She explained as best she could.' If Rose needed an ally, she seemed to have found the right one in Ralph, and Bea wondered whether this was, in the long run, a good thing. They were thrown together almost like people marooned on a desert island, in an artificial situation where judgment could easily be impaired.

Rose cradled her wineglass dejectedly. 'I don't suppose,' she said, 'it sounded a very likely story.'

'Well, they must have more-or-less accepted it – they've let you go,' suggested Bea.

'Not really.' Rose shook her head. 'I have to stay here till further notice, or inform them of any plans I might have to go anywhere else.' She put the glass down on the old stone fender and leaned towards the fire, burning merrily now that Ralph had thrown some small logs on. 'I just wish there was something I could be doing to prove where I was – but I can't think of anything.'

'It's not really the best time to be trying to think, Rose,' Bea said gently. 'Let's see if we can get a bit of sleep and do our thinking in the morning.'

'You're right. I'll go up in a minute. You have the bathroom first, if you like.'

Bea nodded and said goodnight to them both. Rose turned in her chair and took her hand for a brief moment and Ralph got up from the fire. 'Goodnight Bea,' he said, 'and thanks for all the washing-up!'

Bea had not expected to sleep well. Her restlessness was not helped by the headache which had been developing during that last hour. At half-past two she looked at her watch, sighed and went off in search of some paracetemol. She seemed to remember seeing some on the window-sill in the bathroom and she crept across the landing as quietly as she could.

'No point in being stealthy,' she thought as she passed Rose's door. 'Sounds as though she's not asleep either – but for a different reason.' She found the tablets, then paused a moment at her door from where, looking through the archway towards the main landing, she could see the moonlight shining through Ralph's wide open door.

'A good idea?' she wondered. 'Yes – on the whole... God knows she needs comforting, though it's to be hoped it doesn't cause more complications.' Bea got back into bed after pulling back the curtains slightly – she loved the moonlight – it fascinated her. Unexpectedly, she felt less tense than she had been and she was able to remind herself philosophically that Rose was old enough to know what she might be letting herself in for. 'If everyone was as careful and prudent as I am,' she murmured aloud, 'I don't suppose anyone would ever do anything.'

She lay very still, waiting for her head to clear. She watched the moon's delicate progress, as it produced a continually shifting pattern on the walls and ceiling and then she felt for the first time since that quarrel, a longing for Philip. Up to now she had not acknowledged that she missed him so much, even to herself. The developing tenderness between Ralph and Rose had steered her mind back to the time when she and Philip had first met. She had been twenty-three, he around twenty-seven.

She had been doing a post-graduate course in Leeds and studying had got her down a bit. She had been trying to work all that Sunday in late Autumn and nothing seemed to stay in her head. Towards evening, she had set off for a boring walk on her own in Roundhay Park and it had started to drizzle, which just about suited her mood. Perversely, she had sat on a damp bench, gazing absently at the lake, while vaguely patting the head of a moist, spiky-haired dog which had appeared from nowhere and which had apparently mislaid its owner.

'He looks about as fed up as you!' said a friendly voice. She had not noticed his approach, but now she looked up at a rather thin face with dark eyes, grinning quizzically out of a fur-lined hood. It was an interesting face, appealing, though not in the least conventionally handsome. The rest of him was of average height and well-built (so far as Bea could tell, under the bulky clothing). He pushed his hair impatiently back from his forehead, disturbing the hood and revealing a white streak that stood out among the dark brown.

'May I?' he asked, perching on the bench beside her and introducing himself to the delighted dog, asking its name. Bea explained that the dog wasn't hers.

'He suddenly materialised – and he reminded me of one we had when I was a child. We called him Muddles – a sequel to "Puddles", which he started out with for obvious reasons.' Bea smiled ruefully. 'I'm afraid I've done the wrong thing in talking to him – he'll probably follow me home now.'

'Don't worry. If he does you can give the police a ring, and you'll have done the owner a good turn – there's no-one in sight, so he must have escaped.'

Bea stood up and said she would set off and keep a lookout for the owner. If nobody appeared, she would do as he suggested, though she would be unable to hold on to the dog for long as she lived in a rented room.

'Well, I could take him to the police station, if you like – unless you've got a car handy?'

In the end, they had walked together to the man's car and he had taken the dog with him. Bea had gone back to her lodgings, feeling somehow less depressed in spite of damp hair and wet feet.

She had learned the name of this man, who was quite easy-to-know, though perhaps rather serious in outlook. He told her that he was in Leeds to visit his parents and said he had just joined a legal practice in Darlington. So of course, Bea explained that it was her home town and she had lived there until she went to university.

Philip had found the weekend in the parental home rather trying, hence the lone walk in the rain.

After this, they had made vague noises about other Sundays when they might be walking by the lake – possibly in the early afternoon – and it had not been long before they met again and began to go to concerts and films together. They found they had a lot in common – books, music and their fondness for hill-walking.

They shared something else too: each had a slightly difficult relationship with one parent. In Philip's case, it was his father. When at last, Bea came to know Philip's family she recognised almost immediately aspects of her mother in Mr. Lander (she always found it an effort to call him Tom and he was still "Mr. Lander" in her mind). What Philip had later told her bore this out; his father was inclined to be intrusive, with a need to dominate. But in conversation, he also gave her the impression of a blusterer, opinionated and probably a bigot. Bea could well understand Philip's need for fresh air during his visits home. On the other hand, she would have described his mother as "a sweetie".

Life had gradually fallen into a pattern – together but apart. Bea finished her course successfully and landed the very sort of job she had been aiming at, right there in Leeds. Philip progressed in the Darlington practice, although there had been a period a couple of years ago, when things seemed not to be quite right. Philip clearly didn't want to talk about this and Bea had wondered if some crisis in his family was draining his resources. He had appeared to be short of money for a period, although quite adequately paid. Bea did not feel tempted to question Philip. His reluctance to discuss such things might be an odd quirk, but it was one she understood. Reticence – even a measure of secretiveness – were qualities that tended to develop as a shield, when a parent was over-involved and a bit inclined to domineer.

The crisis, whatever it had been, soon passed and Philip's finances had improved markedly. They continued to respect each other's privacy and worked hard at building an enduring relationship, though separated by their work during the week. But how time had drifted by! They had talked of settling down soon and agreed that marriage was what they wanted – a conventional background for the children they hoped for. Friends had regarded them as a serious item for years, but each had a career that mattered, and it never seemed to be quite the right moment.

I wish we'd not let things drift so, Bea thought now. We might have resolved the problem of our jobs long ago, if only we'd got down to it. Heaven knows we've had enough time to be sure we're suited in the ways that really matter. Reluctantly, Bea had realised that her mother had a point when, unasked as usual, she had reminded Bea about her biological clock. No panic yet, of course, but Bea would have liked a little time to settle into marriage before the responsibility of children took over. 'Surely,' she murmured to herself, sleepy at last, 'Surely it's not too late....'

CHAPTER 8

Mrs. Holroyd was already at work washing the kitchen floor when Bea came down at almost nine o'clock. She introduced herself and found that she was making excuses for her lateness. Damn, she thought. There I go again – no need to apologise. Why should I get up at crack of dawn on holiday?

'Nay love, don't you worry!' Mrs. Holroyd's voice was as comforting as her person. She was round, pink and wholesome and had on a flowered overall – she might have walked straight out of a cartoon depicting the very best and nicest stereotype. Being set in the traditional village mould, she seemed at first middle-aged. But Bea realised quickly that Mrs. Holroyd was in fact no older than Bea herself. 'I'm here early when I get a lift from Mack,' the soothing voice continued. 'It saves a mort o' trouble if I don't have to be fetched up from t'village.' Squeezing out her mop, Mrs Holroyd took her bucket to the drain outside the back door, and carried on talking as she poured away the dirty water.

'I thought best get t'kitchen done with while you're all out o' road. Most of it's dry already, so I'll leave t'door ajar to finish it off, and leave you to have your breakfast in peace.' She came in again, clanked her bucket (also of the traditional type) down in the big walk-in cupboard and then set off purposefully with the vacuum-cleaner and an ancient box of polish and dusters, to start on the living-room.

Bea made herself a mug of coffee and sat down by the window, enjoying the streamers of sunshine that were weaving through the early mist.

'Any coffee going?' Rose had come downstairs noiselessly.

'Oh – hi! Sorry, I only made a mugful, but the kettle's boiled…
I didn't feel like anything to eat.'

'Really?' Rose sounded amazed. 'I'm starving. I'm sure there's
some bacon in the fridge. Bacon and mushrooms, that's what I
could eat.'

'For someone just recovering from a police interrogation, you
seem remarkably sprightly!'

'Oh – I think interrogation's putting it too strongly. Anyway, it
doesn't do to let those officious busybodies get you down!'

Bea decided that any doubts she might have had about Rose
and Ralph last night were now resolved. Obviously, it *had* been a
good idea.

'Mrs. Holroyd's here,' she said by way of preventing her
thoughts from showing through. 'She's doing the living room at
the moment. She seems a very nice person.'

'Yes, Ralph was telling me about her.' Rose had the grace to
avoid Bea's eye for a second or two as she mentioned him. 'He says
her husband's first name is Makepeace! Isn't that lovely?'

Bea chuckled. 'No wonder she shortens it to Mack. I'd assumed
there was a Scottish connection somewhere.'

'PC Makepeace Holroyd!' Ralph came in to the kitchen, grinning.
'It's all right, she's got the 'vac on – there's no way she can hear.'

'Would you like a cooked breakfast? Bacon and new-laid eggs?'
Rose was standing by the Rayburn with a large pan at the ready. 'I
thought I saw some mushrooms – '

'In the larder … I'll get them. I bought them yesterday.' Ralph
brought a box of open field mushrooms to the sink and started
preparing them.

'Change your mind, Bea?' Rose held the bacon tongs up enquiringly before wrapping up the remainder of the bacon.

'OK, go on then … I never do at home, but I think if I smell
the bacon cooking I'll weaken. Can I help? I'll scramble some eggs
if you like?'

'Good Lord! I'd no idea you had the technical know-how,' laughed Rose. 'Yes – great, thanks.'

Nobody mentioned Rose's current problems during the meal, which was relaxed and good-humoured. Bea found that after all, she was quite hungry. She and Rose offered to clear up afterwards, since Ralph said that he must spend the rest of the morning working in his room.

'I badly needed to get away for a bit,' he explained. 'And as I never managed to finish my work on Thursday night, I brought my laptop with me. It just needs finishing off and then I can Email it and forget about it. I'll try and catch Mrs. Holroyd when she comes upstairs,' he added. 'She might give me an idea of what the police are doing.... . she's not supposed to, of course.'

'You haven't forgotten it's the inquest this afternoon?' Rose called after him.

But Ralph hadn't forgotten anything and said he would be going with them.

*

Barbara was wondering if she could possibly get away for a bit... just until things had quietened down. She could go to her Mother's for a day or two, but that would mean going sick and she had already taken last Friday off work. True, she had telephoned Marianne on the previous evening, saying she had a chill and Marianne had agreed to give the message to the head teacher. She'd done her best to let them know, hadn't she? Not as if she were leaving them in the lurch.... though Marianne hadn't improved things by ringing her at home to ask her about some work their two classes were sharing. Rod of course, had said she was away for a couple of days –but at least Marianne had had the gumption to act dumb on the phone and say that she'd forgotten. So at least there was no crisis on the domestic front.

It looked then, as though she would have to stick it out, keep her head down and hope no-one started prodding around in matters that didn't concern them. Today was Tuesday. The longer things went on quietly like this, the greater the chance that it had all blown over. It was a bit unnerving, though:

one or two people had drawn attention to the news, now that the victim's local connection had been published. There had been some quite detailed information in the local press and radio – rather less on TV. Barbara was having trouble suppressing feelings of guilt. She told herself that she wasn't an irresponsible person, given normal circumstances. But her initial annoyance at her involvement had given way to a feeling of remorse and it was all the worse because there was nobody she could discuss it with. Bottling up worries could affect your judgment if you weren't careful.

*

'I'd like to go to the village this morning,' said Rose, hanging damp tea-towels on an old-fashioned creel. 'That's assuming the fuzz will allow me to travel that far... would you mind giving me a lift down there? It's mainly the Post Office and that sort of thing, not masses of groceries or anything, so I can walk back. I'd like a walk.'

'That's fine.' Bea was by the window-seat, looking at the back garden. 'I thought I'd spend the morning in the garden – there's plenty to be done.'

They set off as soon as they had finished in the kitchen. The mist had cleared completely and it was a lovely sparkly morning. The peaceful village seemed to guard its private life, taking little account of events in the bigger world beyond. Bea left Rose outside the Post Office and then came back and changed into the oldest things she could find.

'Gloves,' she thought, remembering her blister. 'Damn, I could have got some in the village.' But then she recalled seeing several pairs somewhere around. She asked Mrs. Holroyd, who was just finishing her coffee break.

'In there, love – that big cupboard.' Mrs. Holroyd indicated the walk-in broom cupboard, which housed the boiler and where cleaning tools were kept. 'And if you're wanting overalls, there's a pair that should fit, just about – you're a tall lass.' She was now making her way upstairs and called over her shoulder, 'Have a look in the shed.'

Bea fetched her boots from the utility room and then went to see what she could find. As she opened the cupboard door, she realised that the transmission of sounds between kitchen and bathroom was much clearer here, directly underneath. She noticed that the central heating pipes ran through another aperture. Now she was inside, she could hear quite distinctly. Ralph must have "caught" Mrs. Holroyd as he intended, probably as she was taking some cleaning products out of the bottom of the airing cupboard. Bea could not resist eavesdropping – something that hitherto she would never have admitted wishing to do.

' … put his car,' said Mrs. Holroyd's voice. 'There's a clump of trees close to the old drovers' road – "the top road", you know – only five minutes or so from here. That footpath over the fields brings you out just there. Well, they reckon that's how he could get over here without anyone seeing, but the car wasn't there any more … been stolen, they reckon.'

Bea was amazed to think that she had not really considered how Guy had travelled to the caravan – she had been so much preoccupied with *why*. But if he had used that footpath, then someone must have told him about it. Fascinated now, she had no intention of removing herself from the cupboard and she imagined Mrs. Holroyd poised, spray cleaner in hand, as the voice continued, presumably with Ralph nodding his encouragement.

' 'Course, there's talk going round the village that he came to meet *her*. But there's always that sort o' talk…. our Mack says it's a strong possibility though – and you know who they'll go for in that case, don't you?'

There was a non-committal grunt from Ralph as she continued. 'They'd have to break his alibi, though. And they've taken him apart, between you and me … Rhona and her mum say they've not bothered Geoff again, but then they would say that, wouldn't they? And Mack knows different.'

'Well, it's difficult to see any other explanation for the man being up here – never mind getting bumped off…'

'Oh, don't be too sure. Another idea is that he might be caught up in this racket that's been in the news from time to time … it seems that it's a sort of spying. Sounds daft really, but they say these big companies send people to spy on other firms …'

'Doesn't sound very likely to me. That sounds like something in a film … whereas we all know about the other business. I'd have thought it was just waiting to happen – '

'Hasn't even tried to cover it up much – there's one or two have seen her coming up in this direction you know. They even wondered if she was looking for you – used to run after you a bit one time, didn't she? Except you've not been here for quite a while now … '

'Glad you noticed that, Mrs. Holroyd! Well, I'd better not hold you up any longer.'

'No, that's right. And I've said far too much as it is.' Mrs Holroyd's voice became rather fainter, as apparently she turned to go. 'Our Mack's always saying I never learn to keep me mouth shut. He'd be ever so mad with me and he could get into trouble. Still, it's quite all right just telling you, isn't it?'

At this point Bea thought the time had come to grab a pair of gardening gloves, which were indeed on the shelf, have a look in the shed for the overalls, and make sure she was in the garden where she was supposed to be. It was quite likely that Ralph, along with the family and regulars, knew all about that useful cupboard. She didn't want to advertise the fact that she was prepared to eavesdrop like the proverbial parlourmaid. She picked up some tools and the wheelbarrow from the shed (but there was no sign of the overalls) and prepared to waste no more time. She could chew over all that she had heard as she worked. By the time Rose returned, she would have her ideas in order.

*

Bea broke off her task only to take Mrs. Holroyd home at eleven-thirty. She was surprised that Rose hadn't returned by now, and she kept a lookout in the village, just in case she had changed her mind and wanted a lift. However, she didn't see her and in all she had put in a good two hours' weeding, not counting the interruption, before Rose returned. Bea was quite willing to put down her trowel.

'It's getting on for lunchtime,' said Rose, as Bea stood in the kitchen doorway. 'Though I shouldn't think any of us is really ready for it.' (Speak for yourself thought Bea – weeding's hungry work.) 'Do you reckon we should disturb Ralph – ask him if he wants coffee or a beer or something?'

'I can't see why not. If he was working in his office he'd be used to plenty of interruptions.'

'OK. Well, if you're going up to change out of your gardening gear, will you ask him? I'll get on and make a sandwich or something… coffee for you?'

'Oh, I'd rather have a beer – or a shandy, if we can find any lemonade. It was pretty warm work.'

Bea kicked off her boots and padded across the flagged floor in her thick socks. She could hear Ralph's keyboard clicking steadily as she went upstairs and she tapped on his door and opened it a crack.

'Oh, hang on!' he said, looking round. Bea thought he looked rather flustered. 'Ah, it's you, Bea. Look, can you give me a minute to tidy my stuff up and I'll be right down?' Bea was still poking her head enquiringly round the door, but Ralph made no indication that she should come in.

'Rose says do you want a beer, or some coffee or something? We're thinking of having a sandwich for lunch if that's enough.'

'Fine. A beer and a sandwich will be plenty, thanks.' Ralph sounded more his usual placid self, as he grinned at her and she nodded and retreated. I'm over-reacting to everything, that's what it is, thought Bea as she went downstairs. Getting quite neurotic, thinking people are behaving suspiciously all the time … a bit like that thing in "Three Men in a Boat" about reading a medical book and convincing yourself you've got all the ailments in it.

'Everything except housemaid's knee … ' she added, without realising she had spoken aloud as she entered the kitchen. Rose looked up and asked her what she was on about.

'My knees – after all that weeding,' Bea lied and she thought – not just neurotic, but talking to myself! And now I'm even finding it necessary to cover up. Better get a grip.

They all took their drinks and a plate of sandwiches out into the garden. The weather at least, was in holiday mood, although the sharp little breeze was still there and caused them to seek the shelter of an ancient ivy-hung wall. Rose made them all keep quiet, as she was certain she had heard a cuckoo. To townies such as they were, this was a rare event and sure enough, after a few moments of expectant shushing, they heard the strangely evocative call as they stretched their ears towards the spinney. They all agreed that this was a wonderful spot and Rose said it was a shame to have to work indoors on such a day.

'Yes it is,' Ralph replied. 'But it'll take less than half-an-hour now. I don't suppose we'll be all that long at the inquest – it'll be a formality.' He helped himself to another sandwich and looked at Rose. 'You all right?' he asked. 'Not worrying about this afternoon?'

'Not really … I'll be OK once I've done the bit about the official identification, I think. I wish there was someone else to do it, and of course everyone will know … will know things that are *my* business, not theirs. And I keep having a bad half-hour about the situation I'm in – just wish I could prove where I was.' Rose passed the plate over to Bea in response to her signal. 'Did you find anything out from Mrs. Holroyd?'

'Oh yes. Sorry, I'd forgotten – got a bit wrapped up in the paper work. She was quite chatty, bless her. Then she got conscience-stricken afterwards. She really does get carried away … Mack would have a fit!'

'Well, yes,' put in Bea. 'But it's his own fault. You'd think he'd have learned not to tell her anything, knowing that she's going to talk.'

'I don't think he *does* know – certainly not the extent of it,' Ralph answered. 'After all, people aren't going to tell him!' He reached for another sandwich. 'These sandwiches are very, very good, by the way … I think,' he went on, 'that the people she talks to take good care that he shouldn't know she can't keep her tongue still … that way, they'll go on finding out lots of useful things.'

'Well, it's certainly handy for us – what did she say?'

'Oh – a few things the police haven't mentioned. They seem to know where he hid his car, for one thing.'

'Guy's car? I've been wondering how he got here without the whole village knowing.' Rose pointed to the last sandwich on the plate and, when the others shook their heads, she took it. 'Where was it?'

'There's a footpath that runs from the corner of the paddock and it skirts the fields that once belonged to this farm. It leads to the old drovers' road – the one I sometimes come in on, actually. Apparently a car had been parked up there among some trees, but someone had removed it later. Goodness knows how they can tell, but the police seem pretty sure that was the car he used. Footprints round it, maybe.'

'So the idea of his being taken to the caravan against his will is unlikely,' said Bea slowly. 'And the murderer must have know where his car was, unless that was moved by a third party … I wonder what he was after.'

'Or who? That seems fairly clear. Sorry, Rose, but he seems to have been – well, in the habit of running after whatever was available.'

'Oh, don't worry! I found out what he was like very soon after we were married. Within weeks. What I can't understand is why he wanted to get married at all, since he never intended to make even the slightest commitment to our relationship.'

'I expect he couldn't resist you!' Although Ralph made it quite clear that this was a joke, Bea couldn't help feeling that it wasn't entirely tongue-in-cheek.

'The idea,' Ralph went on rather hurriedly, 'seems to be that he'd arranged some sort of assignation with Rhona. He knew of a suitable place where they could meet that was very handy for her – knew where the key was, because he'd made a point of asking you, Rose.'

'My God, what a fool I – '

Bea interrupted her. 'I don't think so, Rose. It's not your fault, love. How could you possibly know he'd make use of the 'van like that? You'd only just married the bloke, for Heaven's sake … you'd hardly be suspecting him of planning to meet someone else.'

'Thanks, Bea … but if the police know all that, and if they can see what's obvious to us – that Geoff came and caught them there – then why haven't they arrested him?' Rose frowned at her coffee cup, which she was cradling in both hands.

Bea shook her head. 'It's not that simple, is it? Presumably they haven't any firm evidence. And then, Carmen said he'd been at work at the critical time, so that'll have been checked.'

'You said he works at the hospital in Blaeborough?'

'He's a porter there I think, Rose.' Ralph looked at her thoughtfully. 'It would be interesting to know exactly what kind of proof he has that he was there all night, wouldn't it? I wonder how we could find out.'

'You mean, it might help my situation if they could nail him?

'Mine too,' answered Ralph. 'Don't forget I'm still trying to prove my alibi as well.'

'Yes, but the police don't seem quite so bothered about you, do they?' As she said this, Bea realised that something seemed to be pointing the police away from Ralph. Perhaps it was lack of motive. Then she remembered that Mrs. Holroyd had spoken of another possibility.

'Did your leaky source suggest that there were other suspects we don't know of? I mean, if there was another motive for the murder – a strong one – it would widen the field a bit, wouldn't it?'

Ralph looked at her as if he was weighing her up. 'Well, you can't widen it too much, because local knowledge is implied. They reckon the murderer must be someone who knew that the 'van wasn't likely to be used – and then after the killing, thought that the body wouldn't be found for ages ... that's about all she said, so far as I recall. Oh – and there are wild rumours flying around... ridiculous speculations. But it seems clear to me that after years of putting up with Rhona's behaviour (and the Dysons have said he's been incredibly patient) – he just cracked.'

'But if he has a sound alibi...'

'I've heard that people with the very best alibis can be the most suspect, Bea. If you don't know you'll need an alibi – well, so often that's just the night you're spending a quiet evening at home. Whereas, if you were planning a murder, you would make sure people have seen you around – though obviously not for the entire period.'

'Yes you would.' Rose nodded vigorously. 'After all, people don't keep a log of your movements, so you'd have a good chance of getting away with it, if it depended on your colleagues at work. It's the oldest trick in the book – to tell one group you're in another department ... and vice versa. I think we should try to find out what the basis of his alibi is and see if there's a loophole.'

'I expect that's exactly what the police are doing,' said Ralph. 'Still ... you never know.'

'Well, I don't suppose the Inspector's going to give us any hints.'

'Carmen ought to be our best bet,' said Bea. 'But though she seems to need to talk, all she'll say is that none of it is true.'

'That's the sort of conversation to encourage, though. She's probably keen to explain why Geoff couldn't possibly have been anywhere else but at work ... that might guide us to find every reason why he was somewhere else!' Ralph stood up as he said this and began to gather the remains of their lunch and head for the kitchen.

The women brought the rest of the crockery in and felt quite surprised to see that they had eaten the lot. Rose and Bea started to wash up and Ralph went to fetch the big log basket to fill for the evening.

'I dropped in at the farm shop on my way home today, as it happens,' said Rose. 'We needed eggs and bacon and I thought I might hear something.'

'And did you – hear anything?' asked Ralph, as he paused in the doorway with the empty basket. Bea thought there was a slight edginess in his voice. He put down the log basket and leaned on the door jamb.

'She wasn't going to talk to me, of course – Carmen, I mean – she doesn't really know me and anyway I expect the news has spread in the village by now, that …that Guy …'

' 'Fraid it will, love. But in any case, it will all come out at the inquest.' Bea smiled encouragingly. 'I think you'll feel better, not worse, after that.'

Rose nodded and grinned ruefully, and Bea felt that the old easy long-standing friendship was beginning to revive.

'But I *did* hear some of the locals talking before they noticed me waiting in the queue. Not much … apparently that shovel had been identified as the weapon. They reckon Guy was hit from behind as he was going into the 'van. Goodness knows how they can tell. Then, of course, his body was moved inside the 'van afterwards.'

'Wouldn't be a woman then – the murderer,' said Bea. 'It would be quite difficult to drag a body up the step and through that narrow doorway … then through the bedroom door and on to the bed – '

'Well, they aren't looking for a woman, are they?' Rose protested. 'Then,' she continued, 'they said Mr. Goss who owns the farm and the shop is saying that he doesn't recall ever having a shovel like that, now that he's had time to think it over.'

'But he'd tend to say that in a any case, I suppose.'

'Oh, I don't know, Ralph,' put in Bea. 'He's no reason to be concealing anything – I mean, he's not a suspect, is he?' She dried her hands on the towel hanging behind the door. 'It doesn't help Geoff, either way though, does it? He'd not be far from that shed – he'd pass it both coming up and going back.'

'If it *was* Goss's shovel, it was certainly handy. Funny choice of weapon, though.'

'And if it *wasn't* his,' argued Rose, 'someone obviously got rid of it there – on the principle that the best place to hide a tool is in a tool shed.'

Ralph picked up the basket after Rose told them she hadn't heard any more, and he headed for the log pile.

'Time to be moving,' he said as he staggered through to the living room with a heaped-up basket. 'I've never been to an inquest. I hope I don't sound ghoulish, but I think I might find it interesting.'

*

In the event however, it was anything but interesting and it was over very quickly. Rose was clearly upset at having to give formal evidence of identity, but once that was over there was minimal time spent on questions about the discovery of the body, and those were directed mainly at Bea. The medical evidence and the police report were also extremely brief. They agreed afterwards that it wasn't nearly the ordeal they had been bracing themselves for – although none of them had admitted feeling apprehensive. The Coroner had pronounced the expected "murder by person or persons unknown" and adjourned the proceedings for two weeks.

They were all rather quiet on the way back, each feeling undecided whether to be relieved that there had been so little to it, or disappointed at such a damp squib. It was only twenty-five to four when they returned and Ralph said he would finish his work quickly, so that he could send it and forget about it.

'Tea and bun in half an hour or so?' queried Rose. 'I picked up some Yorkshire curd tart while I was at the farm shop and it looks delicious.'

'Great. See you later then.' He went off upstairs and Rose asked Bea if she was going to be gardening again.

'Mmm. Yes, I expect so,' murmured Bea absently.

'Think I might go for a short zizz – I didn't sleep an awful lot last night.'

Bea kept a perfectly straight face, as she said that she was not surprised at that in view of all the stress. She decided to get changed and have a short session in the garden. She looked ruefully at her second-best jeans ... gardening wasn't improving them, but of course she had never originally intended doing anything other than tidy up the shrubs around the caravan. Perhaps she should have another look for the overalls Mrs. Holroyd had mentioned. She hadn't found them last time, but maybe she hadn't looked thoroughly enough. They might be ideal for a warmish afternoon, worn with very little underneath.

The shed was packed full of the usual sorts of things people hang on to and rarely use again – as well as tools, a hosepipe, the lawn mower and the wheelbarrow that she had forgotten to put away – presumably Ralph had seen to it later on. No sign of overalls, though. Junk fascinated her and she had to make a conscious effort to leave its charms and get back to her project. As she made for the door, she noticed an old bicycle, coyly hiding under a tattered tarpaulin – never to be used again, she supposed.

Pity, really, she thought. I wonder how difficult it would be to make it roadworthy? Rose might have liked to use it to go to the village. But I suppose it's hardly worth doing a lot of work on it at this stage ... Nevertheless, she pulled back the tarpaulin and, examining it more closely, saw that the tyres looked all right. Instead of the rims sitting depressingly on the ground as she had anticipated, with the rubber beginning to crack, they looked – operational. She pressed one with her thumb. It was quite firm. There were also signs that the chain had been oiled.

If we're going to be here for a few more days, Bea decided, it might be worth digging it out ... I'll see what the others think.

Back at work on the weeds, having resigned herself to the sacrifice of the second-best jeans, Bea tried to sort through the jumble of events and make some sense of it all. A number of little oddities that didn't seem to add up to much must have reasons and explanations – but were they purely coincidental? If so, they were merely serving to muddy the water. But the main question was why had Guy come here, apparently furtively. If she could get Rose to give her a picture of what Guy was really like ... all she had learned so far was that he couldn't leave the girls alone, even when newly married. But was he trustworthy in other ways, apart from his philandering nature? From Rose's story about the visit to the caravan, she had the impression that Guy was manipulative and opportunistic.

But surely, even if he had flirted a bit with Rhona (and everybody flirts with Rhona, it seems) that wouldn't be enough to bring him all the way up here and risk using someone else's caravan, where he couldn't be certain of remaining uninterrupted? This was a man who was obviously very attractive to women. He didn't have to go to the inconvenience of running after the Rhonas of this world. She was neither particularly beautiful, nor the kind of bright and amusing companion who could hold his interest. She was simply one of those women who have some kind of unquantifiable magnetism which keeps a bunch of blokes round her (it must be pheromones!). But it was instant come-hither, not long-term enchantment.

Bea was so lost in her contemplation of all this, that she did not notice the footsteps on the gravel and she was startled to find a figure standing close to her. She straightened up, still on her knees, to confront Geoff Collins. She noticed that, as well as being tall, he was very muscular and it felt as if a giant was looming over her. To cover her confusion (for she felt as though her thoughts about his wife were written on a placard hung around her neck) she made a great show of brushing soil from her knees as she stood up.

'I brought you these up,' he said. He had a shy smile and there was something very open and appealing about his features which had a healthy outdoor glow. 'I've been doing a bit of shooting and I thought you might be glad of 'em.' He held out for her approval two good-sized rabbits and then went on: 'If you want, I'll skin and joint 'em for you – I don't know as Ralph's used to that?'

'Thankyou – thankyou very much indeed.' Bea had now recovered herself. 'Yes, if you wouldn't mind, it would help if they were skinned … it's really very kind of you to think of …'

'No trouble. When I'm working nights, I like something to do for part of the day and I sometimes get more rabbits than we want. I'll find a knife in't farm kitchen, don't you bother – long as you don't mind me helping myself.'

He went towards the back of the house with long, unhurried strides. Bea was rather relieved that the rabbits, next time she encountered them, would resemble what she had seen in the butcher's and not something furry, cuddly – and dead.

It didn't seem to take him more than a minute or two and then he strolled back with an air of ease that Bea found impossible to reconcile with the accusations everyone seemed to take for granted.

'How are you all, Geoff?' she heard herself say and hoped as she said it that he didn't take her interest the wrong way. 'I gather the police have pestered you a bit … we've had them around too.'

'They've been a right pain, haven't they?' he grinned. 'You just had that Inspector Dove, from what I've heard … I had to talk to his boss – at first you think he's a pussycat, but really he's got a way of looking through you, as if he knows everything you're thinking. Even the Super stuck his nose in once when I was down at the station. And they've been up at the house – the Sergeant and the Inspector … I was a bit fed-up, like … but there's no point worrying about what can't be changed, is there?' Bea couldn't help admiring Geoff's good-tempered stoicism and lack of resentment.

'Still,' he went on, 'I think it's died down a bit now. They've been round everybody at work, you know, asking who'd seen me and when – all that sort of thing.' He chatted easily about his predicament and certainly he didn't seem to have the smell of guilt about him.

'So they know that you were at work then? That's good – you must be relieved.'

'Well, up to a point,' replied Geoff. 'It wasn't really straightforward though …thing is, in the night, well the work's done different – not so organised, like. Them as could remember would say they'd seen me, p'raps early on … then I was with a different lot later, and then when I was going off shift of course, there were other folks just starting theirs. But, any road, in the end they reckoned I couldn't have moved my van in the night. The staff car park's got a barrier and you have a card to open it, and it's time recorded, so they've got a check. They know I didn't take the van out, so I think they'll leave me alone now.'

'Well, you can put it behind you now, can't you?' said Bea, who felt that Geoff sounded completely sincere.

'Aye, I'll be happy enough to forget it. Just hope other folk will too.' He turned away towards the lane. 'Nice talking to you Bea – hope it all gets sorted out for your sake too.' He nodded his goodbye as Bea thanked him again for his gift and he went off with that same deliberate, unhurried walk that echoed the way he talked.

Bea felt ashamed at how readily they had all assumed he was a killer. She herself had fanned the flames, with her willingness to suspect his behaviour. She had never had a long conversation with him before this and she found him gentle, open and forgiving. She picked up the trowel and began savaging a flower-bed she hadn't touched before. She would talk to Rose again as soon as she got the chance – there must be things Rose hadn't revealed. Then, Mrs. Holroyd had hinted at "a sort of spying". Why had Ralph been so dismissive about that, and why hadn't he mentioned it in the first place? Somehow, she didn't feel she wanted to ask him about that at the moment – at least until she knew more about Guy's business life.

Bea carried on until thirst and her aching back reminded her to look at her watch: just after four-thirty. She would go in and see if Rose was up and make sure that Geoff had covered up the rabbits properly.

Putting the tools away, she glanced thoughtfully at the bicycle. 'Ralph must know about the bike – surprising that he never suggested it to Rose,' she thought. 'But then, we've all had a lot to think about.'

*

Rose was in the kitchen, examining the rabbits which, duly skinned and jointed, had been put in a large bowl and covered with a tea-towel. Geoff was clearly very domesticated. Bea explained where they had come from, as she heaved off her walking boots, which looked rather the worse-for-wear, after the session in the garden.

'Geoff! He's been up here again!' Rose sounded horrified – as though Bea had been entertaining the Yorkshire Ripper or Hannibal Lecter. 'Whatever for?'

'To bring rabbits for our supper,' Bea replied calmly. 'I hope you know how to cook them, because all I know about rabbits is that their domestic life seems rather hectic, but they're not very good at games.'

'Well, I've not often cooked them,' Rose sounded rather doubtful. 'We could have a rabbit pie – or, I think my Mother makes a casserole and serves it with a herby Yorkshire pudding … it would have to be tomorrow, though – I meant to tell you, I got some haddock from the fish van in the village for tonight's supper.'

'Oh yes, now I think of it, I intended telling you about Nutty the fish man on Tuesdays. Nobody seems to know why he's called Nutty. I think the fish comes up to Leeds from Bridlington or Grimsby or somewhere. It's always very fresh, anyway.'

'But didn't it bother you – Geoff coming up and bringing rabbits?'

'Well, I was a bit taken aback … I wouldn't have known what to do with them at all, if he hadn't skinned them and so on.' Bea knew that she was being deliberately perverse, but something in Rose's air of conviction about Geoff's guilt needled her. And that's not fair of me because I was just as bad, she thought, until I'd spoken to him.

'Bea, you know what I mean. It's serious. I feel very uneasy to think he might come round at any time – a man like that – '

'Look here, Rose, I'm not at all convinced that he's involved. Now that I've had a chat with him I feel quite different – he told me the police have accepted his alibi – his van was in the staff car park and it gets clocked in and out … '

'Well, honestly Bea! You're usually the sceptical one … I'm the one who's supposed to swallow anything! But *really* – he's hardly going to say they suspect him, is he?'

'Fair enough,' Bea conceded. 'But the fact that they haven't got him in custody surely means they can't find any evidence.'

'Well, I don't know … the police nowadays have to be so careful before they go around arresting people. They might be on the point of arresting him right now, for all we know … and remember what Ralph said yesterday about alibis that are a bit too perfect!'

'Yes, I suppose you're right,' Bea admitted unwillingly. 'It's just that … well, he strikes me as a particularly genuine type. He didn't even seem tense or worried either. Honestly Rose, he talked as if it had all been an awful nuisance, and that it was more-or-less done with now.'

'He might just be a very good actor.'

'Yes, he might. But I don't think you'd ever imagine him to be anything other than a very straightforward, rather naïve sort of bloke. Even his job – a hospital porter – suggests to me a … well, an uncomplicated man, probably with a caring nature.'

'It could equally well suggest that it was the only job available in a rural area where opportunities are as rare as hens' teeth.' Rose spoke with a most unexpected sharpness. 'Why – I bet this farm must have been one of the most prosperous round here, with plenty of employment for local people – but it isn't a farm any more, is it? The traditional jobs just aren't there.'

Bea put on the kettle. 'Do you want to give Ralph a shout?'

Rose went up the backstairs and Bea got out mugs and plates, reflecting wryly that she and Rose had exchanged their usual roles. She wondered why Rose had been so keen to believe Geoff guilty – and why, for that matter, she herself had been so eager to defend him.

'He'll be down in five minutes,' said Rose, closing the pine door at the foot of the stairs. 'If you'll make the tea, I'll have a look at the rabbit. I might put a herb marinade on it and then tackle it in the morning.'

'Rose ... don't think I'm just asking out of idle curiosity: will you tell me a bit about Guy's job? What did he do at the paint factory?'

If Rose was surprised or reluctant, she didn't show it. 'He was on the technical side, rather than sales – his degree was in chemistry I think.'

'I see. And, forgive me, but it's an idea that's been nagging me – did you ever find him ...devious, or sort of secretive? About his work, I mean. I don't mean in his social behaviour.'

'He didn't talk about his work a lot, in fact I never quite got to grips with what his job really entailed.' Rose went to look in the larder for ingredients and then began mixing them together. 'But I do remember once or twice, he had to meet some people connected with his work in the evening and each time, he got terribly edgy. He wouldn't discuss it. Is that the sort of thing you mean?'

'Yes, exactly that. Did you know who these people were?'

'Haven't a clue. He never said. I probably never asked though, since it wasn't important to me and he hated me to probe. But anyway, he was probably on edge because something he was working on wasn't going well – that would be the most likely thing, wouldn't it?' Rose spread her mixture over the rabbit joints, covered the casserole dish and put it in the fridge. 'Why do you want to know all this, Bea?'

'Oh, I don't suppose there's anything in it. But I was just considering alternatives. If Geoff didn't kill Guy in a sudden fit of jealous rage, then there must be someone else who had a reason to –'

The backstairs door opened and Ralph appeared with an envelope in his hand. 'Could you hold the tea and curd tart for two minutes? Do you mind?' he asked. 'I've got my Emails off, but this has to go by snail mail – I'll go in the car to post it, so I won't be long.'

As he shot out through the back door Bea caught sight of the envelope, noting that it was addressed to Glasgow, but she couldn't see any other details. 'Kettle's boiled … I'll make the tea,' she said. 'By the time it's brewed, he'll be back.'

'Fish for supper tonight,' Rose called through the open window as Ralph was getting in the car. 'But we've got rabbits for tomorrow!'

'Great!' Ralph shouted back. 'Always knew you'd be a good shot.'

Bea didn't feel she could go back to the subject of Guy again just at the moment. It would probably make Rose defensive and uncooperative. Also they were likely to be interrupted again. She wondered how she could find out more. Rose had mentioned a conversation about industrial espionage which, taken with Mrs. Holroyd's remarks, had started up a fresh line of thought. The person who would be able to help, ironically enough, would be Philip. He was employed by a firm of solicitors with a large commercial practice and he had often said, with a rueful grin, that he met a few dubious characters from time to time. Sometimes, he said, it was difficult to decide whom to trust, since most big firms were keen to know what their rivals were doing and some were none too scrupulous.

I can hardly get in touch with him to ask him about it, thought Bea wryly. She was surprised to find that thinking of Philip gave her a sudden ache and a longing to see him – to be held and reassured. He had a wonderful way of overcoming her anxieties. Perversely, she occasionally found this irritating, since she sometimes thought him almost complacent. But just now, it might have been very acceptable.

*

The curd tart was all they could have wished for. It was something that Bea associated with her early teens. One of the rituals her family had always observed during the summers at the caravan, was buying one in the village. There was an old-fashioned bakery there in those days, long since closed and the farm shop was now the place for such delicacies. Bea had learned to appreciate this unique regional tart, after her initial refusal to taste it, as a child.

As they drank their tea, Ralph, who seemed in high spirits and glad to get his work out of the way, suggested that they all go to see a film that evening. He had found out from the well-informed Mrs. Holroyd that a comedy, currently enjoying overwhelming acclaim, was now on at Blaeborough's small cinema.

'It's just what we need,' said Ralph. 'Light-hearted – escapist. I could ring up and book if you like – save a lot of hassle.'

'It's a nice idea,' Rose said. 'Only it always makes it awkward to get a proper meal done in time. We've got this fish and it should be eaten today.'

'Can't you pop it in the freezer,' Ralph suggested. 'We'd have time to get something to eat in Blaeborough as long as it was fairly quick – Chinese or something?'

They agreed on this plan, but Bea said she had recently seen the film in Leeds and so she would bring her car and make her way home after the meal. This arrangement suited her very well, as she had a plan in mind for later in the evening.

Rose said: 'We'll have to be off soon after six then – glad I didn't have a second piece of tart. It's a bit soon to eat again ...'

'You'll manage it! Let's get organised then. We've got three-quarters of an hour.' Ralph turned to Bea, looking at her grubby state after the weeding. 'If you want a bath, there's plenty of hot water.'

CHAPTER 9

They settled for an Indian restaurant in the end. They discovered that they all had a passion for Indian food and they agreed that the meal was remarkably good – especially for a small market town out in the sticks. Afterwards, there was very little time before the start of the film, so Ralph and Rose headed straight for the cinema and Bea went to collect her car. She set off for the outskirts of the town, towards a building she had been to recently and reluctantly. Although still known locally as the Cottage Hospital, it had grown into a fairly extensive complex. The mortuary was in the rear wing – all that remained of a grim old labyrinth, demolished as unsuitable for modern purposes and now replaced by a modern brick pile.

First, Bea drove right round the hospital, eventually joining the main road again. She had noted that round the back, on the farthest edge of town, was a quiet road, flanked by some scrubby woodland. The hospital had only three entrances, two near to the main road and one for staff and deliveries at the rear, between the mortuary and the former nurses' home that was now the admin. wing.

It was through this back entrance that the staff car park could be reached, through a barrier with a machine for scanning permits. Around the parking area the walls were high, but in a corner, she had spotted a wicket gate, leading on to the road. This interested Bea, as clearly the other entrances would be far too public even at night for any furtive comings and goings. She now started on the circuit once more, this time pulling up close to the rear of the building in the little-used road. She got out of the car, feeling conspicuous and rather stupid. The small gate was clearly in use, as its hinges and latch seemed in good repair and oiled. It was locked, as she expected – but keys could be borrowed, copied ... there seemed to be a staff entrance directly serving the car park too. All that was needed was an alternative means of transport and the chance to leave it in a convenient place nearby.

She returned to the car, sharply disappointed. She had not come here hoping to disprove Geoff's alibi, but rather to convince herself that he had indeed been unable to leave unnoticed during the night shift. She could not explain to herself why this should be important to her. After all, it would be better by far if Geoff were guilty – for everyone except him and his family. Otherwise, she thought, suspicion is thrown back our way.

She started up the car and headed back towards the village, wondering why she had been so sure that Geoff was not the murderer. I only came to prove it to myself, she mused, but now it seems as if he could have come and gone during his shift – possibly using a bike which he could have brought in his van and then concealed in the bushes. Perfect cycle route too, she concluded, as she drove along the level road which followed the long ridge – he could do it in no time!

However, she comforted herself, that was a very long way from proving that he had done so. No need to think up wild theories and anyway, if she could work all that out, so would the police.

They would also know whether Geoff had a bike at home and would be aware if he had pinched one locally. They'd have arrested him by now if that were so, wouldn't they?

Bea drove up the lane to Shawhead Farm and turned into the gravelled yard. Silhouetted against the setting sun was a figure coming towards her. She wound down the window, as she brought the car to a halt.

'Good evening, Sergeant,' she called, recognising now the bulky, no-nonsense shape of Sergeant Bamford. 'You've missed the others. They've gone to see a film. Or did you want me?'

' 'Evening Miss Roebuck. It was Mr. Norman I came to see. Just tidying up a few loose ends.' The Sergeant seemed to be trying to make up his mind. 'Well,' he said at last. 'Maybe you can tell me. You remember those glasses you found in your caravan when you were there with the Inspector?' He leaned his arm comfortably against the roof of the car. 'Er … during the interviews we've been conducting, we've been told that Mr. Norman has a similar pair. I just wondered if you'd seen him wearing them?'

So they *were* following up such small details then! 'No,' Bea answered without having to think about it. 'I certainly haven't seen him with glasses on, but he has mentioned losing a pair like that … he thought he'd had them on Saturday in the yard, and had put them down while he was chopping wood, but he could only find the empty case afterwards.'

'I see. Thankyou Miss.'

'But Sergeant – it doesn't make sense, does it? I mean – if somebody's seen him with the glasses, then it would have to be since – since it happened … he only arrived at the farm on Friday night and you've had the caravan keys in the meantime.'

'That's right Miss,' said Sergeant Bamford woodenly.'

'So they can't be that same ones?' Bea persisted.

'That's how it would seem, Miss Roebuck. But the Inspector's not one to overlook anything, however far-fetched it might seem to be.'

With this ambiguous remark, the Sergeant turned towards his vehicle which had been parked under the trees and, after thanking her and saying he would call back sometime the next day, he drove away.

If Bea had been hoping to develop a flair for detection she was disappointed, as it seemed that she had learned very little and had probably failed to grasp something significant. She put the car away and went inside. She decided to telephone home – for home was what she called it, despite the comfortable and long established flat in Leeds.

'I've been trying to ring you.' Her mother's complaining voice seemed to suggest that Bea should really make an effort to be in when she rang. 'And there's no answering machine either … '

Bea didn't bother to explain that an answering service would be of no use where there were long periods with nobody there to check it. Instead, she told her mother about the meal they had had and that Rose and Ralph had gone on to see a film.

'Why ever didn't you go too? You need to be taken out of your-self after all that's happened!' Mrs. Roebuck was now apparently upset to have found her at home … you never could win with Bea's mother.

Bea said quietly that she had already seen the film. 'Thing is,' she went on hurriedly, while she had a chance to speak. 'I can't go on staying here forever and I imagine the police can't insist on our sticking around … anyway, I think Rose needs to be back on Friday. So I just wondered whether to come up myself – she'd be glad of a lift back to Darlington.'

Mrs. Roebuck erupted into joyful exclamations at this sugges-tion, so that was agreed upon. A weekend at home would be a comfort and would give her a chance for a good long talk with her father. Bea would welcome that; the only trouble with going to Darlington was that it was where Philip worked and lived during the week. Bea was in such a muddle about her feelings. Until she had sorted them out a bit, she was still reluctant to talk to Philip.

' … won't you dear?' her mother was saying.

'What's that, Mother? Sorry,' she lied. 'A crackle on the line – I missed all that.'

'I was saying I could invite Philip up on Sunday. You two need to talk things over …'

'No! Please do *not* make any arrangements,' Bea said firmly. 'I'd much rather make my own plans.'

'All right dear, just as you like.' Her mother sounded sad to encounter such ingratitude. After a number of messages had been exchanged, Bea said quite truthfully that she had run out of change for the pay phone. She told her mother that she would phone again to finalise times and rang off. She felt flat and disappointed not to have spoken to her father on this occasion. She had forgotten that he usually went to the meeting of the local photographic society on a Tuesday evening. She had also forgotten to tell her mother about the inquest.

The dialogue that had just finished was a wearying reproduction of dozens of conversations she had had before. They were endemic in the Roebuck household whenever her mother was involved. They always left Bea feeling somewhat drained, even though she knew it was foolish to let such things get to her. There was something in the way Mrs. Roebuck took it for granted that others shared her point of view, which Bea felt bound to challenge. If she resisted the urge to do so, she ended up feeling she would explode and if she remonstrated, she was left feeling guilty.

Philip, on the other hand, managed to handle her mother with great tact and patience – helped, of course by her mother's strong partiality for Philip. Right from the start, when Bea had first taken him home, he had made a hit with her mother. He didn't flatter her though, but used the skills learned in court to lead her gently away from her more extreme statements. The rapport that he had developed with Dr. Roebuck was of a different calibre. It had taken its time to ripen and was altogether a quieter, more soundly-based friendship.

Philip's court work was the part of his job that he liked best. Bea knew that he had hoped to increase his time spent as an advocate and was ambitious, but during the last year or so, he had complained that opportunities in this area had become rather scarce. He told Bea that lately, although he had done the spade-work in quite a number of cases of industrial espionage, when they came to court the representation fell to someone else. This had worried Bea, who knew that Philip sometimes reacted badly when his aims were thwarted.

When Bea visited Darlington, Philip would spend time at the Roebuck's, but he never stayed there. He and Bea allowed Mrs.

Roebuck to preserve her fiction that, whatever other people's daughters did, her daughter did not share a room with her boyfriend. Bea marvelled at her mother's ability to re-write the facts to suit her own preferred scenario.

She turned on the television in the hope of catching up with any further information put out by the police. However, the initial spurt of excitement appeared to have faded, and with no further sensations to report, the public's interest had probably flagged. Bea found it difficult to concentrate on other news at the moment, so she turned off the set and dipped into a book on local history that she found in the living room.

*

At about a quarter to eleven, when Bea was just thinking she might as well go to bed and read one of several books she had brought with her, the sound of wheels on gravel told her that Ralph and Rose were back. Both seemed to be in remarkably good spirits and police inquiries seemed to be the last thing on their minds.

'Nightcap, Bea? Rose?' asked Ralph. He had laid the fire in the living room stove before they went out and Bea was glad that she had put a match to it before phoning home. Ralph brought drinks and they sat round it now. Bea asked how they had enjoyed the film.

'It was great,' Rose answered. 'The meal was good too, wasn't it?'

Bea almost found herself remarking, with an edge, that it was turning into quite a jolly holiday. What's wrong with me? she wondered. Why do I always want to be so sarcastic and spiteful?

Instead she said: 'Sergeant Bamford came up this evening. He wanted a word, Ralph, but I don't think it was very important.'

Ralph seemed quite sanguine about this. He smiled, almost indulgently, as if to say, well they have to keep themselves occupied, don't they? 'Did he tell you what it was about?' he asked languidly.

'He said it was about the glasses left in the 'van … wanted to know if I'd seen you wearing any like them.'

'Wonder what made him think of me?'

'Oh, apparently someone he'd interviewed fancied they'd seen you wearing some. I said I'd not seen you in sunglasses, but that you'd mentioned mislaying a pair. I hope I didn't say the wrong thing.'

'No … no that's fine.' It sounded as though Ralph was quite pleased about it.

'Well, they can't think you left them there, can they?' asked Rose. 'Because *if* anyone saw you wearing them, it must have been after … after Guy was killed and of course the police had taken charge of the 'van by then.'

'Quite right,' answered Ralph. 'In fact, I was thinking about my sun specs earlier today …I've got a theory that I'd like to test out.' Ralph stood up and, picking up the empty glasses, he went towards the kitchen, saying over his shoulder, 'I'll test it first thing in the morning, just in case our friend the Sergeant turns up again early.'

*

Breakfast was a lazy and prolonged affair, since they had not made any plans for the day. Bea noticed that Ralph did not seem in a hurry to carry out his test, or whatever it was, in spite of what he had said. As they were clearing away the dishes however, Rose asked if had changed his mind.

'Not at all.' Ralph brought the cafetière to the sink and started to rinse it out. 'But when I thought about it, I saw there was no rush, because if the Sergeant turns up I can show him what I mean.'

'Are you going to stop being mysterious and tell us what it's all about?' asked Rose, as she ran the hot tap into the bowl.

'Oh, don't spoil the fun.' Bea said. 'We all like to have a chance to build up suspense and then reveal all – including the power of our "little grey cells". Why don't you give us a few clues, Ralph and see how we get on?'

Ralph seemed quite happy to adopt her spirit of competition and they quickly finished the washing up. Ralph said he would go up for a pullover – he had overestimated the warmth of the morning. 'Then I'll take you to the site of my investigation and you can probably see what I'm getting at.'

'Do we need the key to the caravan?' Bea said, wondering what she could have missed – and more surprisingly, what the police could have missed.

'Yes, OK … not essential, but it might confirm my theory.'

'I'll get mine from upstairs. The police might not have put the spare one back – and anyway, we don't want to dig for it, do we? Wait there,' she added, as she headed for the backstairs. 'Don't start without me – it wouldn't be fair!'

As she ran up the stairs, she realised that they were being very childish and treating it like a game. She felt rather ashamed of her willingness to do so. Perhaps it's just our way of handling an unpleasant situation, she thought. Probably healthier than brooding over it.

She joined the others as they walked towards the paddock. Ralph was looking down at Rose's attentive, upturned face. Looks a bit heavy, thought Bea. For all the world as if he was assuring her of his honourable intentions!

They moved apart as Bea approached and Ralph beckoned her as he walked round to the far side of the caravan.

'This is the idea.' He stopped about halfway along the caravan's side, on the opposite side from the door. 'Does it suggest anything to you?'

Both the women stared at the side of the caravan and waited for inspiration. Rose looked up at the windows – two large ones in the living area and a smaller one higher up, belonging to the end bedroom. Apart from the bathroom window, with a small air vent over it, there were no other features. A large gas bottle stood between the two smaller windows with its pipe attached somewhere under the 'van.

'Well, nobody could get into the 'van very easily,' said Rose. 'Those windows are tightly sealed. But in any case, if we know that the key had probably been copied, he didn't have a problem getting in.'

Ralph smiled. 'Bea?' He stood back, as they walked up to one end and then turned round and simply stared.

'No idea. It's too much like one of those maddening brain-teasers – you know they have a terribly obvious solution, if only you would indulge in a bit of lateral thinking. But I imagine it's got something to do with the glasses being just where they were … and also it depends when there was an opportunity to put them there?'

'Mmm. I've a mental map of the layout of the 'van, Bea. I was staying with the Dysons at Christmas once and there was a very hard frost. I came over with John to help him drain the water system.'

'Oh yes, he always did that if it looked likely to freeze up. I'd forgotten about it …' Bea was frowning over an idea that was so simple that she couldn't believe it hadn't occurred to her before. 'Do you mean – something to do with the position of the bath-room shelf?'

'Hey! This isn't a fair contest at all.' Rose laughed. 'You've for-gotten that I've scarcely set foot in the caravan and I was in no fit state to take in the geography – anyway, I never saw the bathroom.'

'Sorry Rose. Well, let's stop playing silly buggers, anyway. This whole thing isn't a game, is it?' Ralph pointed to the vent above the bathroom window. It had a plastic cover made of some opaque material which projected from the wall of the caravan by perhaps an inch and a half.

'I've never really looked at it before,' Bea said thoughtfully. 'You don't normally notice that there's quite a gap at the bottom end of the cover, do you?' She put her hand under the plastic shield. 'I can get my fingers in a little way and I can feel two – sort of slots. Do you mean …?'

'Exactly. Quite a convenient way to "post" a pair of sun glasses!' Ralph took from his pocket the thin envelope-type spectacle case that he had taken out of the drawer and pushed it easily through the gap. 'There are two vents under the cover, and if you push the object upwards you can then bring it down through the lower slot.'

'Yes of course,' said Bea slowly. 'And you reckon somebody put your specs into the 'van –'

'To incriminate you!' gasped Rose.

'Well, to create a diversion,' replied Ralph. 'I wouldn't put it stronger than that.'

'But – *after* the police had done their search, inside and outside the 'van … what would be the sense?'

'No sense whatever, Bea. Someone clutching at straws, I imagine. They must have thought it might be some use and they couldn't do anything while the police were around.'

'And you were the handy scapegoat!' Rose looked horrified. 'I suppose if he was in a panic, he might seize on any opportunity –' They didn't need to ask Rose if she had anyone in particular in mind.

'It was still of some use.' Put in Bea, looking at the vent as though it could tell her something. 'If he hoped I'd find them, as I did, perhaps the idea was to suggest the murderer returning to the scene, as long as he was careful not to get his fingerprints on them.'

Rose shook her head. 'Well, but *your* prints would be on them, Ralph – and the police have got those, haven't they? So you'd think they'd come straight to you about it, instead of making a vague inquiry.'

'Exactly! But the police *haven't* come to me, have they – because the person who planted them hadn't thought it through properly. They made one big mistake.'

'Go on!' Rose looked expectantly at Ralph and Bea scratched her head thoughtfully.

'I don't think I'm going to tell you just yet … shall we go into the 'van and see where the case landed?'

'Well, OK, but you've got to tell us, now you've gone so far,' protested Rose.

'I'm not just being bloody-minded, Rose – honestly. I'd like to talk to the Sergeant and test my theory on him ... open up then Bea, will you?'

They had to take turns to peep into the tiny shower room, where they could see the spectacle case wedged at the back of the shelf in much the same position as the glasses had been.

'But how could he be sure they would tuck themselves away so convincingly?' asked Rose. 'He wouldn't know where they'd land – and he can hardly have practised beforehand.'

'He wouldn't need to – that was just luck. It wouldn't have mattered if they'd fallen on the floor, they'd still be found ... into the loo wouldn't have been so good, but he'd have a good idea of the layout from the pipework under the 'van.' Ralph looked suddenly grim. 'He's going to need a lot more luck though, if my guess about the fingerprints is right.'

'You think they'll be Geoff's fingerprints?'

But Ralph only grinned and shook his head. Bea thought he was being a bit triumphalist. That was excusable, she supposed, if he believed this was an attempt to frame him, but she could hardly believe Geoff to be so devious and so – well, spiteful.

As they left the caravan, Bea offered the key to Ralph. 'Then, when the police turn up you can show them.'

'I don't think I'll wait for them to come round,' Ralph muttered, as if he was weighing up the possibilities. 'I think I'll go down there and see them right now.'

On the way back to the house, Bea was thinking about the bicycle. She really shouldn't be sitting on the fence like this. Ralph had put forward a very good argument – what other explanation was there? It looked as though everything pointed to Geoff, so why keep quiet about her own small investigation?

'I've been doing a bit of sleuthing myself,' she began. She told them about her exploration of the hospital perimeter. 'I don't know what made me do it,' she went on. 'I think I really wanted to prove to myself that there was no loophole in Geoff's alibi, but instead, what I saw made me wonder … I'd seen that old bike in the shed – '

'That old thing,' put in Ralph quickly. 'Is is usable?'

'Well, it certainly looked so to me – oiled, tyres OK, everything,' she answered. 'Anyway, it wouldn't have to be *that* bike … any bike would do. He could take it in his van, hide it in the bushes behind the hospital and then all he'd need is to pop out where he wouldn't easily be seen. Then the fact that his van was in the staff park all night is irrelevant.'

Ralph seized on this possibility. 'Right,' he muttered. 'No alibi then … yes, I see. It wouldn't take long at all. Not as if it involved pushing it up hills – the road along that ridge is as flat as an airstrip.'

Bea could have wished he didn't sound quite so delighted at the thought of Geoff's guilt. But you could hardly blame him, she thought – still under police scrutiny himself and now possibly the victim of a trick. And anyway, if Geoff *was* the murderer, then he deserved none of her sympathy. If not, she felt sure this would easily be proved.

'Shall we have a look at the bike?' she heard Ralph say to Rose, as they turned into the back yard just ahead of her. 'Though of course, he could have a bike at home, which the fuzz would know all about, or he could have taken one belonging to a neighbour.'

They uncovered the bicycle and Ralph was about to pull it out from the wall, when Bea suggested that he shouldn't touch it, just in case it *had* been used, because of fingerprints. Ralph, however, took no notice, but wheeled the machine into the yard to examine it.

'Doesn't matter about prints,' he said. 'If it did turn out to have been used by Geoff (and I think it's unlikely myself) they'd know which were mine, wouldn't they?' He pulled his socks over his trouser bottoms, saying, 'Chain's a bit oily!' and rode tentatively round the yard. 'Most probably one of the Dyson grandsons uses this. They were up here the other week, so my Aunt says… . saddle's highish though, for youngsters – and I don't think they're very tall.'

While he was speaking, something flashed through Bea's mind so fleetingly that she could scarcely grasp it. 'Breathalyser,' she found herself murmuring aloud.

'What's that?' asked Rose, who was watching all the proceedings, but taking no part.

'Mmm? Oh, sorry. Thinking aloud, that's all.' She saw Ralph turn into the lane to continue his trial ride – or perhaps he was just enjoying himself. 'I suddenly thought of a neighbour of mine. The police caught up with him after he'd been drinking – just as he was parking his car outside his house. He dashed into his kitchen and drank off a large Scotch before they could stop him.'

'But what on earth has that got to do with anything?' Rose looked as if she was beginning to wonder whether all this talk of crime and guilt had knocked Bea a bit off balance.

'I haven't the remotest idea,' admitted Bea. 'It simply came into my head from nowhere …I'm merely explaining what I was muttering about,' she added with dignity.

Ralph reappeared and pulled up abruptly in front of them. 'Brakes work!' he grinned. He looked at the bicycle afresh. 'Well, he could have used it – it's perfectly up to the job. But I reckon it's a long shot, myself.'

'What about getting into the shed?' asked Rose.

'Oh, no problem there. Nobody ever locks anything up. People round here are used to trusting their neighbours – not many places like it left …'

'Until they started murdering one another, you mean?' asked Bea pleasantly.

'Ouch!' Ralph pulled a wry face. 'Anyway, it's a possibility, I guess … worth considering. I might as well ride down to the incident room on it and they can take a look. But I think we shall find they are ahead of us on this one.' And without another word, he swung his leg over the saddle and pedalled off, leaving Rose and Bea to stare after him.

'That bike could be evidence,' said Bea severely. 'I don't think he should have been riding it.'

CHAPTER 10

'Want a coffee?' asked Rose as they went into the kitchen.

'Mmm – certainly do.' Bea flopped down on a chair by the table and told herself not to get her knickers in a twist about Ralph doing a takeover job on the bike. But she was curious to know what Rose was thinking. 'He certainly scuttled off in a hurry, didn't he?'

'I think he was just relieved that this cloud over us looks as if it might be clearing, you know.' Rose spoke gently. 'It's worried him quite a lot I think, even though he isn't showing it.'

'Well, I suppose you'd sense that quicker than I would.' In seizing this chance to say what she had had in mind for some time, Bea hoped it would come out sounding as she intended. 'You're getting quite close, aren't you?'

Rose glanced quickly at her as she reached for mugs from the dresser. 'Does it show?' she asked calmly, but with a diffident lift of her eyebrows. 'We're not an item, or anything, you know ... but yes, I – he – we're very much attracted,' she ended stiffly, and she sounded as if she was giving a news handout to an avid tabloid reporter.

Bea felt for her. Rose was bound to be self-conscious about confiding in her, after the fiasco that had happened barely a year ago.

'I can understand that,' Bea did her best to make it easy for Rose, who had no reason to feel ready to trust. 'After all, we're all in an artificial situation, and you two are both in a bit of an awkward position with the police – '

'I know what you're going to say – and judgment gets distorted!'

'No love, actually I wasn't going to say that at all. I was really thinking that things just happen faster – almost like those war novels or movies …everything kind of telescopes.'

'Yes, that's exactly it. Only, I really am trying to take it slowly this time, Bea.'

Bea, relieved and gratified that Rose was prepared to discuss this, chose her words carefully in an effort to appear positive and helpful.

'Yes, well of course you don't know each other all that well yet …but a bit of a fling and no bones broken might be really good for you – you need an antidote to Guy.'

To Bea's surprise, Rose's greenish eyes were filled with tears. She brushed them away impatiently and grabbed a piece of kitchen roll.

'This is so silly. I realise now that I never did love Guy … and now I can't really mourn him. And that's sad, Bea, isn't it? My husband has died and I don't even want to mourn him.'

Bea got up and went to give her a hug, warmed and gladdened to be once more in that happy and important friendship they had always had up till last year.

'I should think it's right to have him in mind just a bit. You don't want to become inhibited, so that he can't be mentioned. But you could enjoy a bit of er … "relaxing dalliance", shall we say … with Ralph, then put the past in its place and wait and see what happens next!' Bea supposed that this had been an acceptable mix of the sympathetic and the banal, because Rose's face had that typically open smile that said her mood had lightened.

They sat and sipped their coffee companionably and Rose asked Bea whether she was going to be gardening, or whether they should perhaps go out somewhere. The weather was still very good and Bea said she could hardly remember a time up here when it had been so settled.

'Yes, we should go while we have the chance … in fact, I've been thinking: it's Wednesday today and it will soon be time to go home (if they let us).' Bea reached to the dresser behind her for the biscuit tin and tugged off the lid. 'We've hardly done anything with all this going on and I don't see why we should lose out entirely on the holiday.' She pushed the tin towards Rose. 'What would you like to do? More local walking? Or should we suggest taking the car somewhere a bit further afield? Ingleborough Cave, perhaps – or to those wonderful waterfalls near there – or Malham, or the White Scar Caves …'

'I don't mind where – I'll love it wherever we go. But I was wondering if perhaps you and I should go together – this afternoon or tomorrow? I can't imagine Ralph minding, because he hadn't planned to have us here anyway and it might be a good idea to slow things down a bit. But the main thing is, it's what you and I had intended – not a threesome, which could be a bit tedious for you.'

'Rose, I'd love that!' As Bea drank up her coffee, she felt elated that Rose had been the first to make the suggestion. 'It's great that you thought of it – but let's play it by ear, shall we? See what Ralph wants to do and we can decide then on a short trip this afternoon or to go after an early lunch tomorrow – we'd have a bit longer that way.'

'Fine. Well then, I'll get some salad together for lunch now. There's cheese, various, and some ham – OK?'

'Right. Well then, if you can stagger along without my expert help for this one, I'll nip down to the village for a newspaper and perhaps a magazine – anything you need?'

Rose made a few suggestions, adding that the drinks cupboard needed replenishing too. Bea took the kitty money from its hiding place and set off blithely for the village. For once, she was not lost in thought as she drove.

*

When she passed the old schoolroom, Bea noticed the bicycle, propped up close to the road. However, just as she approached, a constable came out and wheeled it away towards the outbuilding at the side of the school. Evidently they considered it worth inspecting then. Bea wondered how Geoff (supposing their idea was right) had managed to take the bike to the hiding place in readiness, without anyone seeing him put it in the van. It would be risky, surely, to drive up to the farm for it. Easier if he was taking the bike from his own house – if he had a garage, or even a car port, it might give enough privacy for loading it.

Curiosity once more got the better of her and she made a small detour to take in the estate where Geoff and Rhona lived. She wasn't certain which was their house, but she had been to Carmen's once or twice on errands for the church fete and she knew Rhona was only a few doors away. She had slowed down to a walking pace, when she was startled and mortified to see Rhona coming out of her door (well, presumably *her* door), probably on her way to work for the lunchtime stint.

Waving in what she hoped was a friendly and casual manner, Bea sped off up the road, turning purposefully into the next crescent, where she parked the car and waited until Rhona had had time to disappear. She felt thoroughly shabby – as if everyone on the estate knew why she was there and thought her a nosy old bag.

After all, she thought, what difference will it make if I do find out more about the Collinses? It's up to the police – they don't need my help. Nevertheless, she once more passed the house that Rhona had emerged from and saw that on the side of the modest ex-council semi quite a big car-port had been added. Its sides and back were made of some opaque material. In it she recognised Geoff's van, a smallish blue one – but plenty big enough to transport a bicycle. Discreetly.

Impatient at her own preoccupation with the crime, Bea drove away as soon as she reckoned it was safe to do so without catching Rhona up and she left the car in a side-street close to the middle of the village. In the friendly post office, she bought a newspaper and chose a magazine that she thought would appeal to Rose as well as herself. Then she remembered that she needed a birthday card for her brother. She had almost forgotten about his birthday, but it wasn't too late to send it and enclose a cheque – always popular, even though lacking in inspiration. It wasn't easy to find a card for this most difficult category – the late teens male. She picked the one least likely to offend and handed her purchases to the post-mistress, who had been in charge there ever since Bea's childhood. After the usual warm greetings had been exchanged, Mrs. Gledhill – the name suddenly sprang into Bea's memory – asked after the family and offered sympathy for the distressing events.

'A lot of folk are hinting that it must be you-know-who! But you know, love,' Mrs. Gledhill shook her head and her soft voice sounded sad. 'I've known that family – both sides of it – all my life. There's no harm in *her*, not really. Silly, mebbe … bit worse than silly now and then.' Mrs. Gledhill took the money that Bea had counted out and looked across toward the door to check that they were still alone. 'It's just … well, having a Mam that's that bonny, it can sometimes make a lass have to – sort of *prove* something.' She opened the till. '*He*'s very good, you know. Takes no notice of her most o't time. Not the sort to knock her about like some would.'

Bea hastened to agree with this charitable assessment. But an unpleasant doubt was niggling away as Mrs. Gledhill was speaking: wasn't it exactly those long-suffering, *accepting* people who finally reached breaking point? Then even a placid man might be violent?

*

Philip heard no more from the police after he had supplied all the details they'd asked for. He hadn't expected to. It was natural that they would speak to all Bea's contacts, but according to the news gleaned from Dr. Roebuck there were some likely suspects locally. Even so, he was glad to have their visit behind him. Apparently, they had also telephoned his boss at the office, just about some trivial detail of his work pattern it seemed – nothing to mean anything. But a respectable solicitor does not welcome such attentions. On his way to work in the early morning, he had wondered if he was becoming a bit stuffy. Should he be bothering about his image?

Well, he thought, if I *am* getting into an old fogey, Bea will soon tell me so … if she ever speaks to me again she will, anyway. But he was convinced that there was too much in their relationship for it to founder over a disagreement on future plans. The more he thought about it, the more optimistic he felt. He was determined to get in touch again somehow, especially as he had had time to analyse what had gone wrong and he felt that what he now had to say would start to put things right. Leaving the past behind was vital. In future he would aim for harmony in their ambitions and a solid basis in his chosen profession … and most important of all, he would learn from past mistakes.

Philip suddenly felt light, elated. All he had to do was go for it – grasp the thing he now recognised as the central core of his life, before it had the chance to slip away.

*

Rose had the lunchtime salad all ready by the time Bea returned. 'But Ralph's not back yet,' she said. 'He's been gone a long time, hasn't he? Do you reckon that's a good sign or a bad?'

Bea, who thought it impossible to say, was preparing to sound casual and reassuring, but there was no need in the event, as Ralph appeared at the kitchen door at that moment. There was no sign of the bike.

'Hi – oh, food … good. I'm quite hungry.' Ralph threw his pullover over the back of a chair and glanced at the newspaper that Bea was reading, spread out on the table. 'Must be all this interrogation. Very stimulating, you know – not to mention the walk back.'

'How did it go?' asked Rose. 'You've been quite a time, so I suppose they must have been interested.' She put a big bowl of salad, a loaf and a plate of assorted cold foods on the table.

'Oh, they're interested all right. Odd reactions though, the police seem to have sometimes ... that is, when they show any reactions at all. A lot of the time you get that dead-pan look, have you noticed?'

'Ralph, that's just what we've been telling you, if you remember – '

'What sort of reactions?' queried Bea.

'Well, when I took the bike in, they seemed quite put out.'

'Because they hadn't thought of it themselves!'

'Don't you believe it. They'd already had a look at the bike and I expect it'd been gone over for prints ... oh, thanks.' Ralph took a plate and cutlery from Rose. 'But when I arrived and told them why I'd brought it they just looked at me – I don't really know how – as if they were weighing me up and not liking the result much.'

Some of Ralph's ebullience seemed to have subsided, Bea thought. It was interesting to see a more vulnerable side of him than hitherto.

'What did they think of your theory about the sunglasses?'

'Oh,' Ralph laughed, but he did not actually appear amused. He handed the plate of food to the others and helped himself to a chunk of bread. 'Seems they were ahead of me there, too. At least I was right about the fingerprints though: there weren't any.'

'Well, everyone knows to avoid leaving fingerprints – ' began Rose.

'Yes of course,' answered Ralph. 'But if the glasses had been left by mistake – well, their owner wouldn't have wiped them, would he? Whoever put them in the 'van should just have avoided handling them – then it would look as if they had just been forgotten.'

'But did they think it could have happened as you said?' Rose wanted to know.

'Mmm ... they seemed to think it very likely ... is there a beer in the fridge?' he added.

'I'll get it – I'm nearest,' offered Bea, getting up. 'Sorry, we forgot all about a drink.'

'Well, there's a first time for everything!' Ralph grinned as the bottles and glasses were passed over. 'But although they agreed,' he went on, as he fiddled with the opener, 'the police didn't seem to think it made much difference to anything. They seem to be on another track entirely.'

'Yes, but you can't really tell what they're thinking, can you?' Rose gave her beer bottle to Ralph to open. 'You were quite a long time, if that was all.'

'No, it wasn't all. They've been chasing up Pete … d'you remember? He was the guy who went to Nepal. They managed to get an itinerary from the agent who booked the trip for him and with a bit of luck, there'll be a message fairly soon, even if they can't contact his mobile.' Ralph drank his beer thoughtfully. 'Then they took me over all the things I'd told them already, which was very boring.'

'Have some more cheese!' said Rose.

Ralph accepted some more of just about everything. 'Let's forget it all for the moment … I'd like to get out into the fresh air this afternoon. Shall we go for a walk? I could arrange one with a good pub at the end of it.'

'What do you think, Bea?'

'Pity to waste the weather.' Bea wondered as she spoke whether she ought to opt out, instead of playing gooseberry. But if she did it would probably look terribly obvious and it wasn't as if they were seventeen, after all. That settled the question of when to explore the Ingleton area – or wherever. They could get off in good time tomorrow afternoon.

So they decided on the route Ralph suggested and wasted no time getting their things together, as they were later than usual in setting off. Ralph drove them for a few miles until they had left the tilled fields and scattered farms behind and they could look at open country all around. The walk followed a well-chosen circular route, scenic and just sufficiently taxing.

The pub, close to where they had parked, was the sort of place Bea liked best. She was glad there were still a few like it left: isolated, but probably very well-know for miles around, solid and definitely "unimproved" – offering as a matter of course every simple comfort and very well-kept beer. They stayed longer than they had intended and the low sun was in their eyes on their journey back. Bea felt as they drove back to the farm that she would remember the afternoon for a long time as an outstanding period of tranquillity among a turbulent few days.

'The minute we get in,' Rose said, as they drove up the lane, 'I'll get that rabbit casserole into the oven. It's all ready and I've part cooked it, so it won't need – oh, there's a car! We've got visitors.'

As Bea caught sight of the indigo-coloured Golf, her mental processes seemed to go into slow motion. She stared at it, thinking vaguely that it reminded her of one she knew well. Then realisation dawned.

'That's Philip's car,' she said in flat, quiet voice.

*

He had been waiting for her for a couple of hours, sitting in the garden. As he came up to her, she wanted to run to him and be held. Instead, she gently held out both hands and he took them equally gently and pulling her a little closer, he kissed her lightly on the lips, then let her go with no attempt to prolong this initial encounter.

'Shall we take a walk?' suggested Philip. Bea nodded and led him through the little spinney, without mentioning that she had been walking all afternoon.

Funny, she thought as she strolled beside him, I haven't been able to visualise his face while I've been up here – after all these years! She glanced up at him to remind and reassure herself. He was not a great deal taller than Bea, although solidly built. He was darkish and generally unremarkable, except for that little stripe of completely white hair on the top of his head. Bea understood that it was the result of some youthful ailment, but she had never enquired too closely, since Philip was slightly self-conscious about it. She actually found it quite attractive, but she thought his eyes, which were dark and deep-set, were his best feature. She turned to look into them now as Philip began to speak.

'I couldn't stay away any longer,' he said, though she had given no sign of requiring an explanation.

'Well, but I'm coming up to Darlington at the weekend … '

'Yes Bea, I heard – from your mother. But you know what it's like when you're staying at your parents' – difficult to find a bit of space. I had to know how you are and what's going on. I took some time off work – just for today… and Bea, I'm *sorry*.' He caught her hand for a moment and stared hard at her. 'I'm so sorry, my love.'

'Can we …?' Bea pointed to a log and they sat down.

'There's a lot I want to say,' began Philip, once more capturing her hand, which still bore earthy stains – she tended to fling off her gardening gloves almost unconsciously. 'But it can wait … just tell me how you're coping and whether the local fuzz have left you alone now.'

She told him as best she could, all the events of the last five days. Philip's knowledge of the area and even some of the people, saved a lot of explanation. She went into some detail about Ralph and the budding relationship with Rose. 'I've had a few uneasy thoughts about him,' she confided. 'I even wondered if he'd handled that bike simply in order to account for any fingerprints … rather like that man who took a quick swig from a whisky bottle before the police could get him to blow into the bag! I'm glad Rose didn't realise what I meant when I was thinking aloud about that, because I've accepted – reluctantly – that Geoff's probably guilty. It's strange that the police haven't made a move there – but they may be waiting for a particular piece of evidence.' Bea had tried hard not to leave anything out of her narrative, though as she said to Philip, there was sure to be something she'd forgotten.

'What made you so sure it wasn't Geoff?'

'Nothing! Nothing at all. There's no concrete reason … that's what's so silly. There's every reason why he *should* have done it – it all adds up.' Bea shifted her position, as the log was not designed for prolonged sitting. 'Even sillier, when you think that the next likeliest candidates are Ralph and Rose! So why on earth have I been clinging to this ridiculous urge to exonerate him? It was just a feeling, but I'm facing the facts now.'

'I don't think it's unreasonable to listen to one's instincts,' Philip replied, frowning a little. 'It's a matter of keeping instinct in proportion … sounds like what you're doing now.'

'I think so, Philip. It's been a bit difficult this week … I felt as if I couldn't be completely open with Rose. I could hardly start telling her of my doubts – or even queries – about Ralph. They *do* seem to have fallen for each other.' Bea looked up quickly at Ralph. 'Which is great,' she added hastily. 'Except that it does complicate things a bit.'

'I should think it would.' Philip grinned. 'But it seems to be the sort of complication Rose thrives on!'

'Mmm.' Bea's gaze was drawn towards the farmhouse, just visible through the trees. 'I've felt I was walking on eggshells all week. So frightened of sounding "I told you so" – because of Guy, you know. But then this morning we talked freely and we suddenly found ourselves back just as we used to be, and that was wonderful.'

'Bea, love … I'd give a great deal for *us* to be back as we used to be … Do you think there's a hope?'

Her eyes still on the distant scene, Bea nodded softly and she made no protest when Philip pulled her towards him and held her – safe, comforted and with no imminent prospect of release.

*

A chill breeze, that had been less noticeable in the sunshine, eventually coaxed them from their place on the log and they hurried back, realising that the others would need to know their plans – and whether they included rabbit casserole.

'I should think there'd be plenty, if you want to stay for supper,' said Bea.

'I'd like that, but it would make it a bit late by the time I've driven back – and I've got to be at the office early tomorrow.'

'Do you want to stay? Could you leave in the morning?'

'I'd have to leave very early … would there be room for me?'

'There'd be room for you, Philip.' Bea smiled. It was important that they didn't gloss over all their past difficulties, but she felt it would help if they talked in a loving atmosphere without pressure of time.

Rose and Ralph were both in the kitchen when they returned and, judging by the enticing aromas, supper was nearly ready.

'You timed that well,' said Ralph. He came forward to introduce himself, since he and Rose had somehow managed to fade away when they had heard who it was. Philip hurried in from the threshold to respond.

'Philip Lander,' he said, offering his hand to Ralph and grinning across at Rose, who had just put the seasoned Yorkshire pudding into the oven.

'Hello, Philip.' Rose shut the oven door and straightened up. 'Good job you've come in now, or you'd have missed this masterpiece of English provincial cooking! Can you be washed and brushed up in about twenty minutes?'

'Great! Thanks . . I'll just – '

'I'll show you,' offered Ralph. 'That way I get out of any further duties.' And he led Philip up the backstairs.

Bea had made quite a performance of washing her hands at the sink, to cover the slight embarrassment she felt. Philip's sudden appearance and the way he had then scooped her up without so much as greeting her friends, might have looked rude – or at any rate, strange. Rose would understand, of course, but she felt rather uncomfortable about Ralph.

'It was the right time for him to come, wasn't it?' Rose said, showing that she understood things well.

Bea smiled at her, as she started to collect cutlery, condiments and a pile of napkins. 'Yes,' she replied. 'There's a lost of sorting out to be done. But Philip seems as if he truly wants to work out a compromise. He's staying tonight,' she called over her shoulder from the living room. Hope that's OK?'

'Of course ... he'll share your room? Or is he to be made to sleep in the bath?'

'Well, I gather there are other rooms available ... but no, I reckon we really are back together.' Bea returned to the kitchen for glasses and side plates, piled some warm bread rolls into a basket, and put them all on a tray. 'I seem to have realised that there is so much that's worthwhile – so much that we need each other for – that the sacrifices each of us makes will pay dividends.'

'That's how I'd feel, I'm sure.' Rose was busy at the cooker, with pans of vegetables. Bea stayed at the kitchen table for the moment, with one hand on the tray, watching her friend's deft movements.

'And you know, you might not find it so much of a sacrifice in the end.'

'Perhaps not. I shall tell him that wherever we find ourselves after we've got married, I'll look for a job there.' Bea went back to the big table in the living room and finished laying it. She sat there for a moment or two, mulling over the dramatic change in her situation, before returning to ask: 'You're wondering, aren't you, what caused this major change of heart?'

'Well, I'm glad, Bea – whatever we've said about it before – because you both seem so right for each other ... but yes, I did wonder.'

'I can't say exactly. But it's had something to do with the way, this week, I've not just missed him in the obvious ways – I was feeling all that before we came here. But I've realised that he is the person I should be going to with my worries ... oh, I don't know – just that he should be *there*.'

'That's absolutely obvious to me,' said Rose. 'You've sometimes got to let your heart rule your head, you know! OK, you and I have completely opposite views on this … but there *are* times when it's right to cast out logic and follow your instinct.' Rose said this with an air of finality. 'Oh, by the way, we brought all your walking gear in and put it in the utility room.' As Bea murmured her thanks, Rose grabbed the oven cloth, opening the oven door, looking as if she meant business.

'Now, I'm ready to dish up, so if you can get your act together with the table – make sure there are plenty of table mats and then take these hot plates through … '

'OK, I'm going. You can be a real despot when you're let loose in a kitchen! It won't take a minute – and here come the men, right on cue, when the work's done.'

*

It was a wonderfully clear night, though it felt quite cold, when Bea and Philip grabbed their jackets and wandered outside after Rose's splendid supper. Bea marvelled afresh at how gazing at the stars can help to restore a more realistic perspective. Ralph had volunteered to wash up with Rose, stressing the very short time Philip had to spend there. Bea suspected that Ralph probably meant "you'll need a chance to have a nice row and then make it up."

But Bea did not intend to force the issue. At the moment, she didn't want to break the spell – they had been so in tune, so content with each other. However, the subject must be broached, or it would lie in wait, ready to ambush them in the future.

She looked at the magnificent sky, and then nodded to Philip, who pulled her arm through his and seemed quite relaxed. 'It makes you think of priorities, doesn't it?' she said at last. '… Philip,' she went on. 'As to my own priorities … I know what they are now. My job in Leeds – well, it's a job, isn't it? That's all. It isn't *life*. I've realised that what I want is to be married to you – wherever it takes us. I'll give them my resignation as soon as you like, and – '

'You don't have to do that, Bea.'

'But I want to, I'll be happy to – '

'Will you shut up, woman and let me explain!' Philip grinned. And she looked at his face, clearly lit by the stars, and at his hair, with its white stripe that caught the light. 'If you were to get a job in Darlington it wouldn't solve anything!'

'You can't mean you want me to stay at home!' Bea was about to erupt in a forceful protest, as she assumed that this meant he wanted children straight away … surely not – they'd agreed to get settled first.

She was about to draw breath, but the chance never came. Philip grabbed her with his free arm, and, drawing her to him, he stifled her potential outburst with a violent kiss. Then, pushing her away from him a little – more gently than he had seized her – he began to speak quickly, while she was still recovering her breath.

'Ever since we had that awful row, I began searching for a post in or near Leeds. I certainly didn't hope for anything very soon – but this post turned up almost straight away, in a very respected firm. It absolutely fell in my lap: one of their specialist staff had a heart attack. He should be taking care of a tricky case that's due to come on quite soon. Rotten luck – but good for me, as it's the sort of stuff I've got plenty of experience with.' He took her hand and led her towards the end of the garden where they both leaned on the tall dry stone wall. 'It's long-term (I hope), and there's plenty of scope in my particular field to develop the range of work … there might be the hope of a future partnership too.'

Bea looked for a long moment into his face, wondering at the way the miserable deadlock had been resolved so easily, once the will was there.

'You'd do that?' she murmured. 'You're not afraid you might regret it?'

Philip's smile, in that unreal light, seemed rather mysterious to Bea and she asked herself why she had never noticed that particular expression on his face before and what it signified.

'I've thought it through, don't worry,' he reassured her, as if he had read something in her gaze. 'The new job will be more challenging than I could have imagined ... and there've been a few – er, undercurrents developing recently that I'll be glad to leave behind.' Then he looked down at her and this time his smile was the warm and straightforward one she had always been used to. 'It was my own choice you know, it wasn't a last resort.'

They turned away and headed back towards the house, Philip holding her closely. 'But Bea, we mustn't overlook the – the damage we do to each other, but remember it and not let it happen again.'

'The irresistible force and the immovable object? Yes, I suppose that could be us if we're not careful. But if problems crop up, we'll have had some practice now at handling them. There's usually a compromise – '

'We Brits have always been good at compromise.'

'You Yorkshire folk haven't!' muttered Bea.

Good-naturedly, Philip pointed out that the further North one went, the more stubborn the inhabitants became. And laughing at themselves, they made their way to the kitchen door, completely absorbed in their own happiness.

'Do you want to join the others for a nightcap – I think they're in the living room?'

'Not really.' Philip took off his light anorak and found a hook for it. 'If you just tell them we're in, so they can lock up or whatever, I'll sneak up the backstairs and find your room.'

'That's what backstairs are for!' agreed Bea.

*

When Bea came down to breakfast, Philip was long gone. He had insisted on going off as quietly as possible and said he would stop for breakfast on the way rather than disturb the household. Bea knew how important it was to him to get away really early. He needed to go back to his flat to shave and change before work and he was one of those people who are infuriatingly punctual.

She imagined that her face would have told them the story, but she quietly went over the plans she and Philip had made. Bea was careful not to make a big thing of this, being mindful of the clouds that still hung over Ralph and Rose's budding relationship – no matter how much they appeared to be unconcerned.

'He's on three months' notice before he can move to Leeds … well, two and a bit now.'

'Then you'll get married straight away?' asked Rose, and she spoke so enthusiastically, that Bea realised she need not play things down. 'What sort of wedding will it be?' Ralph busied himself making more coffee and toast, as if to dissociate himself from this feminine chatter, but could be seen smiling indulgently.

'We haven't got as far as planning it … I think we'd both prefer an informal, unconventional sort of ceremony – but you know what my mother's like! We'd probably have to elope to get away from the biggest state occasion you ever witnessed … Durham Cathedral … York Minster? She'll want the lot, with bells on.'

'Quite literally,' said Ralph, as he brought the refilled cafetière. 'But it's surely up to the bride and groom to decide – '

'You haven't met Bea's mother, Ralph! She's … a rather determined lady.'

'Ah, that's where you get it from.' But Ralph's analysis of Bea was not well received and she suggested that he change his tactics unless he wanted hot coffee spilled where it could do most damage.

In this relaxed way breakfast continued and they started to discuss plans. For Rose and Bea it would be their last day at Shawhead Farm.

'It's a strange feeling,' said Rose thoughtfully. 'I've sort of got used to the situation while we're here, but back home … well, there will be a lot of adjusting before I can pick up the threads. To start with, I've got an appointment tomorrow … do you remember my saying last week, Bea, that I had to see the solicitor late on Friday afternoon?' Bea nodded. 'Well, that had been arranged a couple of weeks ago to discuss a legal separation – or divorce.'

'Oh dear.' Bea pulled a wry face. 'That does seem ironic.'

'Well, what's even more ironic is that the meeting's going ahead! I rang up to cancel, but my solicitor wants to discuss the settling of Guy's affairs – his will, or whatever.'

'Hell, I hadn't thought of that,' Ralph said. 'Do you think there'll be much to settle?'

'I don't know. He never seemed short of money, though he spent it as fast as it came in. Every now and then, he was quite flush,' Rose said, frowning as if she suddenly remembered something. 'He got bonuses, you see.' She stared at her plate thoughtfully. 'I don't even know whether he made a will and I don't care either … but of course there will be odd legal bits and pieces to sort out. When I was on the phone to them, they told me that it was quite important to tie up the loose ends, and after that I can try to put it behind me.'

'I see.' Bea nodded again. 'Well, you know I've promised to go home to Darlington for the weekend (it'll be unbearable, with Mother making a drama of everything – just hope she keeps off the subject of weddings – I'm not ready to cope with that!).' She spread honey on her last bit of toast. 'But that means I can give you a lift back and – oh, will you be all alone at home if your parents are abroad now?'

'I'd be very glad of the lift. I'm not sure exactly when they return – it'll be in the next day or two. But I shall be fine at home … I need a chance to think and to catch up with events – that's if the police are OK about me going.'

'They can't stop you, you know, Rose,' put in Ralph.

'No, perhaps not. But I've got to inform them of my intentions at any rate. I don't want to get across them again.'

'Any ideas about today? What shall we do?' Bea asked.

Rose hadn't forgotten their conversation of yesterday and suggested that she and Bea should have the trip that they had long planned (a slight exaggeration here) – possibly after an early lunch. Then she would be back in time to cook their final meal together.

'No, I'll do that,' said Ralph firmly. 'If you trust me, that is.' As the women started to clear away the dishes he turned towards the back door. 'First I've got to go to the village to pick up Mrs. Holroyd. I forgot to mention she's expecting to come today and she hasn't got a lift this morning. I'd better go right away, or she'll be around the place all day.'

'I'll fetch her, Ralph,' offered Bea. 'I know where she lives, of course.'

'That's great – thanks. Then we can have an early lunch and I'll take her back and do any shopping I need for tonight.' Bea fetched her jacket from the hall, as Ralph continued. 'Maybe we could have a lazy morning in the garden together, since the weather's holding up … there's an old croquet set in the shed – how about a really evil cut-throat contest!'

Bea however, said she would like to spend some time sketching, so they need not wait to start their game. She knew that croquet often brought out the worst in people and hoped they wouldn't have taken the mallets to each other by the time she returned. Picking up her keys from the hook by the back door, she got into her car and set off down the lane. Mrs. Holroyd was ready and waiting at the front door of the police house and she was as chatty as ever from the moment she got into the car.

'He doesn't usually go in to Headquarters on a Thursday, Mack doesn't, so I don't get a lift up,' she told Bea. 'Thankyou for fetching me, love. Only trouble is, I'll be there till nearly lunchtime, doing it this way – but I'll be upstairs by then, so I'll not get in your road.'

Bea assured her that, as far as they were concerned, the arrangement was fine. 'We're going home tomorrow, Mrs. Holroyd – Rose and I that is.' Bea changed gear as they climbed the steep lane out of the village. 'That's if they let us go, of course! It's been a rather peculiar week.'

'That it has, love. Still, I think they might be getting somewhere now – you can usually tell, because they clam up – nobody'll say owt about the case once it gets to a certain stage – not even our Mack knows the whole story yet.' Mrs. Holroyd seemed undeterred by this embargo and sounded very confident as she continued her summing up of the case. 'The way it's turning out will be bad for the village, though – I don't know of anyone as won't be fair sickened for Margie Dutton …aye, and that daft girl of hers as well.'

'Yes, it seems to be pointing that way, doesn't it?' Bea tried to keep her reply reasonably neutral and to say as little as possible in case Mrs. Holroyd remembered that "our Mack" would not approve and then this useful source of information would dry up.

'All but at an end, I reckon it is – though they'll never say so, of course … that bike out of Dyson's shed – they've had their suspicions about that, you know.' Mrs. Holroyd chuckled, as she went on: 'Weren't too pleased when young Ralph brought it in, either. Seems they wanted it left where it was – some plan they had not to mention it, or draw attention to it, like – p'raps for fear of gossip getting about. And I hear they've had one of the young constables doing timed runs – all sorts of different places – on a bike just the same as that one.'

They turned into the lane and Mrs. Holroyd began to collect up the shopping bag and cardigan that she always brought with her. 'It'll be a terrible thing in this village if it turns out the way it's looking, though they seem to have hit a bit of a problem with the shovel – the one that's supposed to have been used … doesn't seem to belong to anyone round here. Mebbe the Dysons will be able to clear that up – they'll be home this weekend – oh, here we are, then.' Bea drew to a halt and Mrs. Holroyd's flow of information did the same – she needed to pause for breath, in any case.

Bea pulled up in the yard and guessed that was all she would get on the grapevine this morning – not a bad haul, really. She went upstairs to look out her sketch-pad and pencils which were somewhere among her luggage. Then she chose a quiet corner of the garden at the side of the house furthest away from the scene of battle, where she could imagine the furious skirmishes of that nastiest of games.

'Do them good,' she muttered to herself with a malicious grin. 'That'll help them decide whether they can get on together!'

She found a good spot to put down her camp stool, after picking her way to avoid the nettles and brambles that had taken over the further corners of this little-used area. A stand of birch trees not far away interested her; behind them she could pick out a hint of hills, hazy and tantalising.

Just the thing for water-colours, she thought, as she arranged her pencils and rubber on a nearby log. Pity she hadn't brought her paintbox – but then there wouldn't really be time in any case. At peace with herself, she found her sketch growing quickly and was pleased with it. Sounds of the croquet game came and went. It did not sound to Bea like a very serious game, after all – the noises were far too polite and friendly. More like billing and cooing, she muttered to herself.

Eventually, she came to a natural pause and she was surprised to find that it was a quarter past twelve. She stretched, collected her things together and set off in search of the others. They appeared to have finished playing and she found Rose in the kitchen.

'Oh, good. I was going to give you a shout,' said Rose, putting salad and an egg mayonnaise on the table. 'We're not having very much – saving up for Ralph's speciality tonight.'

'What's that going to be?'

'No idea. He's not telling, but I don't think he's going to use the fish that we froze. I packed some fruit and cake for us along with our water bottles, so we shan't starve …'

'Who won then?' Bea brought the cutlery and plates to the table. 'Or was it just a friendly – to the point where it didn't matter?'

'Rose won!' Ralph was grinning as he came in from putting away the mallets, hoops and balls. 'She's so cunning – you'd never suspect it to look at her, would you?'

'P'raps not,' agreed Bea. 'But haven't you always known it's those innocent-looking ones that you should watch out for?'

*

'What did they want this time?' enquired Rhona, as Geoff came home after another session with Chief Inspector O'Neill.

'They're on about a bicycle, for God's sake!'

'Well, you haven't got a bike. I can't remember you ever having one.'

'No. I know. They keep going on about my alibi … there were spells during the night when no-one saw me around – I mean, there always are, on night shift – '

'I thought we'd had all that before?'

'Yeah, well they're still on about it – I suppose they reckon I could've done a trip back here if I'd had a bike with me.'

'You couldn't know you'd not be missed.'

'I expect that's a chance you'd take if you … if … '

'And you'd have to be able to fly over the wall, as well. But I suppose,' Rhona said reluctantly, 'there's always ways and means in a place like that, without using the main entrance for all to see.'

'Aye, that's right enough. They won't find any problem proving someone could go out if they'd a mind to,' answered Geoff miserably.

'You don't want to go round saying that! Sounds as if you've given up.'

'Don't talk so daft! Of course I'm not going round saying it – I'm saying it to *you*, aren't I? Because it's true and there's no point in pretending it's not.'

Suddenly, she put her arms round his neck. 'I'm sorry Geoff … I *am* sorry.'

'Nay lass, it's not your fault,' came his muffled reply. Then, pushing her gently away, he brightened a little. 'There *was* one thing, ' he said, frowning as if trying to work something out. 'Towards the end, just before they sent me home, there was a phone-call for Mr.

O'Neill and he looked very surprised while he was listening. And then he looked across at me as if he was – well, sort of weighing me up, like. And after that, when he said that's all ... well, he were a bit different – in his manner, like – as if something had changed.'

'You mean – p'raps they'd just heard about something else that's nothing to do with you?'

'Aye, could be ... but I don't rightly know! Just wishful thinking, mebbe.'

And later, when he was alone, he wondered. Was she really sorry because she had caused him to be suspected, with her flighty behaviour that everybody seemed to know about? Or did Rhona believe she'd actually driven him to seek out the man, after finding out where he was going to be?

He didn't want to think about it.

CHAPTER 11

After a very quick lunch, Rose and Bea left Ralph clearing up and set off, delighted that the weather was still holding up, after a misty start earlier on. They had decided on Malham Cove, which probably wouldn't be so off-puttingly busy as in the height of the season.

Bea had passed on what she had heard from Mrs. Holroyd, which didn't come as much of a surprise to the others. Ralph said he didn't think the shovel could belong to the Dysons, since there were already two shovels as well as a spade and fork in the shed, all in usable condition. It was a bit of a mystery, since it surely wasn't the sort of thing you would choose to bring along with you if you were going to need a weapon.

'It's terrible to think it's probably someone you know – the killer, I mean.' Rose settled herself comfortably in the passenger seat as they turned into the main road from their lane, and she started to study one of two ordnance maps they had brought with them from the farmhouse. 'But, to be honest, for me … and for Ralph too, it can't help but be a relief if it turns out that way.'

'Of course. I can see that. And it *is* looking fairly certain, isn't it?' Bea shook her head sadly. 'I must say, I find it pretty upsetting – but my own reasons are completely illogical.'

'Odd, isn't it?' Rose looked thoughtfully across at Bea. 'I mean, you are usually so rational – far more so than I am. Do you want me to do any navigating, by the way?'

'I think I know the way, but you'd better check. That road map stuck in the door-pocket might be more help at this stage.' Bea slowed down and pulled in close to her side of the road as a huge lorry loaded with sheep in an upper and lower "layer" approached them. 'I'm looking forward to going there again ... I haven't been to Malham since we spent a week there on a Field Study Course in the last year at school. I know you weren't on that trip, but you'll have been there at some time, I expect?'

'Oh yes, my parents took me when I was too young to appreciate it. Unless it's very sensational or it includes a fair with rides and that sort of thing, you don't get too excited by natural phenomena at eight or nine.'

'Well, of course, the cove *is* sensational – but not perhaps what we were looking for as kids.'

*

It did not take long to reach Malham and they found they had time to visit Gordale Scar, as well as taking a look at the Cove.

'Perfect weather to see places like this,' Bea said as they returned to the car. 'Everywhere looks so fresh, and you don't feel so hot and grubby as in the height of summer, not to mention avoiding the crowds.'

'It's been completely unmissable.' Rose stowed her walking gear in the boot with Bea's things and fished out a tin of travel sweets to put into the glove compartment. 'That extraordinary cliff face, then the river, the gorge, the waterfall, the birds – we didn't go to the Scar when I came before, so all that was new to me.'

'There's a very good pub not far away as well – it's near where the school was camped. We've time to pop in on our way back if you fancy a drink.'

'Yes, great. But I shouldn't have thought you'd have known much about the pub, coming here as a school-girl.'

'Actually, it was just what interested us most! I suppose by then I'd be seventeen ... the chief attraction of pubs was that we weren't supposed to go into them – and then the groups from boys' schools were likely to be found nearby. We told the staff we were going for an evening stroll and we girls were very good at making ourselves look older. Pubs didn't do much checking-up in those days. More difficult for the boys … '

'Mmm, yes. Mind you, the bar staff must have been a bit dim if they didn't guess that the sudden influx of young people was from a school trip! Do you know, Bea, I'd almost forgotten about all that. It makes me feel quite old when I think how long ago it was. But I do remember that one of the main reasons for wanting to go on courses like that was the hope that we'd find some boys around!'

'I reckon that's the meaning of extra-mural studies! We were plunged in at the deep end as far as sex education goes. It's not really all that long ago, but they didn't seem to give us as much information then – or was it just our school that lagged behind?'

'I think the Head dragged her feet as far as she was able to.' Rose giggled suddenly . 'But we used to enjoy asking embarrassing questions in biology … do you remember that mistress – Miss Ackroyd, it was – '

'Oh, I know who you mean – she used to go puce in the face. It was very satisfying! Weren't we cruel?'

'Yes, it was a bit cruel, but I think it's just what all children do if they see a weakness waiting to be exploited.'

'Ready then?' asked Bea, fastening her seatbelt. 'Let's go and see if the place has changed … I hope not – it's quite nostalgic.'

*

When they got back to the farmhouse, they found Ralph in the kitchen, with a glass of wine near at hand, well on with his preparations for the evening meal.

'Get yourselves sorted out,' he suggested. 'Then come down and do the table and the drinks for your exhausted staff!'

'You'll be trying to tell us you've been slaving here since we left,' Rose said.

'Well I have – most of the time, anyway. What was your afternoon like?' Ralph settled the lid gently back on to a large pan of something that smelled very good and then flopped into the big old chair at the head of the kitchen table. 'At least the visitor attractions aren't too busy yet … and you'd have the roads more-or-less to yourselves.'

'It was really lovely. I wouldn't have missed it,' said Rose, throwing her jacket over the back of the ancient settle at the far end of the room.

'We found a pub you'd have liked as well,' Bea added, as she gathered up various items that she would want to pack later. 'You should go and look at the place for yourself sometime, if you haven't been.'

'Well, I have been to Malham – but it was years and years ago and it was on a – '

'Field Study Course!' chorused Bea and Rose and they left him wondering what they were finding so funny, as they went to tidy up for supper.

*

Ralph had cooked beef olives, which he now served out, much to the appreciation of the women. He told them that half the battle was to get the beef cut correctly.

'I went down to the butcher in the village. He's nearly as good as the one in Blaeborough – he really knows what you're asking him to do – and the vegetables are from the farm shop. I have some news from the village, as well,' Ralph went on. 'Thought I'd wait till we're able to talk without distractions … apparently, they've had Geoff in for questioning.'

'Arrested him?' Rose sounded horrified, but with an undertone of excitement.

'No, not arrested. They might even have let him go home again by now, but it looks as if they took him in to "help the police with their enquiries".'

'I suppose it might suit the police for the moment to keep it voluntary, so they aren't tied to the rules that apply once someone's arrested ... ' Bea felt very sad, even though she had been anticipating this, just as the others had.

'Yes, it might be something like that,' agreed Ralph. 'I gather it's a question of what kind of evidence they've got and in any case they'll make sure they know where he is if wanted.'

'Did the butcher tell you about it?'

'No. As soon as you two left, I ran Mrs. H. home and Mack was there when we got to their house. He told me – said there was going to be a statement on TV today anyway, so it didn't matter if he talked about it. But he said that we mustn't think it's all cleared up, because there's a lot going on under the surface – whatever that means '

Rose glanced at her watch. 'The news'll be starting in five minutes – we'd better put it on ... did this Mack tell you anything else?'

'Well, he couldn't say much, of course. He's not going to gossip like his wife – unfortunately for us! But he indicated that the evidence against Geoff is all circumstantial.'

'I never quite know what that means,' Rose murmured.

'Doesn't it mean,' said Bea, frowning, 'that the indications point towards him, but they don't *prove* that he did it. Not like a direct link, such as a hair or a fingerprint might be ... '

'Or a bloodstain!' put in the irrepressible Rose.

'Er – yes, I think that's more-or-less it. I mean, if a suspect appears to have had a strong reason to be at the scene and then they think a bicycle has been "borrowed" ... that's the sort of thing I imagine might make the police re-interview him.'

'Mmm. That's what I thought. It isn't absolute proof, is it? OK – it looks very likely, but unless someone saw him on the bike ... ' Bea looked across at the other two and thought: hell! – I still want to think it isn't him!'

'Time to watch the news,' said Rose.

'OK – there's a pudding, but it's cold, so we could see if anything's mentioned and then finish later.'

'Good idea. That was pretty filling, so I could do with a pause,' said Bea, pushing her chair back from the table and slewing it round to face the TV. 'Fantastic meal! I'll have to take lessons one day. And to think you've made a pud as well ...'

'Actually not,' Ralph smiled. 'I had thought of trying to convince you that I'd made it myself – but I knew that you'd never buy it.'

'But *you* did!'

'Did what?' asked Rose as she fiddled with the remote.

'He bought it.'

Rose and Ralph groaned and Ralph suggested sardonically that, instead of training as an assistant chef, Bea might learn to be his stooge and they could work up a double act. 'I picked the pud up in the Farm Shop – '

'Sssh.' Rose moved her chair nearer to the set and indicated that the news was beginning.

As before, they had to sit through several items of general and global interest before the report began, but at last there was an interview with a Superintendent. They hadn't actually met anyone as senior as this in their several encounters, and he was quite an imposing figure. However, he spoke only briefly, to sum up progress to date. He particularly stressed that, although a person had been voluntarily to the police station, helping to clarify certain aspects, an arrest was not imminent, and a number of different leads were being followed.

'He's even more cagey than Constable Makepeace Holroyd,' laughed Ralph, getting up and heading for the kitchen. 'Let's clear the table a bit and then I'll fetch my celebration pudding.'

He brought in a tarte au citron that managed to look handmade and at the same time professional. The Farm Shop was beginning to acquire a reputation for these "home-baked" items.

But Bea, though she tried to join in the mood of end-of-term light-heartedness, felt she had not really been infected by it.

*

When Bea awoke on Friday morning, she was quite surprised to hear a steady patter of rain on her window. It seemed incredible that the break in that exceptionally fine spell of weather should come on the very day she and Rose planned to leave.

Over a leisurely breakfast, they decided to have a light lunch and then set off. They wanted to spend some time after packing up, making sure that Mrs. Holroyd should have no extra work to do in their rooms and bathroom. Then they would go down to see the police to inform them of their proposed whereabouts and for Bea to supply her address for the weekend.

'Shouldn't think they'll be too bothered about Rose and me now,' said Ralph confidently. 'If they reckon they've probably got their man, they'll be more relaxed ... look, Rose, there's something I want to ask you about – '

Accordingly, Bea suddenly found that she had something urgent to do about her luggage and, muttering her excuses, she went up to her room. It seemed clear that Ralph wanted to make plans to meet Rose in the future and she felt *de trop*. The obvious thing was to start packing, but instead she found herself sitting in the window seat, gazing at the hills. She began to think about the caravan. She had intended to do something about it, though she had no idea what. Too late now, she thought, and came to the conclusion that it would be best to talk to her father before making a decision. Why, she wondered, am I in this strange mood? I ought to feel huge relief that the whole business is over, but I don't – I just feel uneasy ... something doesn't seem *right*.

Oh, it's ridiculous, she thought, giving herself a shake and getting up from the window. My friends have just had a terrible load lifted from them ... do I know what it feels like to have a murder charge looming over me? Even if it's only a remote threat, none-the-less it's demoralising. I'm letting my own illogical reactions take over, when I should be more concerned about them.

195

She dragged her large bag out and plonked it on her bed. Uncharacteristically, and with scant respect for silk blouses and her best underwear, she hurled clothes into the case, along with shoes, her sketching things and her slightly muddy fleece.

*

'You coming?' Rose put her head round the door of the bedroom. 'Oh dear! Who's rattled *your* cage? You're normally the world's tidiest packer, but this looks like the last day at Debenham's sale.'

'Oh, it's nothing. Take no notice of me … it's just – I feel sorry for the Collinses, and particularly for Carmen. But of course,' she went on hastily, 'I'm very glad that you and Ralph have most probably seen the last of the police. It's a bit muddling, that's all … look, I'll be down right after you – tell Ralph I'm on my way.'

Bea closed up her bag, ran a comb through her hair and hurried downstairs and out to the car. She automatically took her place in the back. Although Rose had never made a move to claim the front passenger seat, somehow this had become the norm – a symbol of her growing relationship with Ralph. Bea wondered what plans they had in mind, now that they were on the point of separation. As if she had spoken aloud, she received her answer.

'We've been discussing plans for the weekend,' Rose said. 'I've just managed to phone Mum and Dad – we had to go up the hill to get a signal. But after all that I could have rung them on the landline anyway. They were back home! They got back last night from Canada, a bit earlier than I'd thought and they were just going to try and contact me. Anyway, Ralph says he'd like to meet them, so he's coming over to Darlington.'

Bea carefully allowed no surprise to show on her face, though she thought that things were moving along far too fast. 'Are you staying at Rose's then?' she asked. 'It would be just one long car trip if you were to go straight back to Manchester from there.'

'Yes, it would be – and it might be a bit much to stay with the Downeys on my first visit … but as it's turned out, they're going over to see Rose's sister today and staying till Sunday.' Rose's sister Emma lived in Newcastle, and she had given birth to her second child just before the Downeys left for Canada.

'So it seemed best,' added Rose, 'for Ralph to come over tomorrow, and then he can meet my parents briefly on Sunday before he goes back to Manchester.'

Ralph smiled at Rose and said: 'So we wondered if you want to give Philip a ring and see whether he'd like to come over to Rose's with you tomorrow evening for a sort of celebratory meal.'

Rose said: 'Now that it's all over, it would sort of round things off … '

They had reached the old schoolhouse now, and Bea was thankful that they were all busy getting out of the car, so that she did not have to reply straight away. I expect they're right, she thought, as they made their way to the door. But somehow it didn't seem quite the thing – to be celebrating, before it was all made official. She thought that Philip would probably agree with her and say it's never over till it's over. However, she murmured as they entered the big old-fashioned porch, that she would try to get hold of him.

Ralph spoke to the sergeant in charge – one they hadn't seen before, who said that the Inspector would have to be informed and he went off to telephone Headquarters.

'That will be in order,' said the sergeant on his return. 'Please give me full details of where you are going to be and any future address … there's a message for you, sir,' he added. 'We've made contact with Kathmandu, and we have details of your friend's itinerary. He's due to return to Kathmandu briefly and he will be asked to contact us when he arrives – that should be very soon, I gather.'

Ralph said this was most satisfactory. They left all the necessary information and then set off back to the farm. The rest of the morning was spent in cleaning and tidying, with the work shared out scrupulously between the three of them. Part of Ralph's time was taken up with ensuring that a good supply of logs was available and the coke hods filled in readiness. He would do the last-minute things in the morning before he set off to join Rose. Mrs. Holroyd would be in after they had gone, but even so there was plenty to do.

'It's the only thing about self-catering that gets up my nose,' remarked Rose, as she and Bea tackled the cooker and fridge. 'It's annoying that a week's relaxation has to end in drudgery.'

'Bit like washing-up – the only civilised way would be if you could do that *before* the meal, instead of spoiling the occasion.'

*

Rose and Bea set off in good time after a sandwich lunch. There was nothing to hang around for, as it was still raining and in any case, Rose had to be back for her appointment. Bea had managed to contact Philip. She had been surprised to find him in favour of the proposed meal, saying any doubt now was academic. There were no other suspects it seemed, unless you counted Rose and Ralph, which was preposterous.

'I think that after the very strange week you've all had, a quiet dinner together will bring closure – to use the very overworked phrase of the moment. It'll be marvellous to be with you again – I thought of coming round tomorrow morning?'

'Fine.' Bea had looked out towards the front garden and seen that Ralph and Rose were still out there. Quietly and quickly, she had told Philip that Rose was going to introduce Ralph to her parents.

'Wouldn't you like to be a fly on the wall?' she'd laughed.

'That is thoroughly disloyal and unkind … and, yes I would!' Bea had a mental picture of Philip's mischievous grin – so unexpected, as it transformed his rather serious face. He had followed Rose's love life with considerable interest over the years and he'd seemed unsurprised that her recent venture into matrimony hadn't made her more wary. 'By now, the Downeys must have perfected that peculiar brand of long-suffering detachment that's required where Rose's "heart attacks" are concerned.'

'Well, yes and they're right of course. As I know to my cost, if you offer any opposition you only make things worse all round – '

'Well, I think that's forgotten now and I'm sure you'll be happy to leave them to handle things their own way.' Philip's voice had been comforting. 'And we on the other hand, are boringly sensible … I wonder if we're missing something? But I've got to go, love – I shouldn't be gossiping here. See you tomorrow.'

As Bea settled down on the familiar road, wipers monotonously to-ing and fro-ing in rain that alternated between drizzle and downpour, she thought back to that conversation. In spite of her previous misgivings, she now found herself pleasantly anticipating Saturday evening. She was surprised at how excited she felt at the prospect of being reunited with Philip. After all, she thought, it's only two days since he was here. But circumstances were so different now: there was so much to plan and look forward to.

Rose also appeared to be deep in thought and hardly a word had been exchanged for miles. Well, thought Bea, she's got more to brood on than I have. She seems to be heading into the unknown. Exciting, I suppose – but not my scene – nor Philip's. We're too fond of careful planning, too logical … and as he said, too dull, even?

'It must be terribly dull not to act on impulse from time to time!' With startling relevance, Rose had once more cut into her musings, and Bea began to wonder about thought transference.

'I was just thinking that you might find the Ralph and me thing a bit – well, rushed,' went on Rose. 'But I can't change the way I am … I like to feel that, even if it all ends in tears, at least I know I'm *alive* – doing things that I'll look back on when I'm old and decrepit and think My God! Did I do that – was that *me*?'

Bea thought for a moment or two about this. 'D'you know, I've just recalled something that made quite an impression on me, years ago. I went to see a play by Henry James – or rather, it was based on a book by him – it's called "The Heiress".'

'Oh, I know it.' Rose looked keenly at Bea, clearly understanding the point she was making. 'The book is "Washington Square", isn't it? The heiress's father tells her he'll disinherit her if she marries the man she's in love with. She's painfully gauche and shy and hasn't got a lot to attract this charming young man – so her father is certain the man is only after her money.'

'Yes, and of course the father is quite right, because – in the stage version at any rate – they arrange to elope – minus the inheritance of course, but the fiancé stands her up. And then, later on, when the father dies and she finally inherits, it becomes clear that she would have chosen to have known a brief happiness followed by pain rather than the empty misery that her life became.'

'And then, the fortune-hunter comes back and she seizes the chance to turn the tables on him!'

'Which just goes to show how bitter and twisted it made her.'

'So the moral is,' concluded Rose, 'Grab it now and do the worrying later … that doesn't sound a bit like you, Bea.'

'No it doesn't, does it? Perhaps you'll reform me yet.'

'Oh!' Rose suddenly shouted, making Bea jump. 'I've just remembered something. I *can* prove that I was at Howard and Celia's on Thursday night!'

Bea groaned. 'Now she remembers – when it's all over, bar the shouting!'

'I know – how silly is that? But all the same, it's nice to feel completely freed from any possibility of suspicion, isn't it? I do hope Ralph gets his story confirmed very soon, too. After all, they haven't arrested Geoff yet, so far as we know … look how often the police take people in like that, and then have to let them go if there's not enough evidence.'

'So what have you remembered?'

'Well, it's such an odd way for it to happen … it was talking just now about the Henry James novel that made me think of it. I have a feeling that the name of the fortune-hunter was Maurice, or perhaps spelt M-o-r-r-i-s. Anyway the point is, the name Maurice has rung a bell … ' Rose gazed at the road ahead and frowned at the recollection that had just come to her.

'A friend of Howard's called Maurice rang up for him – it was really late on Thursday night and I'd actually gone to bed. I explained of course, about them going off in a hurry … and then I just left a note by the phone, with time and date and Maurice's message. Then I got back into bed and went straight to sleep. I'd taken the call in Howard and Celia's bedroom and I'd no occasion to go back there and see the note or think about it again … I mean it was totally unimportant.' Rose smiled and Bea heard the little light sigh she gave. 'As you say … it probably doesn't matter now either, but it does tidy things up.'

*

If only, thought Barbara, I could stop listening to the radio, turn off the TV, throw out the papers unread! She consoled herself with the thought that at least her husband, who these days seemed to live in his own little world, had taken remarkably little interest. The suspicious death of a man he knew quite well – though they weren't intimate friends – seemed to pass him by with scarcely a ripple. That had been one reason why all this had happened, she reckoned. Rod seemed indifferent to everything these days – apart from his blasted tomatoes. Perhaps that had triggered … well, no use dwelling on that now. What's done's done.

Barbara had been feeling more uneasy than ever since she learned that the police were holding a man for questioning. The tabloids (serves me right for buying them, she thought) had hinted that he had attacked his wife's lover. The newspapers were not a very reliable source at the best of times, and their suggestions were necessarily very vague. But there was enough to haunt her – an innocent man might be convicted. She came out of school at the end of a week in which she knew she had not given her class the attention it deserved and she felt ashamed. Barbara knew she was a good teacher and wouldn't normally behave recklessly. She realised on reflection that she must have been in the grip of some sort of madness … well, she felt sane enough now, and suddenly her mind was made up. She set off in the direction of the local police station.

CHAPTER 12

They went straight to Rose's when they reached Darlington. Rose accepted Bea's offer to drive her to the appointment with the solicitor.

'It's not till half past four, so we haven't got a mad rush. There's time for a cup of tea – and it's nice to have you here, Bea. I feel just a bit nervous about this meeting with the solicitor – well, more upset than nervous, really.' Rose rummaged in the fridge for milk. 'Oh goody! Mum's left us a couple of cream cakes – isn't that just like her!'

'Are you going to be all right for shopping and carrying it all back?'

'Yes, thanks. Ralph's going to be here in good time tomorrow and we can do it all then …I expect we'll make it easy for ourselves with quite few items from Marks & Sparks, but the main part of the meal will be all our own work.'

'I expect it will be wonderful – with two of you who love to cook. I've noticed though, that you competent cooks don't have any hang-ups about the odd bit of convenience food. But we lesser mortals feel guilty if it hasn't been slaved over … and that's absolutely potty, since the stuff I produce wouldn't be nearly as good as a top quality bought-in food.'

Back in the car, Bea asked if she should wait and take Rose home again, but Rose didn't know how long it would take and preferred to catch the bus, which was practically door to door. So Bea deposited her outside the large and imposing building.

'If you're sure … well then, see you tomorrow – we'll bring the wine.' And, wishing Rose good luck with the rather daunting appointment, she set off for her parents' home. Bea had often wondered why Rose had never learned to drive. Whenever Bea had tried to draw her out on the subject, Rose's replies were vague and offered no good reason. As ever, Bea hated not having her curiosity satisfied. 'I'll never find out what's put her off,' Bea grumbled aloud to herself as she drove away from the town centre. 'Something must have happened that she likes to keep to herself … I wonder whether she'll tell Ralph?'

She drove through the suburbs, so familiar to her, yet subtly changed from time to time over the years during which she had become a visitor to her old home. She was aware each time she came that she had been lucky to grow up in an area like this. 'I'm terribly biased – thank Heaven!' she muttered to herself. 'The beautiful region (once you're away from the various industrialised parts), the straightforward, genuine folk who live here … the *space*. For me and for Philip too, there's nowhere to touch the North!'

She wondered whether Leeds would suit Philip as well as Darlington had. Though he came from Leeds originally, he hadn't lived there since he was in his teens. He'd been there on visits to his parents during and since university and of course, in recent years he very often stayed with Bea at the weekend. But it was vital that Philip never came to look on the move as a sacrifice. Although he was enthusiastic now, there would be compromises. Marriage was about adapting and re-aligning oneself … but willingly, gladly, with no sense of obligation, she told herself. Coercion was death to relationships.

She pulled the car into the narrow drive that ran along the left-hand side of the house. This had been her home for four or five years, before she went to college. It dated back to the early 1900's – perhaps around 1910, she reckoned and it was solid and unremarkable. Comfort, practicality, respectability would have been the aims of the builders as well as the buyers of such dwellings.

Bea had always enjoyed imagining what the selling points would have been a hundred years ago. A gas cooker would, she thought, have been a daring innovation and the "range", with its oven and water boiler, still provided as standard. It was still there even now, in the Roebucks' big kitchen – a charming anachronism, hung with bright copper pans, with the modern cooker tucked in beside it. Other important facilities in those days would have been the indoor wash-house – so handy and compact, with its "copper" for the boiling water, shallow stone sink, big square creel and space for several galvanised wash-tubs. There was a convenient larder at the foot of the cellar steps, with a huge meat-safe and marble slab. Bea loved the house and hoped that she and Philip might one day find something a bit similar, though if possible, of a more picturesque vintage – and certainly not quite so large.

Her mother had heard her arrive and was at the door as she dragged her bag in. She greeted Bea effusively, begging her to leave her luggage in the hall – 'Your father will see to it all,' she said, as though speaking of a well-trained member of her staff. Bea disregarded this suggestion and slipped upstairs with her bag to her old room. Her mother called after her that the kettle was on and that she'd want some tea.

'Wonderful,' called Bea, hurrying down the stairs and into the sitting room. It was the only possible reply and in any case, tea would be very welcome.

'Bea! We've been looking forward to this.' Her father had come in, apparently from the garden, since he had removed his shoes and was wearing a pair of ancient cords, of such venerable decrepitude that they would never otherwise have been permitted. 'Rose not with you? I expect her parents will be anxious to have her home.'

'Actually, they're not there today. They had a long-standing arrangement with Emma – there's a new baby, you know, and they'll want to make up for what they've missed while they were in Canada.'

'Oh, Bea,' her mother protested, her voice full of reproach. 'You should have brought her here … she shouldn't be on her own after such a distressing experience – '

'It's all right, Mum. I understand she has a friend staying.' Bea simply hadn't the courage tell her mother that Rose would shortly be joined by a man she had met exactly a week ago. She could anticipate the cries of horror and disapproval, dressed rather transparently as concern. She would never hear the end of it. As so often in the past – and feeling feeble – she took the line of least resistance. Before her mother could begin to enquire who the friend was, and was it someone they knew, Bea hastily proffered the next piece of information, calculated to hold her mother's attention.

'She's asked Philip and me to go over for a bit of supper tomorrow.'

Bea had chosen the perfect diversion. The mention of Philip and the prospect of a resumption of the relationship overrode any other consideration. Even Bea's absence from one of the family meals over the weekend – doubtless planned down to the last roast potato – was instantly excused. The recent coolness between Bea and Philip had clearly been next on Mrs. Roebuck's list of protestations. There had been stern warnings on the phone, when Bea had rung to confirm her arrival time. Bea was being short-sighted and stubborn, according to her mother. 'Poor Philip! How you can *think* of … '

Fortunately, Bea had developed certain skills in dealing with her mother. She had explained why, sadly, the call had had to end just then – she had just found time to ask where her brother was and to hear about the activities which absented him this weekend. .

But now the shadow preventing complete peace of mind for Mrs. Roebuck was lifted and Bea felt she too could relax as she sat down to tea and delicious home-made cakes. There was far more than anyone could cope with and Bea often wondered if reaction to the over-emphasis on domestic expertise and abundance throughout her adolescence might be the cause of her own lack of interest. Philip, on the other hand, was a very capable cook and had sworn to teach her eventually. She thought that might work out quite well.

As soon as they decently could, Bea and her father escaped to the garden. It had been a delight to Dr. Roebuck that Bea had inherited his love of gardening. As they walked around the biggish plot, he outlined his latest plans and demonstrated how his previous schemes were progressing.

'I spent a bit of time in the Dysons' garden,' Bea told him. 'You know how it is when you're worried – a bit of weeding can be really therapeutic.'

'Best thing in the world! And if you're angry, you can be quite vicious with weeds.' They had reached the far end of the garden and Dr. Roebuck indicated the rustic seat, tucked away in a corner among some recently planted willow trees – a birthday present from Bea and Philip. 'Now, bring me up-to-date with what's gone on, will you? I've heard they're holding somebody in custody.'

'Yes,' said Bea with a little sigh. 'Well, he's been in for questioning, apparently … you remember Carmen? Well, it's her son-in-law – but I still keep feeling that all might not be as it appears. The Superintendent on TV last night implied that there were other possibilities.' She went on to describe all that had happened, including her own, not very clever, nosing about and the various doubts and suspicions. She also explained the difficulties Rose and Ralph had had in establishing alibis.

'Actually, Rose has remembered now, that she took a phone message at the crucial time, and Ralph seems to be close to having his story confirmed. It's not important any more, I imagine – and anyway, it's only a matter of an answer coming through from a guy on holiday – but he's in a far-flung part of Nepal, so that's delayed things.'

Bea told her father about the two people Ralph depended on for corroboration and Dr. Roebuck commented mildly that it seemed a pity that both of Ralph's witnesses were not able to help as much as might be hoped.

She mentioned the sun-glasses, and her earlier suspicions. However, she added that on reflection, it was obvious that someone had planted them in the caravan, since Ralph himself had drawn attention to the glasses. 'He had no need mention them – and then, we'd seen Geoff hanging round the place as well. So it looks as though Geoff put them there in a really stupid attempt to incriminate him.' Bea swatted unsuccessfully at a persistent fly around her head.

'I've even wondered whether he might still have put them there if he were innocent,' she continued. 'If he got really needled by all the police questioning I mean, and needed to deflect the search … I should think he's a simple soul who might not even think about the consequences. Or it may be that for some reason he genuinely believed Ralph was guilty.' Bea gave her father a sad little smile. 'All along, I've wanted to think he was innocent, but it seems I may have to change my mind.'

'Sort of explosion, after all his stoical forbearance in the face of his wife's treatment of him?' Bea was surprised that her father was aware of this village saga. She thought that he would have paid little attention to gossip – and anyway, how would it reach his ears? He hadn't been over there for quite a while.

He smiled at her, guessing her thoughts. 'Doctors are trained to observe, you know Bea. They keep their ear to the ground and file away information almost automatically – pay no attention to it unless something crops up. And anyway,' he added, 'that situation has been going on for years and years.'

He shifted his weight about on the none-too-comfortable wooden bench. 'But you know, I wouldn't have thought her clumsy little flirtations had ever gone very deep with Geoff. I always reckoned that he was a particularly well-balanced chap and he seemed to tolerate Rhona in a half-amused, half-irritated way. Shows how wrong one can be! He probably hid his feelings well, but perhaps it was more of a blow to his pride than was ever apparent.'

'Mmm … I expect that's it,' Bea agreed sadly.

*

After eating far too much of her mother's excellent cooking that evening, Bea played canasta with her parents, who were keen card-players and then they watched the beginning of the news – which on this occasion did not mention "The Blaeborough Farm Tragedy". She felt genuinely tired and excused herself after the headlines.

She was grateful that her old bedroom was unchanged since she left home – somehow her mother had resisted the temptation to prettify it. Her unpacking was more in line with her usual fastidious methods, though she was afraid it was too late to expect the creases to vanish overnight. She had taken more care with the little radio from the caravan, wrapping it in a jumper to protect it. As she put it on the dressing table, she checked it to make sure the settings had not been knocked in transit, causing it to start up and spoil her night's rest. Unaccountably sleepy (maybe it was that big meal), she was soon in bed, enjoying the comforting, familiar shape and feel of her old room around her.

She woke later than usual next morning, and joined her mother in the kitchen. Her father, always an early riser, was nowhere to be seen. She agreed to eat a boiled egg – the lightest breakfast she could get away with, as a "full English" threatened to follow her mother's efforts of the previous evening. She then went to survey the wreckage of the clothes she had dealt with so uncaringly on leaving the farm yesterday. As expected, a night on a hanger had been insufficient to improve any one of them. I might have had enough sense to know I'd need something decent to wear this weekend – even without Rose's dinner, she thought crossly. She fished out a favourite dress in a subtle shade of sea-green and, throwing it over her arm along with a skirt and a silk blouse, likewise crumpled, she went downstairs to iron them.

'Whatever have you been doing to your lovely dress?' demanded her mother. Bea bit her tongue and reminded herself that she was here as a guest and it was just for the weekend. Surely, she chided herself, I can control my nastier side at least for a day or so?

But, oh! – if only Mum wouldn't talk to me as if I was still nine years old and had torn my clothes climbing trees!

'Packed in a hurry,' she muttered. 'OK if I use the ironing board?'

'Of course dear.' Mrs. Roebuck took the ironing board from a cupboard and insisted on setting it up and plugging in the iron. However, the bit was between her teeth and she continued: 'But after I've taught you so carefully how to pack properly … there's a right and a wrong way to do everything, you know Bea.'

'Mmm … I'll try and remember,' answered Bea meekly, and awarded herself a very modest medal, as she started on the blouse.

'And then there's your father,' continued Mrs. Roebuck mercilessly, as she stacked the dishwasher. 'The whole of our married life I've kept reminding him to fold his sweater when he takes it off, instead of just dropping it any old how …'

'What an unforgivable waste of all those years together,' said Bea – but luckily she said it to herself.

She was just trying to find a topic that might divert her mother from this depressing and futile train of thought, when the doorbell rang. Her mother shut the kitchen door on the disarray within, but Bea heard Philip's voice in the hall. She felt a leap of pleasure, as well as a touch of relief – for Philip certainly would bring out the best in her mother. (Which takes a bit of doing, she thought cattily). She heard him being waylaid by her father, who had probably been holed up in his study as usual, and then he was taken off to see the willow saplings. It was really lucky that he got on so well with both her parents. Dr. Roebuck and he shared a liking for cricket, gardening and setting the world to rights with their own peculiar brand of non-doctrinaire philosophy. They would happily talk together for hours until Bea, or her mother would put up with it no longer and prised them apart.

She finished the blouse and skirt and had just started on the dress, as her mother came into the kitchen to make coffee. 'Philip's here, Bea – he's gone into the garden with your father. I told him you wouldn't be long.'

After she had hung up the clothes and put away the ironing board, Bea found the men in the greenhouse, deep in earnest discussion. Philip was clearly delighted to be following the familiar old routines that had always marked his visits in the past. They left Dr. Roebuck adjusting the greenhouse ventilators and Philip explained that there was some shopping that he particularly wanted to do. He hoped Bea would come and give her advice, but only smiled and said 'Tell you later!' when she asked what he had in mind. She was a little surprised, as she knew he wasn't fond of shopping and she wondered why he was making a mystery of it.

'Well, yes, OK,' she said. 'Mum's making coffee – so, while you have yours, I'll go and change into a going-into-Darlington outfit!'

'That's fine – there's no rush. It's just so nice to have the whole day free for once.'

*

On the short drive into town, Bea curbed her curiosity, as she realised that Philip wanted to do things his own way. They put the car in a multi-storey and wandered along to the shops at a gentle pace, which Bea didn't normally associate with Philip. He's really left his work behind for once, she thought – perhaps it's because he's working out his notice. After the rain of yesterday, it was sunny again and there was a pleasant freshness in the air.

'Do you know what I want to buy?' Philip asked at last.

'No … how could I know? Is it something you've been wanting for a long time?'

'No – yes!' Philip chuckled and grinned, as he pulled her gently towards a shop window. 'We've never got round to thinking about a ring … even though we've been sort of engaged for ages! I'd like us to choose one today – what do you think?'

Bea gazed into the big window at the mind-boggling variety of rings. Perhaps the cliché "dazzling display" could be forgiven here. She looked up at Philip's eager face. 'I've just never thought of an official engagement, but such things still happen, don't they … what a lovely idea!' She found the vast choice a bit daunting, however and was glad when Philip said: 'Someone in the office told me about a little jeweller's just over there.' He pointed to a narrow side-street across the road. It led down between a wine shop and a camping store. 'I thought you might find those big shops a bit impersonal and overwhelming and this place is supposed to be a little bit out of the ordinary.'

'Oh yes. That would be more our style, wouldn't it?' Feeling slightly self-conscious, she allowed him to lead her to the small and rather unusual shop and there she chose an aquamarine in an imaginative setting, which they both felt was just the right thing for Bea. It fitted without the need for alteration, so that she could enjoy wearing it then and there. They both felt elated and when they called at the wine shop, they found themselves choosing bottles without thought for the price, until Bea came down to earth first and suggested something a little more modest.

She could hardly take her eyes off her beautiful ring – the more thrilled with it because it was completely unexpected. Philip asked her if she would like to eat lunch somewhere in the town, or whether they should go back to the car and find a country pub.

'Oh, let's go to the George!' said Bea. This was one of their favourite pubs, in a nearby village and on a day like this it might even be mild enough to have lunch in its spacious garden. 'It's still barely lunchtime, so it shouldn't be too crowded.'

*

Afternoon tea was taken with Bea's parents in a festive atmosphere. Bea was relieved that Dr. Roebuck had managed to restrain to his wife, reminding her of the dinner engagement, so they weren't expected to consume the sort of feast that was habitually served up. Bea felt strangely shy, as her parents inspected the ring, but her father's delighted face gave her a deep glow of happiness and her mother seemed all approval, although possibly she may have doubted that the ring was sufficiently spectacular.

Bea, felt surprised to find herself behaving so conventionally – a ring … and then a wedding! Well, she was pleased that it had made her mother so happy – it was important that she was encouraged to make the most of this occasion … and then, once these formalities were over, Bea hoped to be free to run her life as she pleased. 'But I do love my aquamarine,' she told herself aloud.

Later on, she changed into the newly-ironed dress and, borrowing a front-door key, they went out to Philip's car. Bea volunteered to drive on the way home. She didn't want Philip to be worrying about what he drank – he needed to relax and she had just had a week's (sort of) holiday.

'Happy?' Philip carefully settled the bag with the wine bottles in it behind his seat.

'Incredibly! All the more so, because last week it seemed as if it could never come right again.'

'Yes, I know. Do you think it's almost worth being utterly miserable, just so you can appreciate feeling this good?' he asked, laughing. 'And by the way, I haven't told you how wonderful you look … you really sparkle! And how clever of you to have a dress to go with your ring – or was it the other way about?'

'Thankyou, Philip,' Bea said solemnly, pleased at one of his rare compliments. 'I guess I had this colour in the back of my mind when we were looking at rings. If you remember, it's one of my favourite dresses – but you should have seen it this morning!' She told him how the strange mood had come over her when she had started packing to come home. For a moment, a little cloud settled over them both.

'It's silly to let myself get too upset, isn't it? After all, there's absolutely nothing I can do to alter things.'

'And if he's guilty, then your agonising is a bit misplaced. Try not to think of it while we're with Rose and Ralph … just remember that Geoff's guilt confirms their innocence. Sorry!' he added.' That does sound incredibly pompous – but you know what I mean?'

'Oh, you're absolutely right, I know that. But I've been a bit bothered about Rose too … she and Ralph seem to have become pretty close in a ridiculously short time. What does she really know about him? I can't help feeling that she might be going to make another serious mistake –'

Suddenly, Philip slowed down and pulled into a lay-by he had just spotted.

'What's up? Has a tyre blown? I didn't feel any –'

Philip didn't answer. He switched off the engine, turned round in his seat towards her and put his finger gently over her mouth.

'Please, love … will you just let Rose make her own mistakes? You can't show her how to live her life – and it nearly cost your friendship last time.'

Bea was silent for a moment. 'You mean,' she said, smiling ruefully, 'I'm an interfering old bitch!'

'No, love,' laughed Philip. 'You don't seem at all old … Ouch! All right,' he added, fending her off. 'And certainly not a bitch … but interfering?'

*

Rose's family had never moved from the house that Bea had first visited in their schooldays. She had been tremendously impressed by it then, as it was a couple of steps up, at least, from the urban villa where Bea had then lived. It was set well back from the road in extensive gardens and was very modern, with a state-of-the-art kitchen (recently refurbished) and plenty of bathrooms and loos. There was a study whose chief function seemed to be to house yet another TV, to ensure that those who were sport-obsessed did not make themselves too unpopular with those who weren't.

Recalling now the times she had stayed for the weekend with the Downeys, Bea was amused at how she had felt – her own home at the time seemed inadequate and terribly old-fashioned. But the Roebuck kitchen had been very practical and had a lovely comfortable atmosphere, while a bath plus shower and a downstairs "cloakroom" had been deemed quite sufficient, at any rate by Dr. Roebuck, who seemed to have the last word when it came to the more important decisions. His office had been a roomy, untidy bolthole where he could usually count on remaining undisturbed. It had grown organically and no-one was allowed to interfere with it. Before Bea was born, and before highly organised group practices became universal, he had held his surgery there, using the morning-room as a waiting and reception area. The present Roebuck establishment was a little more ambitious, but with the accent on comfort rather than status.

Bea was reminiscing about all this as she and Philip approached the rather exclusive area where the Downeys lived.

'What a horrid little snob I was!'

'I think perhaps children often are … well, not exactly snobs, but – natural *competitors.*'

'Yes, that's it. It's part of their yah-boo culture – my house is bigger than your house! But I was certainly overawed when I went to Rose's in those days. I think it was all those bathrooms … funny, because we wouldn't think anything of it now –'

'No, we'd just say "what, no en-suite?" '

'And it wasn't till years later,' went on Bea, as they turned into a tree-lined avenue, 'when we were quite grown-up, that Rose told me how, because her father's a manufacturer, her parents looked up to mine as "professional people"! I suppose it didn't really mean much to Rose at the time and she probably wouldn't have worked that one out for herself … but clearly she was aware of their attitude.' She held out her hand for the car keys when Philip turned off the engine and he grinned at her and handed them over. This was a well-worn ceremony which had started years ago, after that time when they hadn't managed to decide who was to going to drive home – and got halfway through the meal without coming to an answer.

'Seems to me we have to be scrupulous about what we unconsciously pass on to our children. But we won't show our prejudices – we'll be model parents, won't we? That's taken for granted.'

Bea smiled at him. 'We can't even take having children for granted, can we? Fertility does diminish – '

'Let's put the wedding forward, then – if we get married tomorrow, we'll save two or three whole months!'

CHAPTER 13

Rose and Ralph were in high spirits as they welcomed them in. Rose rushed up to embrace them both, just as though she hadn't seen Bea the previous day.

'We've been sitting on the terrace just now. Come and have a drink there – make the most of the evening before it turns too chilly.' Rose led them through patio doors to a sheltered area, very attractively paved, which they considered to be as comfortably furnished as many sitting rooms.

Ralph thanked them for the wine. 'I'll take them through to the kitchen. Back in a moment,' he said, after enquiring what they would like to drink and then he disappeared into the house. He seemed to have become very much at home in the short time he'd been there.

Terribly domesticated, thought Bea. He'd frighten me to death.

'This weather's amazing,' Philip said, choosing a smart high-backed chair. 'It seems to go on and on.'

'Apart from Friday,' put in Ralph, bringing a tray of gin, ice, glasses, some sliced lemons and limes along with small tins of tonic to the table and beginning to mix the drinks. Bea told him she was driving and would like a "pretend one" and he handed it to her, saying: 'I gather you had a pretty grim trip … but that's the only bad day we've had in the whole week.'

'I was reminded during all that sunshine of what strange ideas some Southerners have about us,' said Philip, smiling broadly. 'I was at a conference last week and there was a large contingent from the South … oh, thanks – cheers!' He raised his glass as Rose and Ralph took theirs and then continued. 'They seemed to expect that in the North we would spend the whole time, winter and summer, huddled round coal fires in houses constructed like igloos.'

'Absolutely.' Ralph nodded vigorously. 'And it's not the only misconception, is it? Some people who've never been past Birmingham are convinced it's a sort of stark wasteland, dotted about with mill chimneys.' He pulled a chair into the last of the sun and sat down. 'I've got some friends from Hertfordshire who were considering a promotion to Northumberland. After moaning about the prospect for weeks, they went up on a tour of inspection and they were completely gobsmacked! They'd been visualising a landscape of back-to-back houses and coal tips.'

'Did they decide to move up there, then?' asked Rose.

'Couldn't get there fast enough … and, needless to say, they're now telling anyone who'll listen how misguided it is to make uninformed judgments about places – and particularly about the North!'

Rose moved closer to Bea. 'How are they?' she asked. 'Your parents, I mean.'

Bea laughed. 'Oh – you know. Mum doesn't alter … a lot of fuss about damn-all, most of the time. The fortunate thing is that Philip can do no wrong. Dad and he get on well too – but they're the most sensible people in the world, so they're bound to, aren't they?'

'Aren't you lucky, Bea?' Rose glance across to where the men were deep in conversation and lowered her voice to a confidential murmur. 'Mind you – you've got a nerve, saying Philip's sensible, when less than a week ago you were slagging him off for being so bloody-minded!'

'That was last week!' Bea answered, grinning. 'And yes, I am very lucky. I hope your folks are going to be equally obliging, if and when … Don't see how they can help it,' she added, nodding in Ralph's direction. There, she thought, I can't get much more diplomatic – I'm positively crawling.

Rose beamed. 'Hope you're right, because – no, that's for later. "For everything there is a season" ' she quoted meaningfully, if inaccurately.

'Mmm,' agreed Bea. '*Open season,*' she murmured under her breath, 'when it comes to affairs of the heart.' But fortunately she had waited until Rose had stood up and excused herself, saying she had things to see to in the kitchen.

Ralph yelled after her that she was to call him if he was needed and then Bea remembered to ask how Rose had got on at the solicitor's.

'Oh, I think it was reasonably straightforward – as legal matters go, that is. She may have to wait quite a while before Guy's affairs are sorted. He hadn't made a will and probate can take ages.' Philip nodded his agreement. 'But of course, she's not worried about that,' Ralph went on. 'He's unlikely to have left much, and Rose doesn't need or want it … there's the funeral, of course,' he added. He looked very uncomfortable, Bea thought – as many people do when unaccustomed to death close to the family. 'But we're not going to worry about it until we know that we can go ahead and decide on a date.'

Bea noticed the "we" and looked over at Philip, who had been rather quiet, with a strange, blank expression on his face. He spoke at last. 'Better forget the whole thing for the present and then get the funeral over with the minimum of fuss.'

'I got in touch with the Dysons.' Ralph steered the conversation into another direction with a sudden swerve, which Bea suspected was deliberate. 'When I phoned them, they'd literally just got home.' He turned to Bea. 'They were really pleased that you and Rose have been able to make use of the farmhouse. They sent regards to all your family and hoped that things will quickly be sorted out now, so that you'll be able to forget the reason you stayed at the farm – rather nicely put, I thought.'

'They're such lovely people,' said Bea. 'We've got to do something about payment … it's no use asking them, because they're likely to say forget it.'

'I should just send a cheque, Bea,' put in Philip. 'You can tell us their rates, Ralph, for this time of year and we can work out a suitable amount pro rata.'

'I should think that's fine – oh, I can hear Rose bellow that my expertise is required! Please excuse me.'

'While we've a minute, Bea,' Philip said, bringing his chair closer to Bea's. 'I thought perhaps I could drive you back to ... tomorrow ... you are going back tomorrow, aren't you?'

'Yes I am. That would be great. Mother wants to know if come to us for Sunday lunch, since she was done out of f you tonight. But if we're both going in my car, what about g back here? I don't know if there's a suitable train – or even a suitable one – on a Sunday evening.'

'Well, I could leave by that early one on Monday morn just means getting up a bit earlier.' Philip drained his gin and and, helping himself to a generous top-up, looked at peace the world. 'That's settled, then ... I didn't want to start makin rangements while I'm at your mother's – '

'Because she'd be very likely to do all the arranging for you.

Collapsing in companionable laughter together, they ended i carefree cuddle, which prompted Ralph to offer to throw a buck of water over them when he came out to say they were ready to ea

*

Rose had pulled out all the stops for this special occasion. She had raided her mother's store of table linen and fished out the best silver, till the scene looked like an illustration in an expensive magazine. Bea and Philip, who knew they wouldn't even want to compete, none-the-less were impressed and full of praise.

'But we eat like this every evening!' said Ralph, as he seated them. Rose wanted to be near the kitchen door, so Ralph, after drawing the curtains on the dying light of the spring evening, sat with his back to the window.

The meal was a very unhurried affair. They all wanted to discuss the future plans, so that Bea and Philip had to interrupt themselves as they remembered to supply the appropriate comments and praise for the food. During the first course – guacamole which was Ralph's speciality, Bea and Philip outlined their engagements. Possible dates for the wedding were discussed and both and Rose pencilled them in, to keep them free until the final decision was made. Philip went into a little more detail about the post he was taking in Leeds and Bea talked to Rose about the kind of house they hoped to find one day.

Rose brought in the main course eventually and confessed that she had cheated a bit by using frozen pastry for the salmon en croute. 'The real skill,' commented Ralph, 'is in cooking the vegetables – all Rose's own work ... I just did the peeling and chopping'

As they poured out the wine and raised their glasses to the cooks, Rose said that she had decided to go to Manchester and move in with Ralph.

'Of course, you had to be the first to know,' said Ralph. 'It's a bit quick ... I'm getting that in first! But, honestly, I could wait for a lifetime and never feel so certain.'

'Me too.' Rose looked towards Bea at the other end of the table. 'I just know it's right ... I shall look for a job there – '

'It will all fall into place, as long as we just leave it to fate,' added Ralph.

After this not entirely astounding announcement, it took quite a while for order to be restored. Glasses were raised again and there was much kissing and laughter. Fortunately, a heated trolley was looking after the food. Bea was having to watch her alcohol intake even more carefully as more wine appeared for the toasts. She noticed that Philip seemed to be taking to heart her suggestion that she should do the driving and he the drinking and she was glad that the keys were already safely in her handbag. As he was usually a very moderate drinker, Bea felt it would do him no harm to relax and let his hair down for once.

Later, when they had finished the pudding (crème bruleé, and in this case definitely bought in, though excellent), Ralph made coffee. Then somehow, in spite of their intentions, the conversation drifted towards the unpleasant events of the week.

'I know you feel distressed about Geoff and the people you know quite well, Bea,' Ralph said, quietly. 'But really, I think we've been facing it all along – that it had to be him.'

Bea answered that of course she had come to realise that. 'Everything fits, and nothing else has emerged … I just wish it could have been the proverbial tramp – or lunatic …'

'You're not allowed to say "lunatic" any more, Bea!' Philip grinned as he spoke and, noticing that some wine had been left in the last bottle, decided to finish it off. He was slurring his words slightly, Bea noticed. The others, much preoccupied, probably weren't aware of this – and anyway, it didn't matter.

'Unbalanced – cerebrally challenged?' offered Rose helpfully.

'Barmy!' said Bea firmly. She had limited patience with political correctness. 'But anyway, I've had to accept the logical conclusion, since there weren't any other candidates.'

'Except Ralph and me,' put in Rose. 'I suppose the wife – or ex-wife – is often the first to be suspected, but there was no possible motive in Ralph's case.'

'Oh, come on, you can't say you didn't have a lurking suspicion that I'd been caught in the trammels of the fair Rhona!' Here, Bea had the grace to feel slightly embarrassed.

'Thing is,' went on Ralph, 'she did sort of hang around me a bit at one time. If I'd known how dangerous that might be, I'd have run away even faster than I did!'

'What puzzles me,' Rose said, frowning, 'is why Rhona has this – well – fatal attraction. Literally, it seems. We've all seen the effect she has. It reminds me of that experiment we did in physics at school – just about the first thing you do in the lower forms … with the magnet and the iron filings!'

'Mmm … that's it exactly,' agreed Bea. 'She'd come into a room and suddenly there would be half a dozen men around her, who'd appeared from nowhere.'

'It's not as if she was a raving beauty – ' Rose stared into her coffee cup as if she hoped to find the answer there.

'That isn't the point at all,' said Philip with a smile. 'I've probably seen her a lot less than any of you. But I would say that she's very friendly, warm-hearted, fun … and she could make a bloke feel *great* – you know – bigger, better, more important, more generous. But above all, for anyone who's had his confidence dented a bit by an over-enthusiastic promoter of sexual equality – he'd rediscover his male ego!'

'And all that in one glance!' said Ralph.

'Yes,' said Bea thoughtfully. 'That's got to be it … after all,' she went on, looking round at Rose, 'it's the same the other way round: you might meet a rather ugly little guy, but he has the knack of making you feel like a queen – a man who's attentive, sympathetic, interested. And he makes you feel that *you're* sexy – that you're the one person in the whole world he wants to talk to … that's got to be the secret'

'Well OK,' put in Rose. 'But it does look as though she's carried that rather unsubtle gift a bit too far, doesn't it? Anyway, it is a good feeling to be off that horrid Inspector's list of suspects … oh, Ralph! I forgot to tell you about Maurice – I was telling Bea yesterday.'

Rose repeated her story about the man called Maurice who had rung up on Thursday night.

'Well, that's a handy thing – or it would have been if you had thought of it before! Fancy you not remembering.'

'But I've done that kind of thing myself – more than once,' Bea said. 'You go back into a deep sleep and that's how it gets wiped out.'

'Well, I reckon I'll hear any minute about my own alibi,' said Ralph. 'I mean, it rounds things off, doesn't it? Till then, you're a bit in limbo.'

'But you've never seriously felt – well, treated like a suspect, I imagine?' Philip asked.

'Oh, I'm not so sure.' Ralph explained about his sunglasses turning up in the caravan. 'It was a bit unnerving …'

'Oh Ralph, how rotten of me,' exclaimed Rose. 'I really believed you were treating it as a joke'

'Not entirely, love. To be honest, it was a little bit worrying. You see, I found it really difficult to accept that Geoff would do that deliberately to incriminate me. And so I thought the police might not believe it either and I felt – sort of bewildered.'

'I don't know about bewildered – you had every reason to be bloody furious!' Alcohol had clearly affected Philip's speech more noticeably now and his voice was becoming loud and strident. He sounded quite angry on Ralph's behalf. 'But, speaking objectively, he was probably in a panic because of all the police questioning and that could cause him to act with no thought for the implications … I've known cases like that.'

'Fear drives out reason? Well, perhaps,' answered Ralph. 'But you can see why it'll be good to have Peter Mason speak up.'

'The police know you're here, of course?' Bea asked.

'Yes, this address is among the various ones they've got listed for all of us, so we could have a phone call any time … the icing on the cake!'

'You know, I really should have realised that you were feeling a bit niggly about all this,' said Rose, who seemed still to be weighing things up. 'It was a bit different for me though – but no doubt they could have concocted a motive connected with my "marital breakdown" or something.'

'Mmm. But you'd have needed to be driving a vehicle … and then it would surely take a fair amount of muscle to hoist him up, if it happened as they say it did,' Bea objected. 'He wasn't a lightweight, and those narrow doorways are terribly awkward … '

'Of course Rose wouldn't have had the strength. She's only little – aren't you love?' Ralph said fondly. Funny how idiotic we can appear when we've just fallen in love, Bea thought maliciously.

'She'd need nerve, as well as strength,' added Philip. 'She'd never have kept her cool if she'd suddenly heard that programme – she'd have – '

Bea felt a strange humming in her head. Her heart gave a lurching thump and she felt herself begin to tremble. Somehow she managed to say: 'What programme is that, Philip?'

'Well – TV programmes,' he answered quickly. 'And radio coverage too – all the explosion of reaction – the police and the media … you know!'

'Are you sure?' Bea said slowly and very quietly, amazed at her self-possession. 'Don't you mean an explosion of noise in the caravan?'

Ralph and Rose were puzzled, as they weighed up whether this was some kind of in-joke between the other two. But they didn't look in the least light-hearted. Bea saw her friends looking intently at her and she thought that she might have gone very pale.

Philip answered her calmly, but there was an edge to his voice – of impatience, or perhaps some other emotion. 'I can't think what you're driving at, Bea,'

'I'm very much afraid that you can,' she replied in a voice so filled with deep sadness that Rose and Ralph now looked at her in dismay.

'Bea, I don't know what this is meant to be about, but in the interest of a pleasant evening, may we postpone it, please?' Philip spoke abruptly, barely hiding the disquiet that had sobered him somewhat.

'What's wrong, Bea? Tell us,' urged Rose.

For a moment, Bea could not speak at all. She sat and stared at her empty coffee cup, numbed by her sudden insight. It had been such a small hint – unconvincing in itself. And yet she had no doubt. She stared at Philip in a kind of daze.

'You heard it!' she managed to say at last. 'Didn't you, Philip? My little radio that was set to come on each evening … It spoke to you. You were there. You were – '

'Have you gone completely mad?' Philip stood up, so that now Rose could see how he glared at them all with such a strange look in his eyes that she shrank back and looked towards Ralph for protection.

If Bea needed proof, Philip's demeanour now and his alarming expression were enough. She found a strength which would have astonished her, had she had time to consider it. Mercilessly, she continued.

'What a terrible shock that must have been! Loud and sudden in the middle of that frightful business, just when you needed to be alone and secret … a voice, right there in the room with you – '

'Do you mean – ' began Ralph.

'You can't mean that *Philip* – ' Rose said simultaneously.

'I hope you don't expect me to stay and listen to this sort of rubbish,' Philip managed to say, keeping his voice fairly normal. But he held on to his dignity with obvious difficulty as he started from the table and lurched towards the door that led into the hall.

Bea did not move. She was now frozen in her chair. But Ralph has already got up from the table. He had had time in these moments to take in the situation. Slipping quickly behind Rose's chair, he placed himself strategically between Philip and the doorway, which he now barred by standing across it.

Philip was little taller than Ralph, but he was a heftier figure altogether. However, he had drunk far more than he was accustomed to and as he took a swing at Ralph, Ralph easily dodged out of the way. The women, aghast and unbelieving, backed away from Philip's flailing arms.

At the second attempt however, desperation lent Philip a little more force, if not skill. He knocked Ralph to the floor and seized his chance straight away. With no-one to stop him he was outside in a moment, heading for his car. Then he seemed to realise that the keys were in Bea's handbag, and they saw him set off on foot, away from the house in the starlight.

The starry scene pierced Bea's numbness. Three days ago, on a very similar night … oh, the difference!

Ralph was very quickly up again. He had been caught off balance, but there hadn't been a lot of actual power in the blow. He ran out to his car and started it up, but as he was pulling out of the drive, he was obliged to wait for an approaching vehicle. This car stopped however, as with a screech of brakes it seemed to erupt instantly. What appeared to be a small posse of police (but in fact were only four), chased down the leafy suburban lane into a footpath nearby. There were shouts and the sound of other vehicles roaring up to the scene and then halting abruptly.

In what seemed no time at all, it became clear that they had caught up with Philip before he had got very far. There was no noise or struggling now, as he was put into the police van which had just arrived and it was driven away, followed by one of the response cars.

While all this was happening the women had stood, still and stunned, by the front door. Ralph had backed his car in again and got out, staring at the two police cars that remained.

Rose was the first to speak. 'The police,' she said. 'How could they manage to get here like that?'

Ralph took the women indoors. 'They'll be along to see us in a minute, I think,' he said. He opened a door on the left of the hall and put Bea gently into a chair in the sitting room. 'Get her a brandy, Rose.'

Bea spoke at last. She looked dazed as she took the glass from Rose. 'Arrested!' was all she said. It was neither a statement nor a question; just an expression of incomprehension. Rose sat down beside her, also with a brandy in her hand, and Ralph went into the hall. He left the door ajar, and could be seen admitting the police, who had just arrived.

Bea didn't feel surprised, in her present dreamlike state, to see Inspector Dove. With him was Sergeant Bamford, who explained that they were taking a look around the premises and that they were obliged to search Philip's car. Bea searched in her handbag with some difficulty, her hands shaking so much that she almost dropped the keys as she handed them to the Sergeant. Then the Inspector led her very gently into the study at the back of the house.

'Where are the others?' she asked, as he settled her in the most comfortable chair. Her voice did not seem to belong to her and she had a feeling that seemed familiar – just like that time when she had come out of hospital after an operation – strangely wobbly and with a profound sense of unreality.

'My sergeant's just getting an idea of what went on before we arrived and then your friends will be coming in here in a minute, if you've no objection, Miss Roebuck. I feel we owe you all an explanation of how we came to be here tonight and what we are doing now … the bigger picture will be released a bit later after my reports have been filed'

There was a tap at the door and a constable put his head round it, saying that Mrs. Downey and Mr. Norman were now available. He shook his head in answer to an enquiring glance from the Inspector – presumably meaning that nothing significant had so far been found by the constables.

Rose and Ralph came a few moments later. They sat protectively on either side of Bea and waited.

'I'm sorry about all the disturbance of your home, Mrs. Downey,' began the Inspector. 'We've been watching Mr. Lander closely since the beginning of this investigation, after getting information from an entirely different department. But it was only yesterday that we had a significant breakthrough, and then we could begin closing in. It seems we were just in time.'

'That was my fault,' Bea's voice came in a near-whisper. 'I suddenly saw … saw everything. And I'm afraid I alerted him – oh no, not deliberately … '

'I fully appreciate how painful this must be for you, Miss Roebuck. I gather Mr. Lander is your fiancé?'

Bea nodded and gave a little shudder as she glanced down involuntarily at the beautiful ring on her finger. 'But I don't understand how you came to be there,' she said. 'Just at the moment he ran away.'

'We'd had a man outside your property, waiting to alert the team if Mr. Lander came out. We were just about ready to arrest him, but we were holding back, hoping for one last piece of information. We received that message only moments before you saw us.' When Dove's personal phone started to ring, he spoke briefly into it and then he went on: 'We shall be leaving very shortly – there's no need to disturb you further tonight … may I ask, though, what led you to challenge him?' The Inspector looked at Bea as though he thought this had been the height of folly.

Bea looked stricken as she recalled that scene. 'It was a very little thing,' she answered, her voice flat and very quiet. 'There was a radio/recorder plugged in, in my bedroom at the caravan – you'll have seen it – and last week I found out that I'd previously left it set to come on regularly. It was for an evening programme that I didn't want to miss – I'd been following the story in "A Book at Bedtime", you see … ' Dove nodded. 'Well, I realised the other day that the radio would have been coming on for fifteen minutes each evening – but it didn't matter of course and so I didn't think any more about it. But I did remember how, when I first set it up – oh, months ago – it had really made me jump on the first evening, because I'd forgotten to expect it … and that's how I came to know at once what Philip meant.'

Dove looked at her enquiringly, but waited patiently for her to continue.

Bea paused and drew a deep breath. 'It was tonight after dinner. We started talking about the murder. Philip must have got careless (he'd had quite a lot to drink) and he spoke of the killer "needing a strong nerve when the programme started", or something like that. And I *knew* … straight away. I just saw it in a flash and confronted him – instinctively, without any thought of what his reaction might be. He covered up quite well – said he was referring to the media coverage of the murder … the others might easily have accepted that he meant a radio or TV programme. But they didn't know about "A Book at Bedtime" and anyway, when you know someone very well … ' Bea's voice broke a little. 'Then there was the strange way he began to behave … '

Inspector Dove looked hard at her. 'It looks as if we should have paid more attention to that radio, you know,' he said quietly. 'Although his prints could be anywhere in the caravan quite legitimately … what time was it set for?'

'Quarter to eleven,' she answered.

Dove nodded. 'Yes, that would be it,' he muttered to himself. 'I'm very sorry it's turned out like this.' Bea thought he really did look sorry. Perhaps he was human after all. 'I shall go now,' he went on. 'The Superintendent is waiting for an update and I'm overdue with that already.' He told them that the police would be in touch to tidy up any loose ends and wished them all goodnight.

Ralph and Rose sat without speaking, unable to find anything to say. It was Bea who broke the silence.

'And to think,' she said, as tears rolled unheeded and splashed on to the favourite dress. 'I was so convinced all along that it couldn't be Geoff … but it *had* to be – anything else was unthinkable.' She made no attempt to wipe away the tears as she turned her face to Rose. 'And the unthinkable's happened.'

Ralph told them he would go and make some coffee and went off, as they nodded their thanks.

'Rose, I don't think I can face going back home tonight – and I don't suppose I've got any transport.' With a faint hint of a smile, she went on: 'Mother will stifle me with sympathy when she sees me and I don't feel strong enough to deal with her particular brand of TLC just yet. Or her fury and shame, because that's how it will be. And Dad – Dad thought such a lot of him … '

'You'll be staying here, of course,' Rose answered firmly. 'I'll give them a ring. It's nearly twenty past eleven – d'you think they'll have gone to bed?'

'No, I shouldn't think so. Dad'll be up, anyway – he never does go very early. Thanks for that Rose, but what are you going to say? Can you make some excuse?'

'I don't think I should, really. What if the radio or TV gets wind of it by morning? It would be really bad if your parents learned it that way.'

'Mmm. You're right. I can't think very well at the moment, Rose – so just tell them whatever you think is best.'

Rose went off to telephone, but she was back in a very short time and Bea realised that she must have been very firm.

'It's all right. I said that there had been a distressing development in the police case and that you would tell them all the details tomorrow. I said you were very upset and that I had to get back to you and then rang off! It was your father I spoke to.'

'Thank God for that! He'll give Mother some bland statement to last her till morning and then he'll take the flak when she finds out what it is. He'll understand that it's something that has to wait until we're face to face … oh, Ralph, thanks,' she added as he put a cup of coffee into her hands.

'I still haven't grasped it,' she muttered, sipping the very hot liquid. 'But do you remember, Rose … when you mentioned that Guy and Philip had met? Well, it seemed to me rather odd that Philip never said anything about that, in all the times we've mentioned Guy since. Obviously they'd got some scam going …'

'Yes, and sometimes Guy had seemed rather secretive – about several phone calls, for instance. I told you, didn't I, but I didn't think anything of it at the time. And I think now there were probably lots of other things that I never really paid attention to. They must have had meetings – to plan things, or pass things on, or whatever – but I wouldn't be watching him in that way.' Rose sighed. 'OK, I got suspicious later on, but I just thought of another woman, because that was the way it started to look and that's what he was like … and I still think I was right about that, whatever else happened after.'

'But none of that explains why they were in the Blaeborough area, or why Guy should have been killed, does it?' said Ralph, who sat down, and put his coffee cup on a small table.

'I've got to find out!' Bea sat up and her voice took on an urgent tone. 'Suddenly it seems very important that I find out *why* and how. I've got to know.'

'Of course you have,' answered Rose. 'But for tonight (Bea's staying here, Ralph – I've rung her parents), I think you should try not to discuss it too much or you'll end up going round in circles. Naturally, you can't think of anything else, but sitting here holding an inquest isn't going to help.' Rose stood up and took the coffee cup from Bea. 'I'm going to pinch a couple of Mum's sleeping pills for you and put you to bed.'

Bea managed a thin smile and for once, she was prepared to submit. 'You're starting to sound like my mother!' she said.

CHAPTER 14

Dr. Roebuck had been busy. Ever since Bea had come back on Sunday afternoon with her terrible story, his first priority had been to protect her from the protection of her mother.

Bea had decided to go back to work during the week that followed Philip's arrest. She felt that this was good therapy and she knew that if she left it until later it would be so much harder to get back to normality. Her father, though a little reluctant at first, was soon persuaded that work was the best thing. The last thing she needs, he mused, is her mother fussing over her, or any kind of sentimentality. What Bea *did* need was an explanation and Dr. Roebuck worked tirelessly to seek this out. He managed to get a little information from Philip's solicitor, who told him that Philip had made a partial confession. This did not include murder – but he claimed that he had gone to the caravan and had discovered the body.

Dr. Roebuck took some leave and set off on his own for Lancaster. Mrs. Roebuck, who refused to take Philip's arrest seriously, insisting that it was a case of mistaken identity, was far too busy with her various committees to accompany him. He stayed there two days and by Thursday he was rewarded with some useful information. He hoped if all went well, to complete the picture by making a trip to Shawhead Farm at the weekend and chatting with an old acquaintance in Little Blaeford. He kept Bea informed of all his plans and to his surprise, she wanted to come up from Leeds and meet him in the village.

'I've got to lay the ghost, Dad – the sooner the better. Honestly, anything's better than just wondering what actually happened, with my mind going round in circles – and the police haven't told us anything we didn't already guess.'

So Dr. Roebuck had booked rooms at the Lamb for the following Saturday. He arrived there before Bea was due and went straight up to Shawhead Farm to take a look at the caravan and make it ready to be sold, since Bea had now made up her mind. Then he reported to Bea on his interview with the solicitor and told her about his other reason for the visit to Little Blaeford. They had ordered a tray of tea and were sitting in the snug, which they had all to themselves at four in the afternoon.

'I hope to have a lot more to tell you after my next rendezvous.' Dr. Roebuck poured another cup of tea for each of them.

'I shall have to do this on my own, Bea,' he said. 'I'm going to have a chat with Makepeace Holroyd straight after dinner this evening. I've already given him a ring to arrange it and we're going to meet at the caravan – bit cloak and dagger, but we don't want any wagging tongues. He's our best chance of learning what really went on.'

'But surely,' Bea said, puzzled and doubtful. 'All that is still under wraps – he'll not be willing to reveal police information – '

'When you were little, Bea,' her father replied. 'Mack was also growing up – in the village, of course. I didn't know the lad, but one day, I was walking Muddles (you remember him?)' Bea nodded, with a little jab of pain. She recalled that first meeting with Philip, when she told him of the shaggy mongrel of her childhood. But she must stay in the present, and Dr. Roebuck's voice continued.

'Well, I was walking him over the playing field, when I came across this youngster – maybe nine or ten, looking very miserable and left out of a group who were enjoying an impromptu game of football.'

'Seems funny to think of a young child with a name like that…'

'Yes, well that's just what this tale is about.' Dr. Roebuck put his cup back on to its saucer and stared down at it thoughtfully. 'I started to talk to the child … with a dog it's so easy to get into conversation.'

Bea bit her lip as she thought of the dog that had introduced her to Philip.

'You can guess what the trouble was! He was having a good sulk because they'd been teasing him about his name.'

'And you helped him to get it in proportion?'

'Well, we sat down and talked a bit. I said I thought his name might have come from the Puritans and told him some of the names they invented for their offspring. He ended up being re-lieved he wasn't called "God-be-in-my-head-and-heart" and he cheered up a bit. I suggested that perhaps one day he'd feel proud of his name and maybe he would – make peace, or keep the peace.'

'And that's what he does!'

'That's what he does, but it had nothing to do with my pep talk, because he'd told me by then that he wanted to be a bobby like his father. But he remembered me and he's always been particularly friendly when we've met. I didn't think he'd be unwilling to help – but it's only for your ears and mine, Bea or we'll let Makepeace down.'

'I'd no idea you even knew PC Holroyd,' said Bea. 'You cer-tainly know how to keep things to yourself, Dad – and I shall do the same. Rose and Ralph must be dying to know more, but they'll have to wait.'

'They'll have their own concerns to think about, love. And it just doesn't touch them in the same way.'

Bea was quiet for a while. It was difficult for her not to feel a stab of pain, in spite of being glad for both of them. But their happiness was a constant reminder of what had so cruelly slipped from her grasp, only a week ago.

She reminded herself that there had been pain for others too. As she had driven through the village on her way up here, passing the estate where Geoff lived, she would have liked to be able to speak to Geoff. However, she had realised that whatever she said might well sound insulting. Then she had reminded herself that Geoff had been willing to incriminate Ralph. Clumsy and idiotic though it was, putting the sunglassses into the 'van had none-the-less been an attempt to shift suspicion on to the next convenient person – very uncharacteristic of this man she had come to like. But if he had heard rumours linking Ralph's name with Rhona's, he might have felt he had a score to settle, and failed to take account of the possible consequences – just the impulse of a mad moment. Still, he'd been lucky that the police had only cautioned him, once they knew what he had done. So instead, she had called on the Dysons, to thank them and to leave an envelope on their hall table, before going to The Lamb to meet her father.

The next morning was warm and sunny with a very gentle breeze. They decided to buy fruit, cheese and rolls at the village shop for a simple picnic, with the idea of a gentle walk by the river, while Bea learned what her father had discovered. She had suddenly felt overwhelmed with tiredness on the previous evening and was in bed and asleep by the time her father came back.

They had not felt like talking about the murder while they were packing up at the caravan after breakfast. Dr. Roebuck said he would make whatever arrangements were needed for the sale and also ask the Dysons what they would like to do about the site. Bea decided what she wanted to keep from the 'van and then gave the interior a final clean. Apart from a couple of knives for the picnic, they had left the kitchen equipment, for which she had no use ... Bea felt she did not want another caravan, ever.

As soon as they left the village, Dr. Roebuck began by telling Bea that he had received clear guidelines from PC Holroyd as to what was for general release and what was classified information. The latter, in fact turned out to be about ninety-five percent.

'So many things are completely mystifying,' said Bea. 'I hardly know what to ask about first.'

'Why don't I try to tell the story as I've pieced it together, from the beginning,' said her father. 'You can stop me if you need anything explained.' Bea normally found his quiet voice soothing, but now she was keyed up and thoroughly alert as she concentrated on every word.

'Guy and Philip had met by chance through Rose, as you know,' began Dr. Roebuck. 'Philip had already had dealings in industrial espionage, and was part of quite a large criminal organisation.' Bea winced, but didn't interrupt, except to nod her thanks as her father opened the gate that led into the recreation ground and then on to the river path.

'He was ideally placed, with expert knowledge of methods and contacts. All this had come to him through studying the cases of his clients when he had been preparing their defence. Guy had been recruited because he had useful experience in manufacturing – particularly in research – and he wasn't very fussy about the kind of deal he got involved in.

'The two of them apparently communicated, either by phone or in person, regularly. But throughout their entire association, Philip was being monitored by whatever department it is that deals with commercial malpractice – it would include illegal entry, theft, computer hacking and then of course, selling the secrets to unscrupulous big business. Very large sums of money were involved. Presumably, the police would also be aware of Philip's associates and that would bring Guy into the picture. Then, at the beginning of this year, things were hotting up. The police were getting close to the point where they could pounce.'

Dr. Roebuck glanced quickly at Bea, wondering how she was reacting. She appeared calm and intent on absorbing all that he could tell her, so he continued with his story.

'The two men had been worried because they'd had a tip-off about police activity... or rather, Philip was worried. Guy, as we shall see, was almost certainly becoming a bit of a loose cannon and Philip had received orders to make sure his junior partner toed the line – with threats if necessary. He had finally convinced Guy that their operation must cease for the time being and that any documents or equipment that had been entrusted to him were to be returned.

'They decided to meet at the caravan for two reasons. It was conveniently situated – not too far for either of them – and it would be a lot more discreet than their previous meetings in various pubs. I'm sure Guy would have concealed his knowledge of the area from Philip, but in actual fact, it's pretty certain that Guy had used the spot – and the 'van itself – at least once. He had got to know Rhona at some time – he seems to have craved the excitement of a slightly dangerous affair and the risk of using someone else's caravan just added spice. Philip of course, would have told Guy how to find his way to the 'van and where to find the spare key – unaware that Guy knew that already.' Bea nodded, remembering what Rose had told her.

'He instructed Guy to take the "top" road and park under some trees – perhaps he wanted to avoid the two cars being seen together. Obviously Philip preferred to keep his own visit secret, but that wasn't quite so important, because of course he hadn't come there to kill Guy – just to sort out the present threat to their security. He probably had a cover story ready in case he was seen. But it looks as though he had made sure that the farmhouse had not been let that week (probably by making a bogus booking enquiry through the letting agency) and he would be quite confident that you weren't expected there till the summer.'

They had reached the river by now and they sat down on its tussocky bank to eat their food before continuing along the path. They had brought cans of beer and they sat in silence for a while as they drank them, Bea deep in thought, Dr. Roebuck patiently giving her space. Then Bea asked her father about the other reason for meeting at the caravan.

'The other reason,' said Dr. Roebuck, as he gazed at the placid flow of the river, 'was that Philip was in Harrogate all week at a conference (ironically, one of its main themes was industrial espionage!). So there had to be a change from their usual arrangements in any case. His original idea seems to have been to slip off unobtrusively during the latter part of the evening and sleep in the caravan for a few hours (he had a sleeping bag and could safely use the second bedroom).

'It was probably good thinking – he'd have washed and shaved and could stroll in to breakfast with his colleagues on Friday morning – that way he'd avoid the risk of being seen creeping up to his room in the small hours and inviting ribald comment, which might have repercussions. He wouldn't expect to be missed – but if he was, he'd have a suitable explanation … however, the murder altered everything. All that followed, once that had happened, was swiftly improvised. And it almost worked, despite the premature discovery of the body.'

Bea looked up at her father questioningly and then said: 'Let's walk again.' She found it easier to listen while her body had something to do – even if it was only a gentle stroll. Dr. Roebuck took up the story again.

'I think it must have been his reluctance to let well alone – or to let ill alone – after the murder, that was his big mistake … ironically, his effort to close all loopholes provided the police with some important evidence. But there were also several other factors that would almost certainly have led to discovery in the end. In some ways bad luck came into it, but most of it hinged on one basic misjudgment – Guy was an unwise choice of accomplice. While you might call Philip a professional, Guy was really a playboy – he had been living it up on holiday in the Indian Ocean while the police were closing in. I imagine that threats did become necessary before he accepted that a crisis was looming and that he should return at once.

'The fact that Guy had only just got back after being abroad for a while may well have prompted his current girl-friend to persuade him that she should go along too. This meant that, unknown to Philip, there was now a potential witness who knew about the rendezvous. She's called Barbara Buckley and she's married, which limited their opportunities.'

Bea drew a swift breath at hearing the name. This surely must be the Barbara whom Rose thought she recognised driving furiously away from the Blaeborough area … but that was on Friday afternoon – long after the murder. However, she held her tongue, except to say dryly: 'Poor co-ordination there. He obviously didn't realise that Philip intended to occupy the 'van himself!'

'Correct.' Bea's wry remark reassured her father that the strength of character she'd always displayed from childhood was helping her now.

'And of course,' he continued, 'he wasn't going to tell Philip that he was bringing a girl-friend. Guy and Barbara parked their car at the appointed place. Well, it was Barbara's car in fact, presumably because it was a small dark green one – ideal for keeping a low profile among the trees.

'Philip approached the farm from the main Blaeborough road and put his car in that open cart-shed that he'd often used before. (As I said, he wasn't desperately concerned to keep his own visit secret, but concealing the link-up with Guy *was* important.) So Barbara stayed quietly in her car while Guy went to the meeting place, saying he'd be only half-an-hour or so. Clearly, there was something potentially incriminating to hand over – but nothing has been found.'

Bea looked puzzled. 'Granted that he wanted to keep the cars apart, I still don't see why he couldn't just have walked up to the top road – where Guy was parked. Why go to the trouble of getting Guy down to the 'van?'

'The police don't appear to have the answer to that. But because he didn't trust Guy, it's likely that Philip would want to check something over – a special piece of equipment, say and perhaps a laptop – that Guy had been using to carry out their activities.

It would have been easier to do that in the 'van than in a car at night. They might have needed a power point … and the 'van's well screened from view even when the lights are on. That may well have been the reason, but it's guesswork.'

'Did Barbara know why they were meeting and who was involved?'

'She knew who – she'd already met Philip briefly on one occasion. But Guy had told her that the meeting was to do with a currency racket – illegal of course, but much less serious than what they were really doing and tiny in comparison with the money at stake. Afterwards, Barbara had been very perturbed about what she knew and when finally she realised that a local man might be wrongly suspected, she decided to go to the police with vital details about the meeting. She's appalled now that she knows about the scale of the crime and the ruthlessness that followed when the plan had to be altered.'

'The plan that went wrong?'

'Horribly wrong.' Dr. Roebuck paused as they passed an elderly man peacefully fishing from the river bank with an elderly black Labrador sitting sedately beside him. Bea and her father walked on in silence until they were out of earshot.

'When the police took possession of Philip's mobile they found a text from someone in the organisation, (apparently they used text habitually in case they should be overheard, but Philip was no doubt shocked and had forgotten to wipe it). It warned him that Guy was at best leaky and unreliable – at worst, deliberately betraying him. There was a thinly veiled threat to Philip if he didn't deal with this immediately. That call came only minutes before he was due to meet Guy.'

'Leaving him little scope for improvisation?'

'Very little,' agreed her father. 'But he must have felt very seriously threatened to act as he did. He hadn't time to look around for a weapon, because Guy might arrive at any moment and he had to be ready. So he seized the nearest thing that came to hand from his own car and acted at once.'

'You mean,' said Bea, a tremor in her voice, 'that the shovel was Philip's own?' She explained about their evening out when it snowed. 'We'd taken the shovel along, Dad, and some old sacks to provide a grip, in case we got stuck. It was weeks ago … and you're saying it was still in the car?' She turned to look at her father. 'It's the sort of thing he was always doing, instead of putting things away properly.' She sounded disproportionally upset at this lapse from the accepted standards of housekeeping. 'And so he used it – '

'Yes Bea, that's how it looks. And that proved crucial, as you'll see.'

'Sorry Dad. I shouldn't keep interrupting.'

'He seems to have arrived in time to open up the caravan and to lie in wait so that he could fell Guy with the shovel, apparently just as he was climbing the step. Then, presumably Philip was busy manoeuvring the body into the bedroom when your little radio started up. The sudden effect of a voice must have been terrifying for a moment or two.'

'But Dad –' Bea just had to speak again at this point. 'I can't understand why he left the body to be found like that – found by *me!* And why put him on my bed, for heaven's sake?' She turned to look into her father's face. 'It's one of the things that's giving me courage and helping me to harden my heart.'

'I'm sure he never intended it to be found – least of all by you. That's what the police think too – it's the only logical answer.

'After he'd killed Guy, he had to change his plans completely. It was much more important now to get back to Harrogate quickly. He needed to be back in his room – suppose the fire alarms went off in the small hours? The moor nearby would be the first place he'd think of for disposal of the body, but there wasn't time. Also he had to go there first in daylight and find a suitable place to bury it – so he had to hide it until the next day. Your bedroom is the only one with curtains … those stylish little blinds on the other windows don't fit snugly enough. Actually, the bathroom compartment was the obvious choice. Only – ' Dr. Roebuck hesitated.

'What? You might as well tell me, however unpleasant.'

'There's not enough space to for a body to lie out flat in that tiny shower room. They think he was not sure about the timing of rigor – it varies anyway – which might make it difficult to move the body and put it in the car next day and – and to bury it.'

'I can imagine.' Bea spoke grimly, and her father hurried on with his story.

'So the bedroom was the only option. No-one was likely to come into the paddock, but even so he couldn't bank on it. The curtains fitted snugly enough, except for a small gap at the bottom – '

'I know … I washed them and they shrank. I'd actually bought some material to replace them and Mum was going to … ' As Bea's voice faded away dismally, her father hurried to fill the gap.

'Yes, well he would be quite aware that most of the floor was visible and so it had to be the bed. That couldn't be seen by anyone passing by in the normal way. So he removed the duvet and quilt and laid newspapers – there's a pile of them in the shed – over the mattress. (It's perhaps a bit odd that he didn't cover the body over with newspaper as well – although I suppose it would hardly have helped to conceal it.) I doubt if we'll ever know all the small details … it looks as if he meant to return early on Friday evening as soon as the course ended.'

'Yes, he wouldn't imagine that I could be there – it's something I'd never done … I wonder how he found out, so that he could keep away?'

'That we don't know. It's even possible that he did approach the farm and saw the place swarming with police!'

Bea shivered, in spite of the warm sun. Then she took a deep breath and asked about the shovel. 'The police got it wrong, then – about the shovel they found in Billy Goss's shed at the farm shop?'

'No, actually they were quite right. It was certainly the one that was used. Microscopic traces were found …Philip would know they are nearly impossible to remove from that kind of surface. There'd be no risk of fingerprints of course (he always kept driving gloves in the car, didn't he?). Even so, experience told the detectives that he might be a bit paranoid about the shovel and try to get rid of it straight away. So they did a specific search. The shed was an obvious choice, but the police eliminated the shovels in there … though he'd borrowed other things as we know and a pair of overalls has disappeared – '

'Ah, that's why I couldn't find them,' muttered Bea.

'Traces of that type of material were found on the body. Moving it in such a narrow space would be very awkward and some form of protection was essential. Apparently, Mrs. Holroyd had seen the overalls only a couple of days before, when she was sorting out the garden furniture that's stored in there – to clean it up and so on, at the beginning of the season.'

'Yes, she'd mentioned them to me when I needed something to do the weeding in.'

'They haven't actually been found, but they were a special offer that all the local farmers have been buying from the ironmonger's in Blaeborough, so the police know exactly what they're like. It's assumed that he took them away with him. Once he'd used them there was no question of leaving them in the caravan or the shed – if anything went wrong they'd be exhibit no. 1 for the laboratory and traceable to the wearer. Possibly he might risk keeping them to use when disposing of the body … more likely, he got rid of them in a pond or a rubbish bin straight away, intending to use something else to cover up later.

'But the shovel was a different matter – it was his own property, it was a murder weapon and he didn't want it in his car even for a short time. It wouldn't be used again – it wasn't a shovel he'd need now, but a pick and a spade from among the store of tools, for the digging he'd have to do. So he concentrated on making sure they couldn't connect him with the weapon.'

'Yes, it must have seemed as if it was red-hot to him!'

'It would do, but all the same he would have done better to "leave well alone" until he could dispose of it later. He may have considered throwing it somewhere – on the moor perhaps. But as a solicitor, he'd know that such items often have a nasty habit of being found by a person with an unusually inquisitive turn of mind. And there were already two shovels in the Dyson's shed – adding another one would be unwise. So it looks as though he decided to point any possible discovery towards local suspects. He would have been familiar with that ramshackle old shed down the road.

'But he couldn't risk the car stopping late at night on a lane that has very little traffic at any time. He'd have seen the bicycle. It was in good order and using it would add on less than thirty minutes even if he had to pump up the tyres. Then he'd have to "tidy up", double-check and lock up, but he could still be away by about half-past eleven. So he must have thought it worth a quick ride down there to ditch the shovel. It was unlikely ever to come to light – and even if the worst happened, they wouldn't connect it to him.'

'Safe and silent – and not many houses round there … '

'He used the "back lane", Bea – you know – the one past old Birch's place?'

'Oh yes. I went up that way with Rose only – only the other day,' she faltered, recalling what seemed to be another life, before this nightmare happened.

'You said "safe", Bea … but he was out of luck. He was seen.'

'Seen? But if the police knew someone had seen him on the bike and carrying a shovel, why on earth would they bother with Geoff Collins?'

'They didn't know – not then. He was caught in Mr. Birch's recently installed security lighting. The old boy saw him from his bedroom window – '

'You'd think he'd have been tucked up in bed hours before!'

'More bad luck. Mr. Birch had been taken ill in the night and he'd just been speaking to his daughter on the phone extension – it's on his landing window. When the light flashed on, Philip was immediately below him, riding the bike and carrying something awkward. It seems that the light shone on his hair and on the blade of what looked like a shovel.'

'Oh God!' said Bea. 'Philip's badger-stripe – he couldn't miss it! But you say the police didn't know?'

'That evidence only reached them at the end of last week. The old boy had been whisked off by his daughter in the early hours. Seems he's been staying with her ever since – apparently quite poorly – so he missed the house-to-house questioning.

'Makepeace says there was a bit of a hoo-hah down at the station,' went on Dr. Roebuck. 'The constable might have been more thorough. But to be fair, there's only one neighbour – who said that Mr. Birch had not been at home for a week or more. And he *had* been at his daughter's until the Wednesday – but the neighbour was unaware of his brief return home, before being taken ill again. The daughter's pretty sharp (and the shovel story has been common gossip as you know), so when eventually the old boy casually mentioned what he'd seen, she told the police.'

'Then it was pure chance caught up with him – that and being over-cautious about the shovel.' Bea frowned and nodded to herself, as she considered the irony of the distressing story. 'Philip had acted so coolly, covered his tracks – even covered his clothes when he handled the body …' Her voice tailed off and trembled.

'His experience of "forensic" in a lawyer's office would have alerted him to the transfer of particles between killer and victim. Maybe he'd hoped to find an old coat or something in the shed and then came across the very thing he needed.'

'There's something else that occurs to me, Dad. Wouldn't Philip have had to do something about Guy's car – I mean, he didn't know anyone was there to drive it away, did he?'

'Well, time was too short to do anything about it that night, and he probably felt it was unlikely to attract attention where it was. He'd be planning to dispose of it next day, when he came back – and I'm sure he'd expect to find the keys in Guy's pocket.'

'Mmm. And then, after the body was discovered, he would expect it to look quite natural that the car should be found nearby – except of course, that it wasn't!'

'No. That was a bit of a mystery at first. Philip had admitted to the details of meeting Guy, so the police expected to find an abandoned car. When it was nowhere to be seen, they assumed it had been stolen – quite likely, since the keys weren't found and must therefore have been left in the vehicle. Until Barbara came forward, this seemed the only explanation.'

Bea was silent now, thinking over all that her father had told her. They turned away from the river on to a path that would lead them back to the top end of the village and The Lamb, where their cars were parked. At last she said: 'So Barbara was waiting in the car all this time – what happened to her?'

'Well, in her case, we know exactly what happened, because she finally told the whole story to the police. And you know that I've been to see her in Lancaster. She had been shocked and mystified when the news of the murder first broke. She'd been keeping quiet for obvious reasons, but she was aware of the speculation that the killer was a jealous husband and that a local woman might be involved. Well, she knew that whatever Guy was there for, it wasn't to meet a woman. After the news that a local man was in police custody, she no longer felt she could keep her knowledge to herself …

'She had told her husband she was going to attend a Union meeting on Thursday evening in Manchester and would stay overnight with a friend. She and Guy met, had a meal somewhere on the way and then drove to the agreed place near the farm, from where Guy set off along the field path. Well over an hour passed and you can imagine Barbara's increasing concern when he didn't reappear. She decided to investigate. She had a small torch in the car – Guy had brought a more powerful one for his own use – and she set off to find the path over the fields. It must have been an unpleasant experience, and she wasn't even sure she was going the right way.'

'It must have taken some nerve … but I suppose she didn't have much choice, other than to hang about even longer and eventually drive home alone.'

'She was afraid Guy might have sprained his ankle or something in the dark – she couldn't just leave. As she approached the caravan, she caught sight of a car's rear lights as it was leaving down the track. She was fortunate not to be seen.'

Bea shuddered at the thought of her lover of so many years being now a figure to be feared.

'When she found the caravan locked, she looked around outside as best she could and then shone her torch through the windows. When she came to the bedroom window, the curtains covered it pretty well and she could see only the floor at first through the gap at the bottom. But, by bending down level with the base of the window, and aiming the torch's beam carefully, she saw the foot of the bed. She could just make out a shoe. Then by moving the light around, she saw enough to realise that this was Guy. She could also pick out the newspaper that he lay on and started to have horrible ideas. She tried banging on the window – eventually thumping so hard she was afraid it would break – and all the time with an ear cocked for the car, in case it returned. She didn't know whether Guy was ill, drugged or dead, but there was no way she could get into the 'van and find out. By now her one aim was to get away as soon as she could.'

'I'm beginning to feel quite sorry for her,' said Bea. 'However foolish she'd been, it was a very nasty situation.'

'It got nastier,' replied her father. 'She had to return by the footpath, hoping her torch would last out. She wondered whether perhaps drugs were the real reason for the secrecy – it might account for Guy's being left to sleep it off, if he had accidentally overdosed. She had heard that some drug pushers were also users. She was angry and very frightened … and then when she got back to the car, she found she couldn't start it.'

Bea made a horrified little sound as she pictured the scene.

'She had no breakdown cover, so she sensibly stayed put until the early morning, trying to get a little sleep. But at least she had her mobile. When she heard a tractor in a nearby field, she was able to get details of a garage in Blaeborough with a recovery service and ring them up. Then while the car was being repaired, she managed to get tidied up and fed in a nearby hotel. And when the car was ready for her she set off, getting back just about in time to avoid awkward questions at the other end!'

'And we met her on the road.' Bea described her near miss at the viewpoint. 'She came round that bend in a tearing hurry and she nearly ran into us!' Bea pondered over the coincidence. 'Rose thought she recognised this crazy driver – she muttered something about Lancaster. But I was rather preoccupied by the near miss we'd had and then later we both forgot all about it.'

They paused at the top of the path to draw breath and to look at the peaceful scene.

'So she lay low for a week or so?' Bea mused. 'It must have been a terrible few days – if the only information she had was via the media … it's good that she came forward when she did.'

'Well, it wasn't entirely altruistic, I fancy. The police had been casting their net pretty wide in the Lancaster area – friends and acquaintances of Guy's were questioned, so I guess she just got her shout in before they came to see her.'

'Mmm. Awkward if they'd come to interview her with her husband present.'

'Still, I do believe that she was also very concerned in case an innocent man might be charged.'

'That's something I don't understand, Dad … if they had all these suspicions and had received information about … about Philip – why did they pull Geoff in?'

'Although the police knew that Guy was an associate of Philip's, they hadn't any reason to connect international espionage with a murder in the Yorkshire Dales. Of course it was two or three days before they identified the corpse and even then there was little to suggest a linkage to the espionage. . From my time as a police doctor, I'd say that Philip managed to keep it simple and avoid leaving clues – especially during that dangerous bit, moving the body into the 'van. He didn't have to worry about prints – there'd be old ones all over the 'van from previous visits … and even if he had left *fresh* prints, that alone wouldn't do – too open to professional dispute. So there wasn't much evidence at that stage.

'Meanwhile, there was a clear motive for suspecting Geoff and they had established that he could have left his work during the night. So it wasn't until they knew that the dead man was Guy, that a possible link with Philip emerged – finally confirmed by Barbara … and Mr. Birch'

The long story came to a close just as they approached The Lamb. They decided to go in and order a tray of tea before setting off. Dr. Roebuck was a little uneasy about parting at this point, but Bea's return to work last week had seemed to do her no harm. So he didn't press her about it now, but merely asked gently whether she felt all right about the journey.

'Yes Dad, I'll be fine,' she answered. 'I know I've got to work through this – no-one can do it for me, so I might as well start now.'

'Funny isn't it?' she said, when they were settled once more in their favourite corner of the snug. 'Ever since Rose and I met up again, I've been worrying about *her* judgment where men are concerned.'

She picked up the cream jug and paused, looking across at him with that wry expression he knew so well.

'She was so impulsive … and I was cautious … rational … '

She made no attempt to check the hot, grieving tears that began to flow, and her father carefully removed the jug from her fingers. He set it down and said softly, 'I'm afraid, Bea, that when we're dealing with our choices in life and love, it's really – '

'More luck than judgment!' smiled Bea through her tears.

About the Author

Born in Yorkshire, Nancy Russell has been a riding instructor, market researcher and hotelier. Sailing and writing have long been her favourite pastimes. She brought up her family near Cardiff and now lives in a small market town in the middle of rural Wales.